the
moss

HAVE YOU EVER WONDERED HOW BOOKS ARE MADE?

UCLan Publishing is an award-winning independent publisher specialising in Children's and Young Adult books. Located at The University of Central Lancashire, this Preston-based publisher teaches MA Publishing students how to become industry professionals using the content and resources from its business; students are included at every stage of the publishing process and credited for the work that they contribute.

The business doesn't just help publishing students though. UCLan Publishing has supported the employability and real-life work skills for the University's Illustration, Acting, Translation, Animation, Photography, Film & TV students and many more. This is the beauty of books and stories; they fuel many other creative industries! The MA Publishing students are able to get involved from day one with the business and they acquire a behind-the-scenes experience of what it is like to work for such a reputable independent.

The MA course was awarded a Times Higher Award (2018) for Innovation in the Arts and the business, UCLan Publishing, was awarded Best Newcomer by the Independent Publishing Guild (2019) for the ethos of teaching publishing using a commercial publishing house. As the business continues to grow, so too does the student experience upon entering this dynamic Masters course.

www.uclanpublishing.com
www.uclanpublishing.com/courses/
uclanpublishing@uclan.ac.uk

LISA LUEDDECKE

the
moss

uclanpublishing

The Moss is a uclanpublishing book

First published in Great Britain in 2024 by
uclanpublishing
University of Central Lancashire
Preston, PR1 2HE, UK

978-1-91674729-6

1 3 5 7 9 10 8 6 4 2

Set in 10/16pt Kingfisher.

Designed, edited and typeset by
Eleanor Bowskill, Teddy Khanna and Rachel Robinson.

A CIP catalogue record for this book is available from the British Library.

Printed and bound in Great Britain by Clays Ltd, Elcograf S.p.A.

For Atlas.

And for everyone doing their best.

prologue

WE BROKE THE RULES just once, and we paid for it.

The bog has always been there, lurking behind the house, and we have never been allowed to go near it. Eve, nearly two years older than I am at twelve, lets it hold her curiosity more than I do. She lets the stories about it play in her head over and over again, of missing people and shapes in the mist.

Our dad tells us little, but I think he only knows little.

The fence that runs along it is meant for us, he said. To keep us out. To keep us safe. The reasons are many: risk of drowning, getting stuck in the mire and dying of dehydration. I'm not entirely certain what that is, but I know enough to keep from tempting anything that ends in death.

But Eve isn't like me. Eve loves danger, and danger loves Eve.

The contents of the dollhouse in my bedroom are splayed out across the floor like guts. We have agreed to do some renovations: change out the wallpaper – contact paper stolen from our mother in the kitchen – and rearrange the furniture. The sunlight streams in through the large window, casting criss-cross patterns on the floor around us. I'm dusting off the tiny bureaus and the miniature grandfather clock (spring cleaning, Eve called it), when a sudden and unceremonious *thud* makes us both jump.

We stare at the window, where the glass just *thunked* in a way that settles into the pit of my stomach.

"What was that?" I whisper to Eve, my mind racing with images of ghosts and ghouls.

She stands, slowly, dropping the contact paper and moving towards the window. "A bird," she says softly, a moment later.

I cross the room quickly, staring down to the grass below, where a tiny form flops about, trying to climb back into the air. But something in me thinks it never will.

"Do we leave it?" I ask, feeling a sob fill up my chest. I don't like dead things. Not even the motionless ladybugs that sometimes gather on the windowsills, or the dust bunnies that Mom says aren't alive but gather under my bed like little, fluffy corpses.

"Of course not," Eve says, and she turns for the door. I take another look at the bird, still flopping around, then going still, then flopping again. Its movements are getting smaller, less frequent.

I run from the room behind her.

The sunlight outside is wild and sharp, glinting off the spring morning dew that hasn't yet been burnt away. The ground is harsh against my bare feet, but I think little of it as we cluster around the fallen bird. The brownish feathers remind me of birds I've seen at my mom's feeder outside the kitchen window.

"It's a lark. And he's going to die," Eve says bluntly.

Tears well up in my eyes. I wipe them away sloppily with the back of my hand. "How do you know that?"

"Because he's dying now," she says, scooping it up in her hands. "I think its neck might be broken, or mostly broken." The bird tries to flop in her hands, but gives up, lying still save for its chest rising and falling furiously.

"What do we do with it?" I ask, its little form blurred by tears. "Bury it?"

But Eve turns away from me then, towards the fence – and the bog. I follow her gaze and go still, the tears drying up as something cold takes their place.

"We should give it to the Moss," she says softly, breathlessly. And something in the way she says it makes it sound like a gift. Like an offering.

"We aren't supposed to go near it," I remind her, although Mom is napping, and I know our dad isn't here.

"This is different," she tells me, and she moves towards the fence. I linger a moment longer, debating. Our father has told us at least once a day, sometimes more, to leave the bog alone. To stay on this side of the fence. To let it be. And we always have.

Don't go into the bog.

But maybe Eve is right. Maybe this is different, and maybe the bird lived in the bog and should return there to die. That doesn't seem to be what Eve is thinking, but it makes enough sense to me that I let my steps trail behind her and slip across the fence in my bare feet.

The golden-green grass is damp, my feet squelching as we trail down towards the Moss at a slow but steady pace. Approaching it like we aren't afraid of it, but of course we are. Eve is in front of me, holding the bird aloft like she's carrying a birthday cake into a room at a surprise party. The breeze throws her brown hair around like some wild girl out of the fairy tales our mom sometimes reads to us, and it makes me slow down a step. Put slightly more distance between us.

It's hard to tell where the field ends and the bog begins, but somehow we both know, and we both stop. Pools of water fall beside areas of solid ground, slender bog trees sticking out like long fingers from the ground.

I've never been this close before. That spark of rebellion that brought me here fans into something stronger, something that relishes in the closeness. That delights in being somewhere I know I shouldn't be. Finally.

"Here you go," Eve whispers, kneeling down by one of the murky pools. "This is for you." I don't know who *you* is meant to be, but she drops the dying bird into the pool of water and it goes very, terribly, still.

I can't look away for a long and dreadful minute, and stare at the now lifeless bird floating in the brown water. Can't stop thinking about how only moments ago, it was flying through the air like other birds, its whole life ahead of it, and now it's here, dead, in a bog, and that's just it.

The sobs return; Eve puts a comforting hand on my shoulder.

"Here. Help me," she says, and she walks a few steps away to where a large cluster of bog laurel grows, the small flowers starkly cheery against the backdrop of death.

We pull and pluck until we both have handfuls, then return to the small pool where she placed the bird.

But the bird is gone.

Eve stares at the pool. I stare at Eve, my heart thundering.

"Did it sink?" I ask shakily, but Eve doesn't answer. She just keeps staring, her face unreadable, before her gaze slowly wanders up. I follow it, blinking through the new tears – and if my heart was beating fast before, now it stops.

Through the mist that is suddenly everywhere out in the bog, a shape stands eerily still, watching us. A white deer, with antlers so tall they disappear into the fog, moss and vines dripping from them like an ancient tree. It doesn't move, and I could almost believe it's a painting or a statue – but then a waft of mist drifts in front of it, and when it clears again, the deer is gone.

Eve is frozen in place, staring at the spot where the deer just stood, her knuckles white where they grip the flowers. Then we both drop the bog laurel and run back to the house, our clothes sodden and our legs muddy by the time we reach it.

We never speak of the bird or the deer again.

one

I AM A THOUSAND feet above Maine, and there is a dead girl sitting beside me.

The trick is not to look directly at her. If I do, she's gone before I've finished turning my head. Vanishing like a star in the dawn. But if I don't look at her, she reappears, haunting the edges of my vision. A white gown, dark hair that's matted and mangled, her mouth open in horror. A silent scream.

Breathe. This is not my first ghost, but it is the closest I've come to one, and the cold air tumbling off her feels like the wind on a winter's day. I grip the arm rest as we descend lower and lower over the cloudy state. My state. My home, once upon a time. I have always loved it here, with its wild woods and gnarled coastlines and mist that lies thick with secrets. But for the past 368 days, my home has been far away, on the sun-kissed beaches of California.

"A place of healing," my father had said when he sold me on the idea, immediately after my sister disappeared.

I do not love California, but my aunt does, enough to make it her home for the past fifteen years, and she loved me enough to let me spend a year in her guest room. The change was jarring, even shocking, though I did grow fond of the boardwalks and palm trees, and the sense of *life* and *future* that lights up everything out there. If California is the future, then Maine is the ancient, cob-webbed past. Myth and murk to mint and modern.

And that suits me just fine. I've grown used to my houses having a few ghosts, and my forests a few secrets. Although my sister and I were the only ones who could see the ghosts, and I always felt like we were the secrets.

But the girl sitting next to me now is something else. She isn't like the splintered shadows or threadbare figures that dart across the room in the dead of night. Nor is she like the eyes I sometimes swear I feel watching me when I step outside our house and draw near to the bog that stretches away behind the house for dozens of miles.

The Moss, as it's commonly known. From an old word for British bog land. Uneven earth and pools of murky water, lanky trees in staccato clusters, swampy vines trailing down into the depths. The largest collection of peat in New England, though my father lets no one go near it, even outside of our family.

Click. Whirr. The plane glides closer and closer to the ground. The sun dashes behind gunmetal grey clouds that threaten a late afternoon thunderstorm.

My breath is still tight in my chest, hairs on the back of my neck standing up as every inch of me can feel the presence to my left. The presence that never boarded the plane with me.

I am the only passenger.

It has been a long night and day of travel. The red eye from Los Angeles to Boston. Then an endless wait in the airport because only two flights a day run up to the backwater airport that will save me a five-hour drive into the more unsettled parts of Maine, and I missed the first one. The girl beside me now was not there on the other flight. She was not there in the airport. She was not there when this small, creaky plane first took off.

Watching me with blackened eyes and tangled hair, earnestly, like time is short and I just don't know it yet.

The landing gear thunks distressingly loudly as the ground comes ever closer. Ahead, the pilots chat to someone in the tower. Just another day for everyone. Business as usual. Unaware of the dead girl in the seat beside me.

"Who are you?" My whisper is small but sharp, hard to hear above the high-pitched hum of the engine. "What do you want?"

My eyes keep darting over to her. To take in every detail I can. To understand who she is. Why she's here. But every time I do, she vanishes. Back again in the next moment, when I avert my eyes.

I cast my gaze towards the window. Only a few hundred feet more to go. Glance partially in her direction again, this time she's leaning towards me, wide eyes trained on me. Only inches from my face. The stench of damp earth and mire invades my senses, and I want to pull away, pressing up against the window of the plane, but I stand firm. This is my flight. My plane. My return home.

"Who are you?" Louder this time, but it is still little more than a grating sensation in my throat.

Looking as close to her as her vanishing habit will let me, I wait. I've seen ghosts before. I've seen *her* before. But not like this. Not so blatant and close and *real*. And certainly not so persistent. The two ghosts with which I am familiar are shy, fragmented things, never whole and real and stark like this one. A glimpse, a scrap, a taunt from a corner that you can just manage to convince yourself was a trick of the light.

In the seconds before the wheels at last kiss the runway, a hollow voice whispers in my ear.

Stay away.

Then another voice dances behind it, half-hidden by other noises.

It's cold, Emma. It's cold, and it's dark. Let me out.

And the plane is on the ground, and light misting rain gathers on the front window, and the seat beside me is empty.

She's gone, as suddenly and horrifically as she appeared.

Gone.

My breath comes in gasps now, like catching my breath after diving underwater. I run a hand through the air where she sat only seconds ago but feel nothing save for a pocket of cold air. Part of me starts to doubt if she was ever really there at all, but the stench of rot still clings to the edge of my senses. I've stopped letting myself think for too long about why my sister Eve and I were so . . . strange. Why we could see things others couldn't. Obsessing over the *why* felt useless when I could instead focus on the *who*. Who are they? Why do *they* want to be seen?

One of the pilots looks back at me while we taxi to our gate. He sees my heavy breathing, my hand still clutching the arm rest like the safety of the flight depends on it.

"Nervous flyer, eh?" He grins, showing a piece of chewing gum between his teeth.

"Claustrophobic," I half-lie. I've never been afraid of flying. There aren't that many things that scare me, and all of them are back at my father's house.

Calling it a gate feels rich, when really there's just one small terminal building and the plane just sort of parks right outside it.

The inside of the plane is hardly any bigger than a minivan, so when one of the pilots hauls the door open, I just jump straight down on to the tarmac. My legs sting and ache with the sudden stretch, but I'm grateful to be free. Too much flying and cramped seats and airport gates and not enough fresh Maine air.

"This way."

A moody airline employee, sipping an iced coffee, motions me towards the door of the terminal.

"We'll get your bag in a few minutes."

I move slowly towards the door, enjoying the space to walk, then turn to take one last look at the plane before the door closes behind me.

A girl's face watches me, half-hidden by the reflection of the clouds. Her mouth is open in that dreadful, silent scream.

And then the door closes, and she's gone.

two

California

THERE IS SOMETHING ABOUT the lemon-bright, sequined sunshine of California that my soul gulps down like water.

My aunt and I stop for ice cream along the Venice Beach boardwalk on a perfect summer's day. It's midweek, so slightly less busy than the weekends, but with enough movement and crowds to feel alive. That's what I love the most out here. How alive everything feels. I think Eve would love it, too, but she never got to come out here except when we were very young. It's a shame.

"You said pistachio, right?" Aunt Freda asks me when it's our turn.

"Right," I tell her, watching a group of people whiz by on roller skates. I keep threatening to try it, but I am not good on anything with wheels and I worry I'd end up with at least one broken limb.

We take our ice cream and eat it while we walk. My aunt comments on how she's only come here a few times and always forgets how much she enjoys it. With some beach towels tucked into our shoulder bags, we eventually make our way down towards the water, weaving between clusters of people set up with large blankets, umbrellas, giant coolers and beach games. Coming here is an event, and I feel wildly unprepared.

11

There's a small spot close to the water with enough room for us to lay out our towels. I dropped the empty ice cream cup in a trash can, so I just lie flat with my eyes closed and soak in the sunshine like it can add a little light to my soul. We get heat and sun in Maine in the summer, but it feels different out here, without the constant threat of winter. Like you have to enjoy it quickly or it'll be snatched away.

"Now we just have to get your dad out here," Aunt Freda muses. She adjusts her tortoiseshell sunglasses and finishes applying sunscreen.

"I might have to drag him here myself. He doesn't travel much."

"Maybe for Christmas."

I fall into the sounds of the beach around me: the crashing waves, the peals of laughter, the hum of conversation and the cry of the seagulls. With my eyes closed, I can very nearly imagine that I am back in Maine, lying on a rocky beach somewhere in the summer, and not almost 3,000 miles away from everything familiar to me.

Emma.

I open my eyes and glance over at my aunt, who is reading a crime novel next to me. "What?"

She looks at me, confused, before returning her attention to her book. "What?"

"You said my name."

"No, I didn't."

I sit up and look around us, realising that I might not be the only person on the beach who is named Emma. There are hundreds of people within earshot who could have said it, even though it sounded close at hand.

"Weird," I say, lying down again. I don't let my mind go to the places it wants to go. Telling me I've heard that voice before, and the shadows have followed me across the country.

With my eyes closed again, I can feel myself slipping into a gentle doze, the edges of the world blurring and mixing with a soft dream. The warm sun, the soft sand and the constant hum of noise are enough to invite a nap that I long for. I haven't slept well this week, for no other reason than sleep being a fickle, flighty thing.

Emma.

The word pierces through my sleep like a white-hot poker, and my eyes snap open. I know that voice. I have heard it many times over the years, usually near the Moss, trying to pull me in. Pull me under.

I sit up again, now wide awake, and look all around us to make sure it isn't someone I know. Someone calling to me from across the beach, trying to get my attention. But life drags on as normal, everyone locked in their own little world, and none of them are speaking to me.

"Are you OK?" Aunt Freda asks, temporarily closing her book.

I pick at a hangnail, not wanting her to see my thoughts. To call my dad and tell him it's happening again. That there's something wrong with Emma. "I'm fine," I lie, sending her a big, overwrought smile. "Just a little warm. I think I'll go find something to drink."

Climbing up off the sand, I head in the direction of some kiosks, keeping my eyes on the ground and my thoughts in some semblance of order.

three

SHARP **AFTERNOON** **SUNLIGHT** **SLANTS** through the sombre clouds as I step outside to wait for my dad. There's a piece of paper held tightly in my hand, pulled from my pocket after I climbed off the plane and caught a final glimpse of the dead girl. Holding it feels like home. Like a time long gone, that might never come back. It reminds me of Eve, even if it's the note she left behind before she disappeared. Still, I cherish it, because it feels like a part of her. Her handwriting, written on a scrap of paper pulled from one of her notebooks.

For a while, I stopped reading it. After the police gave it back to me when they were done testing it for anyone else's DNA. Trying to determine if she had run away, been kidnapped . . . killed.

I cannot take it any more, Emma. I've tried for so long, but I miss her too much. I can still feel her, sometimes, but it isn't enough. I want to be with her. I know how to find her, I think. Don't follow me. I mean it. It will break Dad if you do. I love you, Em.

P.S. Stay far away from the Sedge Man. He won't stop, like a hunter, until there's nothing left of you.

14

I have committed the words to memory but I still read them like it's the first time, because they ground me. They were written in the moments before she left, and somehow it feels like when I read them there's still time to stop her.

Stay away from the Sedge Man.

Eve offered little by way of explanation, both in her note and in life in general. She spoke of strange things often, leaving questions in her wake. But that voice I hear sometimes, the man's voice, the voice that asked me to come and play . . . Some part of my soul knows it's him.

I tuck the note back into my pocket, gently, keeping it close.

Dad sent me away within two weeks of her vanishing. I barely had time to catch my breath from all the crying, but now that I'm back, I want to *know*. I want to see what other breadcrumbs she might have left behind that only I can recognise. That might stick out to me, as her sister.

My stomach shivers with nervous excitement at the thought of seeing Dad again, after so much time. A year away is no small feat, especially in the wake of so much tragedy. One disappearance, and then another, which are their own kind of death, only without a funeral. Mom went first, five years ago, and in a way, my sister went with her. She never really came back after that, always locked away in her room, or saying how she could still see and feel her around the house.

If Mom was there, I'd have seen her too.

Eventually, the realisation that Mom was never coming back finally settled in. It took two years, waking up every day and looking out the window in case I could see her walking back down the driveway. Checking her room. Sometimes calling for her out in the garden. But the relentless drag of time was a reminder that, years later, she was gone. *Gone* gone. But there was something about Eve vanishing that always felt so unfinished. And it still does. Maybe just because it was more recent.

Then, after Eve really did follow Mom, in the form of vanishing one day like dew in the morning sun, Dad said enough was enough. He couldn't lose anyone else. Wherever they went – into the Moss, as I secretly suspect – he didn't want me to be next. So he sent me away to California to live with Aunt Freda, and stayed in the lonely, haunted house by himself.

The thought of anyone being alone in that house always made me sad, but especially him. He didn't deserve it.

And yet, despite my absence of 368 days, my father is nowhere to be seen. The parking lot is almost entirely empty, save for a boy sitting in the front seat of an older black pickup truck with the door open. A boy I was not expecting to see right here, right now, and without warning. He watches me for a moment, and I don't look away.

Jordan Sumpter.

The last time I saw him was a week before I left for California. We both grew up in the same town, went to the same school and had many of the same friends. He was always there, like the moon or the stars, in the background of everything even if you couldn't see him. And then, six days before I left, he had showed up on the porch of our house, shaking like I was a cobra that might strike him, and told me the words that had been branded into my mind ever since.

"*I know you're leaving. I should have told you before, but I'll just tell you now. I like you, Emma Carver. I like you a lot. And I wish you could stay, but I know you can't. So there. Now you know. I'm sorry.*"

My face burns seeing him again. Remembering how I'd never mustered up the words to reply to him. I'd said nothing. *Nothing*. Then eventually he had just left, and I hadn't seen him again until this very moment.

Sometimes all the words you never say are enough to give you a sore throat.

I shift from one foot to the other, then back again, nervous. Somewhere, tucked under all the *nothing* I'd said and the guilt that came afterwards, there were soft, delicate feelings that I hadn't let myself acknowledge. That I'd folded quietly into a box and locked tight, because they had no place in my life at the time.

But now, seeing his carefree hair and bright eyes and the way that his smile is always just a little bit crooked, the box starts to crack open once more.

"Your dad sent me. He couldn't get away from work."

There's an apology in his voice, but it doesn't stop the flash of anger that bolts through me at that – I haven't seen my dad in a year and he still couldn't be here. But I know how hard he works, knee deep in plants, pavers and landscaping tools from morning until night. I know if he could have been here, he would have.

"Well, I suppose this will be better than walking," is all I manage, twisting my fingers tightly around the handle of my suitcase until the skin pinches. "Thanks for coming to my rescue."

Jordan scratches the back of his neck, uncomfortable. "It's good to have you back." He has a hard time meeting my gaze and holding it. I don't blame him.

"Here, let me get that." He grabs my suitcase and hauls it into the bed of the truck. "Hop in. The air conditioner doesn't work, but it's not too bad out today. Guess summer is pretty much over at this point." His eyes dart to some nearby trees, where the leaves are turning gold and red and salmon. "The truck is my dad's, but he drives something else for work lately, so I can use it when I need to."

I climb in, silently, and lean as close to the open window as I can. Jordan's words from last year keep taunting me. And then my silence afterwards, deafeningly loud and final.

"It's been a hotter summer than most years," he tells me, but I don't know if it's just to fill the awkward silence, or if he's moved on from our last interaction. "Hot, and dry. We've had less than half the rain we usually get. Everything's a tinderbox."

"Sounds like California," I say, watching as the brownish-green forest blurs passed us. I pull one foot up onto the seat and wrap my arms around my knee.

"I couldn't remember where you went. I thought it was west, but your dad never really mentioned it."

"Los Angeles," I tell him. "But it all basically feels like a desert."

"Well, everyone says to pray for rain." He glances sideways at me, like he's trying to recall something.

"I didn't know you'd gotten religious," I say.

"Not particularly, but everyone else in Scarrow has, it seems."

Hearing the name of the town makes my stomach tighten. So much hides behind the name. Memories, death, ghosts and heartache weighing me down like cinder blocks. I could forget for a time, in LA. But I cannot forget here.

The only good view of Scarrow, some people say, is the one in the rearview mirror. But right now, something is calling to me like a foghorn, from all the way across the country. I could feel it in the moments immediately after waking up. In the liminal time before finally falling asleep. A hand reaching out to pull me back. To bring me home.

My name resonates in my sleep. In the silence while driving or eating breakfast or watching TV.

Emma. Emma.

So here I am.

Jordan rests one palm on the wheel of the truck, and an elbow on the edge of the window. "How long are you planning to stay?"

I shrug, even though he isn't looking at me. "Maybe a few days. Maybe for ever. It depends, I guess."

"On what?"

"A lot of things. My dad. The investigation. How I feel coming back. You know."

There it is. That quiet moment of gathering sympathy before the tenderness shows up in full force.

"I know it was a lot, Emma." The way he says my name makes me look out the window, away from him. "Your mom, then your sister disappearing. I don't know if I ever really said how sorry I was. As we know, I'm not great with words."

Is he referencing that time on the porch? I suspect so, but it's hard to tell.

He shouldn't be so hard on himself. Sometimes the simplest words are the best ones. Unfussy and honest. Most people offer me some variation of *I heard. I'm so sorry. Please let me know if there's anything I can do.* Which doesn't help at all, because unless you can bring them both back, then there's nothing that anyone can do.

"I'm not saying it's the same thing, but I lost my aunt when I was seven. I hated her for it."

I steal a glance over at him, and the wind from the open window is thrashing his not-quite-blonde hair all over the place. "Hated . . . your aunt?"

"Yeah. She didn't tell me she was going to die. Which of course she wouldn't know, but at the time I remember feeling more anger than sadness. Maybe because I was so young."

And out of all the sympathies and drawn-out conversations about loss that I've had over the past few years, that one sticks out to me. "I didn't hate my mom for going. But . . ." I clear my throat, feeling a tightness building there. "But I did hate my sister. I hated the way some part of her followed my mom and never came back, even before she disappeared. It was like I wasn't even here any more, and all she wanted was to get Mom back."

"We all deal with pain differently."

"Yeah. I've heard that a lot." A long pause. "How has my dad been? Have the police given him a moment to breathe?" Having a wife and daughter both go missing tends to bring a lot of scrutiny, even though I know he had nothing to do with it. But without bodies or anything else to go on, it's hard to pin anything on him.

"I think they let up on him eventually, although I'm sure they're still curious. He's good. You know. I think as good as he can be. Definitely better over the last few months. I help him work on the house a lot after school, more over the summer. He pays me cash for gas money and whatnot. Not too bad."

"What sort of work?"

"Oof. A lot. Let me see. Last week I helped him replace some loose stones in the hearth in the living room. I told him he needs to get a chimney guy round before winter, but I'm not sure he will.

I'm not sure he was even listening when I told him."

That sounds like my father. Always distracted. But maybe that's how he copes with pain. Keeping his mind too busy to linger on the sadness for too long.

My dad always likes to joke that he bought the house for a song, but really what happened is that no one else wanted to buy it because most of the sprawling property is made up of the Moss, which isn't usable, farmable terrain. It just sort of sits there, quietly, attracting vultures and carnivorous plants and racking up history that goes back probably thousands of years.

The land is technically protected, to keep us from harming the flora and fauna that make the bog their home around it, but I always felt like there was a different reason we were meant to leave it alone. One that not even the game wardens and preservationists know about.

"Sometimes I help him mow the lawn or trim back growth, which feels vaguely ironic since he's a landscaper, but he works too much to do it himself."

That also sounds like my dad.

To my right, the trees separate momentarily to reveal a wide, open field of tall, greenish-golden grass. It bends gently in the light breeze, rippling like it's a lake and someone just disturbed the surface.

And then – there she is. *Someone*, in a white dress, standing as still as a scarecrow and facing us. Watching us. She doesn't vanish like she did on the plane. We are closer to it now – closer to the Moss. I suspect that's why.

But my glimpse of her is gone almost as soon as it begins, swallowed again by the tall grass and the returning trees, but the angle of her stance and her matted hair settle into my mind like a brain freeze, cold and sharp.

I look forward again, afraid that if I look anywhere else she'll find me.

four

Before Mom

ONLY A FEW WEEKS into seventh grade, and I am at home, sick. Eve hasn't yet come down with whatever viral misery has hit me, but it will no doubt work its way through the family.

The small clock on my bedside table reads half past midnight. It's been hard to sleep with the sweating and shivering from the fever, but I feel calmer now with another presence in the room. A welcome presence this time, unlike so many times before.

My mom sits beside me, on a little stool she brought up from the kitchen, humming softly and occasionally running a hand over my hair. I feel guilty that she is up so late with me and like I should tell her to go to bed, but I selfishly feel better knowing she's here. My mind keeps dancing towards sleep, and even if it is taking a long time to arrive, I know she will eventually slip off to her own room once it fully finds me. She is happy to wait.

I can just make out her blue plaid pyjamas in the faint moonlight. Her eyes are trained on the window as she hums quietly, and more and more I'm pulled towards the velvety soft embrace of sleep. But a rustling yanks me back a minute later, as Mom stands up and moves towards the window. Her hands hang limp at her sides as she stares down *at something – down towards the Moss.*

Pulling myself up onto one elbow, my head swimming, I can see a distant, yellowish light lurking in the bog, drifting up and down slowly. I think it's what's holding her attention, but I can't be sure. Must be a flashlight, or something else carried by someone trespassing into the bog. It's happened before, and my dad usually has to go and chase them back out again.

The light lingers for a few minutes, bobbing up and down, up and down, before eventually turning and retreating into the Moss, where it disappears. My mom doesn't leave the window right away. She just stands there, staring silently, her humming having died away, before she finally returns to the stool.

I keep my eyes closed so she thinks I'm asleep, but now I'm more awake than ever. I see the light burnt into my eyes, lighting up the shadows, waiting and watching like a candle in the dark.

five

THERE IS VERY LITTLE town to the town of Scarrow, but those who live here guard it fiercely. If you are from anywhere else and choose to settle here, you can count on years of effort and hope, trying and failing, before they will see you as anything but a stranger. My family came here when we were small children, both my sister and me. I have no memories of anywhere else, and sometimes that thought is suffocating. Like there is nowhere else but here.

The old brick post office comes and goes, nearly empty at this hour. On a wooden pole outside is a picture of Eve, with the word MISSING printed underneath it. It was actually a selfie that the two of us took together at the top of a blueberry hill, but they cropped me out for a better view of her face. Smiling bright and wide, because it was a good, beautiful day.

The coffee shop sees a few lingering guests enjoying the outdoor tables – no one I recognise. The small park that isn't really a park at all and simply a patch of green lawn holds a smattering of children kicking a ball around while their parents look on.

Nothing has changed. Everything is different.

For the first time in my life, I feel like I don't belong here. I think darkly that wherever my sister went after she vanished, perhaps I'd be better off there. But I'm not the girl who left. I'm the girl who came back.

Wherever she went. It's a funny thought, like she could have gone anywhere else but into the Moss. But they searched and never found her body, and no body often gives the illusion of life. So I've let myself believe that there are other possibilities. That she headed west, maybe, vanishing into some small town that has never heard about the missing girl before. But the Moss is never far from my thoughts. The way it beckoned her, like a bony finger in the night.

Jordan is quiet as we make our way through town. Seeing him there, on the edges of my vision but indistinct, I can half believe it is the dead girl again. That she's here with me, in the cab of the truck, silently waiting for – what?

It's cold, and it's dark.

The air is warm in the late afternoon partial sunshine, but that doesn't stop a shiver from caressing my spine. Jordan glances over at my little jolt and wordlessly points the fan away from me. I'm grateful, but I don't say it.

Our house is called Lark House, and it sits a mile outside of the main part of the town. It takes its name from Simon Lark, the man who built it beside the Moss in 1703 for his family, but later lost his daughter to a tragedy. And that's all the house has been good for since: tragedy.

The road is largely wooded, but the trees soon melt away when the bog land begins to take over. Something in my heart shifts – colder. Heavier. Sharper. The air pinches and throbs, harder to breathe. I can't place it, but I am not the same person I was moments ago.

My chest convulses like I might cry, but I can't. Not here. Not now. Not yet.

It's like Jordan can sense my unease, because he speaks up just when my heart is about to burst.

"It's a curious thing, the Moss. But I guess I don't have to tell you that."

I'm desperate to hear any voice that isn't one inside my own head. "Growing up, it felt like another person in the background of everything, but one you aren't allowed to talk to. The kind that could get you killed."

"Yeah. This whole area is rich with history, but they've never found any old artefacts near the Moss. Pottery, arrowheads . . . nothing. Zilch. Granted, most of it is private property – yours – so maybe people haven't looked hard enough."

My chest heaves again with suppressed sobs as we round a bend. Not far to go now; I know every inch of this road. "My mom used to do a lot of gardening. Never found anything. And the garden never really grew, no matter how hard she tried. Except for vines and weeds." And the thing about my mom was that she could make anything grow. *Buying plants is buying happiness,* she always said. She would rescue the sick and dying plants from the discount section of garden centres and bring them back to their full glory, but only inside. As soon as she planted anything outside, it withered and rotted.

"Bog land can be funny like that. Certain plants grow prolifically, and others die away."

Perhaps he's right, but I've never felt like the bog land was the problem. There was always something else. Some other reason, fluttering just beyond sight. Invisible, but visceral.

The truck wends its way around a bend and then, to our right, the hills die away and the vastness of the Moss consumes the horizon.

It is a great and lifeless thing, yet my childhood years were haunted by how alive it felt. Always watching. Sensing. Waiting, though for what, I was never quite certain. Spindly trees and cloudy water and the maze-like swaths of wet land all stretch away, filling the window into the distance.

My stomach clenches, and I hug my middle.

An ancient post and rail fence runs along the road, separating it from the bog, and every few posts there's a KEEP OUT sign hung askew. They were there when we bought the house, and we never took them down. People are better off staying away. More than one soul has been lost to the water and mud and the hungry, swampy earth that clings on to your feet and limbs and never lets go.

Then the house rises up like a guardian. The white wood exterior is worked over with damp and lichen, giving the farmhouse the feel of seeming abandoned. The chimneys are vacant of smoke or any signs of life, and the windows all look on, soulless. There was life here, once, but that seems long ago now.

Ravenous vines have begun to climb the chimney, and Jordan *tsk*s at the sight of them. "Damn," he says, pulling into the driveway and cranking the truck into park. "I just cut those things back a week ago."

For a long moment, I don't move. Just take in the old white house and the bog behind it and the coldness that settles back in like familiar ghosts welcoming me home. The memories lurch forward, but I smack them down. They will do me no good now.

Jordan climbs out first, but I linger a short while longer. Eyeing the house. The bog. The rose garden that runs the length of the house but is now overrun with weeds. A few peach-coloured blooms still burst forth with colour, but far fewer of them than there once were. Everything feels old, and dead, like the shadowed version of a once-bright memory.

My gaze finds the bog immediately, the scent of rot and damp filling my senses like water. It claws its way into my throat. The spaces behind my eyes. Makes them water.

The tailgate thuds down and Jordan extracts both of my suitcases. Tiredness starts to creep forward at the sights and sounds of returning home after a long journey.

"I'll get these up to your room. You can take your time." He brushes aside some of his hair to send me a look of what I think is understanding, before he gathers up the suitcases and disappears into the house. The screen door slaps closed with an aching familiarity, and all goes still.

The Moss calls for my attention again, and I turn to face it. Memories dance in my periphery, where I've learnt ghosts love to linger. Dead birds and bog laurel and a deer that wasn't a deer. A creature that was nothing to ever walk this world. A cold wind carries up from the Moss, and on it, an invitation.

Come play.

The voice is somehow both in the air around me, and inside my head. A man's voice, unmistakably, and one I've heard before.

So instead, I pull open the screen door and disappear into the house. Some invitations are best left unanswered.

The door drops me in the large living room. Nothing feels different, but there are changes everywhere I can't quite place. The large stone hearth on the same wall as the door. The brown leather sofa we've had since I was young shows even more signs of wear than before, faded and creased and loved. The reclaimed wood coffee table, the antique rocking chair, the cream-coloured wingback chair. It's all still here, haunting the room along with a thousand memories of Christmas mornings and late-night movie nights and feverish naps on the couch.

Old things love old houses, my mother said, so everything in Lark House feels ancient. Like stumbling across a house from the past.

Thumping upstairs informs me that Jordan has reached my room with the suitcases, so I let my feet start to draw me that way. Towards the staircase, the old kitchen lingering to the right. The same kettle on the stove, the same mug rack with a random assortment of thrift shop teacups, the butcher's block island with ten thousand knife marks collected over the years. The kitchen table – the same table where I ate breakfast every morning before school, Eve just across from me with music in her headphones. Our mother buzzing around the room readying our lunches and fretting over the fine details. Every new lunch was a surprise: sandwiches cut into the shapes of flowers, bunnies or hearts. Fruit in vivid hues arranged like a rainbow, tucked in carefully to keep it from moving around. Small notes on rolled paper that were in a new place every time, like a treasure hunt.

All the memories I've kept as bleached pencil sketches in my mind begin to take on colour again, and their weight is crushing. My chest aches.

Everything is the same, but still the subtle changes taunt me.

The third step creaks as I climb, just as it always has. It made sneaking around the house long after dark all the more exciting, reaching out with a foot to try to skip the step without tumbling down the rest of the stairs in the black house.

The shine of the railing is dulled by a thick layer of dust. I run a finger through it as I climb the stairs, and when it bends sharply to the right, my eyes automatically find a painting that has hung there since before we moved in. It came with the house; it's an impressionist painting, ill-defined in that way that suggests more than depicts. But it's clearly of the Moss. The spindly trees, the swampy water and, above, a black, starless sky.

I never liked it.

The turn in the staircase puts me in beams of sunlight streaming in from the landing. The window offers a far-flung view of the Moss, and it's here that I again run into Jordan. He has stopped to admire the view, so I join him.

The horizon melts into the sky, and the bog is there to meet it. The view is only broken by blackened clusters of trees and stumps. So much space. So many ways to die. I think that's what I hated the most about living here when I was younger. The way it sat there, mostly silent, like a warning you could never quite escape. Its presence lurking out every window and on the edge of every glance, and the mist reaching with gaunt, ashen fingers.

"Gosh," Jordan says. "Does it ever end?"

A cold hand coils around my stomach. "Sometimes it doesn't feel like it," I whisper. He glances over at me, perhaps trying to read my thoughts, but comes up empty. I turn away from the window.

"I should get going," Jordan says, moving towards the stairs. "I have to pick up a few things at the store. But your dad said he'd be here this afternoon, so he shouldn't be too long."

"Thank you for the ride." I give him a half smile. The tiniest part of me thinks about asking him to stay, as the house always grows larger and more alone when there is only me here, but I stay quiet.

"Anytime, Emma. I'm here if you need anything." Our eyes meet for just a moment, his catching hints of gold and green in the beams of sunlight streaming through the window. And he leaves me.

Off the landing to the right are two bedrooms – one mine, and one Eve's. I can tell just by glancing in that both have been left largely untouched since I left, and since Eve vanished. It's her room I go to first, drawn along by some invisible string.

I used to envy Eve her bedroom. The deep turquoise wallpaper. The clusters of fairy-tale figurines she collected over the years that now sit coated in dust. The modern art paintings she had found at a flea market that give a chaotic energy to the otherwise peaceful and old-fashioned room. The guitar hanging on one wall, that she played a lot at first and then less and less. Looking back, much of Eve's life at the end seemed to be distraction – distraction from school, from the bog, then from the hole Mom left behind. Everywhere there are signs of a sadness that crept in after our mom vanished and never went away. Never healed, like time was meant to do.

Books she never read, sitting on the old bookcase. A writing desk peppered with spots of salt where her tears fell and dried. The signs are subtle, but they are there. Everywhere. I run a few fingers over a small china vase filled with bog laurel, picked fresh. Eve always loved it, even though I never did. There's a sweetness to it now, my father still thinking to pick some and bring it to her room, in her memory. It gives the sense that she'll be home any moment, and, as I think about it, I fancy I can hear the screen door slapping shut downstairs.

Sometimes, I feel like I hardly remember her any more, even though it's only been a year and a bit. Just the highlights. The birthdays and Christmases. I've always found it strange how memories work. How they fray over time. Go threadbare.

My fingers draw back from the carafe and I brush the dust off onto my shirt.

A creak on the stairs. My head whips towards it, waiting for Jordan or my father to come up from below, but I wait for a time and no one arrives. With slow steps, I back away from Eve's room and peer around the corner, down the narrow, enclosed staircase. But it is as empty as I left it, not a soul in sight.

A coldness brushes past my right arm, and fear propels me down the hall and into my room, where I slam the door and back away one step at a time until I collapse onto my bed.

six

Before Mom

A **GRAPHITE SKY CRUSHES** *down from above.*

A rainy mist clings to the air, threatening to unleash an onslaught at any moment. My rain boots squeak and squelch in the muddy ground as I follow Eve past the dewy roses and towards the fence that holds back the wide field – and then, the Moss.

But unlike other days, Eve doesn't stop at the fence. She takes hold of it, staring straight ahead, then hikes herself up until she's sitting atop it.

"Eve!" I call, running to catch up with her, but my legs are shorter than hers.

She turns a wry smile on me and holds a finger to her lips, her dark hair made curly by the mist falling wildly around her face.

"Don't go into the bog," I remind her, hanging back so a few feet separate me and the fence. "Dad says so."

"Dad isn't here," she whispers back, and something about those words sets me to shivering. Dad isn't here, though I wish he was, and Mom is asleep upstairs. Suddenly, I wish someone other than me was here to stop her.

With a heavy thunk and a small splash of mud, she lands in the field over the fence, then turns to me. "What are you afraid of?" she asks. "It's only a bog."

And she sets off walking, the mist soon swallowing her, while my feet grow roots that cut deep into the ground beneath me. I try to pull them away, but they don't move an inch. I try to call out for my mom, but my voice has been yanked away. So she just goes and goes and goes, and I am powerless to stop her.

seven

DRIP. DRIP. DRIP.

The sound tugs at the edges of my senses, beckoning me forth from sleep, but I am slow to awaken. Still, the sound is there, even as the early evening light filters into my vision and the cream and rose floral wallpaper welcomes me back to the world.

Drip. Drip. Drip.

Like the soft running of a leaking tap, or a faulty shower head, the sound is constant. Incessant. And it was not there when I fell asleep on my bed, above the covers, still wearing my shoes. A day of travel feels like a night without sleep.

Drip.

I sit up slowly, taking in the room. The white metal frame of my bed creaks ever so softly under my shifting weight. Everything feels the same as I left it. The carved mahogany armoire that still holds the clothes I didn't take to California. The small wooden writing desk that faces one large window — a window that looks down over the Moss. It's the desk that holds my attention, because through my blurred, half-asleep vision, I see water droplets tumbling from the ceiling and onto the surface of the desk. A small puddle already sits, staining the wood.

Above, there is no crack or crevice in the ceiling to suggest where the water might be coming from. Just a smooth, white ceiling, with an endless stream of droplets falling like a tiny rainstorm.

I reach out a hand to catch a few of them and they are cold as ice to the touch. Cold like a melted ice pop, or sleet before a snowstorm. My skin burns where it landed and I dry it off on my shirt, over and over again, trying to shake the sensation. When I look up again, the water is gone. The puddle on the desk, the stream of droplets from above. All gone without a trace.

That chill returns, and before I can think too long on it, I leave the room.

I am not alone in the house. Soft humming wafts up the stairs as I make my way down. My dad is here, and suddenly the house feels like a home again. The third stair creaks when I give it my weight, and the humming instantly stops.

And there he is, with his sandy brownish hair in dire need of brushing and scruff I don't remember him having when I left. He steps forward as I reach the floor, arms outstretched, and pulls me in for a hug. It's the kind of hug you long for when you're alone, or when you miss someone, or on those days when the world just needs to stop, and you need someone you trust to tell you that everything will be OK. Not like the goodbye hug from the day he left me at the airport.

"Welcome home," he says by my ear. A pressure builds, and I suddenly want to cry more than anything. Even my dad sniffles when he pulls away.

"How were your flights?"

Without asking, he turns to put the kettle on to make me the peppermint tea I always used to drink after school.

"Awful. Fine," I say, stifling a yawn. "First one was bumpier than hell."

"God, your mom used to hate that. I remember she would always turn white as a ghost and squeeze the hell out of my hand."

My chest heaves with a sigh at the mention of ghosts and planes. I've had enough of both for now. "Aunt Freda sends her love."

"She emailed me once a week, every week, for the entire time you were gone. Like clockwork, on Sundays. Bless her heart."

"She never said."

He shrugs. "You know the local news wants an interview. Did I tell you that?"

I shift, annoyed, but unsurprised. "You didn't."

"They want to check in on the past year. Update the public on the investigation. You know. *A year on, and where are we now?* That type of thing."

"When's the last time the police were out?" I ask. Might as well get the uncomfortable stuff out of the way early.

He sighs. "Not in a few months. They still think I had something to do with it, although they're careful not to say it directly. But it's always there, in every conversation. It kills me that anyone would think that."

Upstairs, I hear a floorboard creak in what I think is my bedroom. My gaze wanders up to the ceiling, but my dad hasn't seemed to notice.

Suddenly I want to be free of the house, feeling a thousand eyes and hands and presences all crushing together around me.

"Actually, I'll have this tea in a little bit," I say, sliding off the stool. "I've had enough of sitting. I'm going to take a little stroll."

Dad drops the tea bag into a cup – my favourite. The one painted with a little toadstool; I love that he remembered. "Sure. It'll be here when you get back."

Outside, light has started to drain from the sky, and the first glimmer of starlight begins to unfurl. An arc of a moon hangs high in the sky, watching as I make my way down the expansive garden and towards the bog. I never decided to go this way, but the memory of watching Eve slip into the bog when we were younger is fresh in my memory, and as long as my father isn't watching, a short visit won't hurt me. I've ventured in a few steps before and lived to tell the tale anyway.

The ground grows soggier as I approach, my sneakers becoming cold and damp. But I still don't turn around. I'm not sure what has come over me, but the feeling in the house, the building pressure, something is pushing me in this direction. And while perhaps I should do more to fight it, I'm tired and wired and feeling ever so slightly mischievous. I was the good girl for years, while Eve broke the rules like they were glow sticks in need of snapping. I'm tired of being the only one to follow them.

I take my first steps into the Moss in . . . years. Even the solid bits of ground that hang above the dark pools are sodden, my feet sinking softly as though the earth is hungry to pull me in. The second I'm inside, the sounds of crickets and owls and whispering grass ceases suddenly. Jarringly. Like someone turned off the sound on the TV. I freeze, staring at the darkening world before me like I've walked into a painting. Cold embraces me, even though it's a fairly warm day.

Ropes of coldness writhe around my wrists, my ankles, my neck. Grasping and twisting.

What was it that kept Eve coming back, time after time? The question is written in the air around me, and one I would give anything to answer.

I thought about it every day while I was in California, reliving all the times she slipped in and came out with a strange look on her face, like she'd caught a glimpse of the gates to either Heaven or Hell.

Two weeks. That's how long the police spent combing through the Moss, searching every pool they could find for her body. Shouting her name. Using dogs to try to pick up her scent. But after those two weeks were up and there hadn't even been a hint of her, they gave up.

But even now, as I look around, I worry that I'll look down into one of the pools and see her floating there. See her distorted face or hair and I will never be able to un-see it again.

A shift in the air.

My feet stop where they are, every muscle freezing.

Something rotten and old, terribly close at hand.

Breath on my neck, hot, and putrid. Out of the corner of my eye, there's the impression of something standing behind me, though there was nothing nearby moments ago. The outline of a pointed nose. Antlers. Long teeth, like sabers. On its back, a rider, though without turning I can make out little of who it is.

My body shakes, head to toe, limb to limb, to the point that I nearly collapse into the water, but I stand firm. I have seen this thing before and lived. I will live again, as Eve did, until she disappeared.

But it still takes me a long minute before I can force myself to turn and face it. And when I do, it's gone. I get only the vague outline of something retreating into the mist, and as it goes, a soft voice like a girl's trills off a few notes.

'Tis the last rose of summer, left blooming alone . . .

My neck prickles, memories churning. I've heard the song before, dozens and dozens of times. My mother used to sing us a lullaby when we were sick or couldn't fall asleep, sitting beside us and holding our hands. But it's been years. Years and years.

It's a song I have tried hard to forget.

Shame burns my face for having come in here at all. I was tired and felt like making trouble, but now I wish I hadn't.

Turning back in the direction I came, I pick my way along, tripping and slipping into the hungry water more than once. By the time my hands find the wooden posts of the fence, I am soaked from the waist down but desperately thankful to feel the splintered wood beneath my shaking fingertips.

eight

Before Mom

IT IS THE DAY *after my thirteenth birthday. I got new pieces for the dollhouse that I've been wanting since Christmas, and I've been waiting to get out of school so I can rearrange the rooms exactly how I want them. Eve always helps me, because the dollhouse used to be both of ours before she stopped playing with it so much. But she still takes the time to give me her ideas and tell me what she thinks of mine, and tonight, Mom promised to have cookies made for us while we work.*

I hop off the bus and skip towards the house, feeling that burst of energy you get when you're about to finally do something you've been looking forward to all day. The screen door slams against the wall of the house when I yank it open, and Mom jumps in her seat on the couch.

"Emma! Easy," she scolds gently, before standing to take my backpack and hang it on a peg. "Good day at school?"

"It was fine!" I call back to her, because I'm already on my way up the stairs. I run first to Eve's room, but she isn't there. Her schoolbooks are on the bed so I know she's already home, but the room is otherwise empty. I check my room next, in case she already started working on the

42

dollhouse, but it hasn't been touched. "Have you seen Eve?" I call from the top of the stairs.

"She went for a walk," Mom calls back.

Annoyance flickers. She knew what time I'd be home, and that I had been waiting all day to see her. I slump down the stairs and out the screen door again.

"Be careful!" Mom says behind me, like she does every time I step out the door.

My eyes move instinctively to the bog, but there are no signs of life. At least not from here. I peek back through the window to make sure Mom is reading again, and then move quietly off the porch and into the garden. To the right of the property is a tree line where a forest starts, and some of the trees run all the way down to the bog. I trot quickly into the shelter of them so that if Mom looks out the window again, she won't notice which direction I'm going. Once I feel safely hidden, I pick my way down towards the Moss.

Some wayward part of me relishes in the sense of wrongdoing. In knowing that I am breaking all the rules and without good reason, other than my annoyance with my sister. I wonder if this is how Eve feels every time she breaks the rules, or if she is so used to doing it that she hardly notices it any more.

My shoes start to squelch as the ground grows soggier, so I hop from high point to high point until I near the area where the bog begins in earnest.

At last, I see movement ahead.

Eve sits on a large rock, braiding her hair and staring straight ahead. I'm directly behind her, so she is unaware of my presence as I creep ever closer.

She is speaking to someone. Not to me, but to someone. Or trying to.

As my feet bring me ever closer on the soft, sodden ground, her voice eases into clarity.

"I know you're out there. I'm here, and I'm listening. I'm sorry for what happened to you. I am."

Through the thinning trees I have a clear view out over the bog, but there is no one else in sight. Just Eve and I, and she is still unaware that I have come up behind her. So who is she talking to?

"You don't have to be afraid. I see you sometimes. I know you're there."

I stop moving and wait, wondering if perhaps someone will come out from behind a tree, but the world is still and quiet. Birds call from the trees, and now and then I hear the skittering of squirrels, but nothing more.

In one of Eve's hands is a cluster of bog laurel. Done braiding her hair, she brushes it back and forth against the ground absentmindedly, and it's this that takes and holds my attention. She seems unaware of it, but where she brushes the flowers against the ground, new flowers spring up. Slowly, but growing up from the ground like a time lapse until the area beside her is riddled with little pink flowers.

My throat clenches like a hand just wrapped around it, and the world seems to tilt. This must be a dream, but everything else feels so lifelike. School. The bus. Coming home to my mom. Walking through the trees to find Eve. None of this feels like a dream.

After a moment, Eve glances down at the ground where the flowers have sprung up. She eyes them, then sighs.

"I'll keep waiting for you," she says to no one, picking some of the new growth to add to her bouquet.

The late spring day is warm, but I am suddenly very cold. The dollhouse and the new furniture all seem impossibly small and far *away, and I can't remember why I was so looking forward to it at all. Moving back slowly, I take quiet, careful steps further into the trees and away from Eve. Whatever she is doing, whoever she is talking to, I want no part in it.*

I make it back to the house without her ever having seen me at all.

nine

MY FATHER IS ON the porch when I return.

"Where did you go?" he demands, taking me by both shoulders. I twist away from him and move towards the screen door, still trembling after the things I saw – heard, felt – in the Moss.

"Into the bog," I tell him, like it's the simplest thing in the world. My body is too weak, my mind still too shaken to think of a lie, and my wet shoes and muddy jeans would give it away if I tried.

It's then that I notice his face is whiter than the mist inside the Moss. "Why, Emma?" he asks shakily, moving to stand between me and the door. "Why would you do that?" He presses his palms to his forehead. "I went in to look for you. You were nowhere in sight."

"I was there," I tell him. "The whole time. Look. You can't fake that." I point down to my soaked shoes, the mud on my clothes. But something about his words gives me pause.

He just shakes his head, his eyes darting behind me. "Don't do this to me, Emma. Please. Don't do this."

"Or what? You'll send me away again?" I regret the words almost immediately, but there is some small bit of truth to them. A worry I harbour quietly.

"If I have to."

I look at him evenly, his answer catching me off guard. "Why?"

"Because I will do anything to keep you safe. Anything to keep from losing you, too."

I finally get past him and through the door, and he doesn't follow. Taking the steps upwards two at a time, I run straight for the shower, turning it on as hot as I can stand, to wash off every last trace of the bog.

It feels like I stand in there for days, time stretching away in a meaningless, dull blur. The bathroom is too steamy to see my hand in front of my face by the time I climb out and towel off. It's as I'm dressing, humming to beat back the silence since I turned off the shower, that I notice something on the mirror. Like an invisible fingertip is tracing out letters in the fog on the glass: A 'c', an 'o', an 'm'. It keeps going, one by one, until the mirror reads *Come in.*

I can do nothing but stare, dumbfounded, before grabbing at the towels to cover up.

I want to have imagined it. I want to wake up in my bed, sweating, to find it was only a dream. I want the cold wash of clarity to come over me, separating me from the nightmare.

And yet, I am awake.

My heart is a bass drum when I finally leave the bathroom and return to the kitchen for food.

My father is seated at the island, working on a plate of spaghetti, when I descend the creaking stairs. He points to another one that's plated and ready to go on the counter, and I take it. I don't say anything for a while, but eat without looking up at him.

All traces of our earlier fight, as least as far as I can tell, have washed away, and we are calm again. Or, rather, he is calm again.

My mind still thunders and races, my heart reckless and wild as the words *Come play* trace along my thoughts.

I find something else for my mind to hold on to. A happier, kinder thought.

"It's sweet that you still bring bog laurel to Eve's room." I take a bite, and then look up at him. He watches me silently. "After all this time. You remembered how much she loved it."

A weighty silence stretches on, and I return my attention to my spaghetti. It isn't like how Mom used to make it, but I'm hungry, and it's a dish that's hard to do wrong.

"What are you talking about?" Dad finally asks, like he's been working out exactly what question to ask for the last few moments.

"The bog laurel in Eve's bedroom. It's nice of you to still bring it to her."

His brows furrow, just a little. I can't tell if he's confused, or worried about me. "I haven't been in her room in . . . God, I don't know. Months."

That coldness creeps in again as my eyes move to the stairs. I can still smell the flowers in my memory – the fresh, floral scent of them filling up her bedroom like they were waiting for her to return. Like she was still there, or would be there, and the next time the screen door opened and closed she would go hopping up the stairs two at a time to go play the guitar or pretend to study while talking to her friends.

"Maybe you just thought you saw it," Dad offers gently. "I know you haven't been back in a while. Some memories are hard to let go of."

He returns to his food, and the mood around us is thick and dark now. Murky, in a way that's worse than before.

"Yeah," I tell him, taking another bite, even though my stomach is turning. "Maybe you're right."

It isn't very late, but the travel has worn me down to the bone and my jaunt into the Moss has left my soul threadbare, so I climb the stairs to sleep when it's only just gone nine o'clock.

My feet take me first to Eve's room, even though I don't remember wanting to go there. The vase on the dresser, coated in dust, is bare of flowers, or even any hint that there were ever any at all.

So much travel. Too many ghosts, following me onto planes. Not enough sensible things, like sleep. So sleep is what I do, after crawling into my bed, kicking off my shoes and rolling over to face the ceiling.

No more bogs and bog flowers and shadows and ghouls riding deer-that-aren't-deer into the fog.

Only sleep.

ten

JORDAN'S OLDER SISTER HAD a baby last year, and she and her husband, along with Jordan's mom, dad and younger brother, are all going apple picking today. I think it was only out of pity because I'm alone so much, but he invited me to come alone, and of course I said yes. It used to be something that my family did in the old days, but now Dad works a lot, and I wouldn't go myself, so tagging along with Jordan's family is a nice way to enjoy the season before it's over.

At any rate, it will serve as a nice distraction before my interview in the afternoon.

I laugh when I climb into his truck to find that we have both donned checked shirts for the occasion.

"It's the autumn uniform," he jokes as we get on the road. "My sister will probably look like a human pumpkin spice latte."

"'Tis the season," I say. There's a certain magic in the way he laughs. One that makes it impossible not to smile. Contagious. Infectious. I hadn't realised how much I had missed it. How healing it sounds, and how needed.

All around us is the only forest fire that isn't dangerous: the flame-red and sunset-orange leaves lighting up the world. They stay this way for maybe two or three weeks before rapidly dying away, but that short time is enough to get you through the winter. The memory of all that violent colour before everything turns white.

The orchard is only a short drive away, owned by the same family for the past few generations. Only a couple of cars sit in the parking lot when we pull in, and one of them I recognise as Jordan's mom's car. She's standing outside with his dad and the others, and she gives us a big wave when we pull in.

There's something freeing about being here, leaving the Moss and the vanishings behind for something simple and sweet like apple picking. I feel like I'm part of a family again, even though half of mine is still missing, and in this moment, things feel good.

"Gosh, I feel like it's been a decade since I saw you last," his mom says, hugging me. "I see your dad from time to time, though. Seems like he's keeping well."

"He stays busy. I think that's for the best."

"Too bad he couldn't come get apples today, but we'll be sure to pick enough for you to take some home to him."

"He'll love that," I say, sending a nod and a smile to Jordan's sister, who is, as anticipated, dressed in an orange sweater dress with boots. Jordan winks at me when I catch his eye. "I'll see if I can remember how to bake an apple pie."

"How very American of you," Jordan says, as we all start drifting towards the orchard. His sister, Cece, her husband and Jordan's younger brother all walk in a small group, while I linger at the back as we pass tree after tree decked out in small red and green jewels.

There's a lightness to the air that gives me room to breathe, and I trail a hand along the green leaves as everyone pauses now and then to pluck a few apples.

"What are your plans for after you graduate?" Jordan's mom asks me, holding a branch still so she can pick a whole cluster.

"I haven't fully decided," I tell her, helping to add a few ripe apples to her bag. "I think I might take a year out to just breathe a little, then study poetry. Or literature. I used to love reading a lot, before things got weird. I think I'd enjoy studying it."

"I remember seeing you carrying books around at some of the games at school," she says with a laugh. "Books are a great thing to make a career out of."

"I don't know what I'd do with it," I admit. "But I like it, and dad says you have to like what you do."

"He's damn right," she says, sending a pointed look to her son. "That's what I keep telling Jordan, since he likes physics so much, but he's worried his dad will be disappointed if he doesn't go into carpentry."

"No, he *will* be disappointed if I don't go into carpentry," Jordan corrects.

"And that's somehow your problem?"

He shrugs and pulls down an apple to eat, as I chime in: "There's enough in life to make you unhappy. The least you can do is find a job you love."

Eve always used to talk about becoming a photographer, because she got that Polaroid camera and had a good eye for framing. She was always having Mom or Dad stop the car when we passed something that was crying out to be photographed. And she was good, too. She got a picture of fog rolling across a lake one time that looked like something from another planet. Pictures don't always do the real thing justice, but somehow she found a way.

"Anyway, I'll stop preaching," says Jordan's mom. "I hope you're coming back with us today. We can bake something for you to take home to your dad."

Jordan sends me a questioning look, and I shrug. "I'll have to check with my people."

His mom laughs, and a crow calls nearby, and a few other families nearby laugh as they try to get the perfect family picture, and this day feels just as quiet and beautiful as I need. I don't ever want to let it go.

eleven

JORDAN IS BUSY IN the afternoon, so I booked a taxi to take me into the next town. It's more of an actual town than Scarrow is, with triple the population and more buildings, restaurants and general signs of life. But, more importantly, they also house a local news station, and that is my destination. I've been dreading this with everything in me, but a girl went missing. People want to follow the story, and I'd rather the story – or the update, in this case – came from me.

I just hate the questions I know are coming. The ones that still don't have answers but people ask anyway, hoping to be the first to hear some unknown tidbit to spread around the town. Like it hasn't just been a year with no leads, no trace and no Eve.

The taxi pulls up outside the studio and I swipe my card, hop out and shut the door. It takes a solid minute for me to gather the strength to go through the door. It's not a fancy building. There isn't even much to give away that it's a studio, other than the sign on the door. But nerves and dread still bubble up, like a carbonated drink in my belly. It's a thick, uncomfortable feeling that makes me want to flag the taxi back down and jump inside.

But this is for Eve.

It's an unfussy room, with a camera, a microphone and a woman named Stephanie who seems tired but like she's trying to be sweet. She has highlighted hair that's curled into beach waves and lipstick that makes me think of cherry blossoms. We all exchange minimal pleasantries as we take our spots, the camera angles are worked out and last minute details are seen to.

I don't look once at the camera, because I'm afraid if I do then the nerves will take over and I might pass out cold. I don't faint often, but I'm also not a stranger to it.

Luckily, this is being pre-recorded for the evening news and isn't live.

"So, it's been a year. Over a year, in fact."

I nod once. "It has."

"What has that year been like for you? I think for so many of us, we see her picture everywhere, and we know the story like the back of our hand, so we feel like we know her. Like we know all the ins and outs. But as her sister, how has the past year been for you?"

I have to muster up a response. Eve lives unending in all of my thoughts, waking and asleep, filling up every corner, every day, but speaking about her out loud sometimes makes the words bunch up in my chest.

"It's felt like a decade. Every morning, I still look outside, still check her room. Still feel like she'll just come walking back into our lives as easily as she left them. I don't think that hope will ever die. I hope it doesn't."

"You two were close?"

"Very close. I always wanted to be her. Or like her, anyway."

"Have you been able to aid in the investigation at all? Provide any details that might help to point law enforcement in the right direction?"

I pull in a breath. Thoughts of the bog rise up. "I wish. They searched the bog, which was the one place I know she loved. God knows why. If she's there, it hasn't given her up yet."

Stephanie goes quiet, and her eyes darken. "That's a chilling thought, Emma."

I shrug. "It's a chilling place. It's very good at keeping secrets."

"Why do you suspect it has something to do with her disappearance?"

The backdrop of my thoughts lights up with shadowy memories. Of Eve's eagerness to give the dying bird to the Moss. Of the antlers that were there one moment and gone the next. Of the ghosts that prowl through our periphery, hiding in almost-plain sight. There is something rotten in the Moss. In the house that stands beside it. And it has always felt like that rottenness had spread to us, too.

"Suspect is a very . . . clinical word. The Moss is a dangerous little corner of the world. People fall in. Drown. Get stuck and dehydrate. And it always fascinated her. I think there was something about the danger that intoxicated her, and she never recovered."

"You believe she went in, and never came back out?"

"I don't know what happened. I wish I did. I would give anything to know. But it felt like a good place to start, so I informed the police."

"And the search turned up nothing."

"Nothing."

"Not even a trace. No scraps of clothing. No items lost along the way. No breadcrumbs, like Hansel and Gretel."

I wince at the way she says it, like my sister's disappearance is some fable the locals read as a cautionary tale. "No. They found nothing to make them believe she went inside."

"Yet, you still believe she did."

It's a question, but it doesn't sound like one. "I don't know what I believe. That's the thing about people who go missing without a trace. There's nothing to go on. But I know she loved the Moss. For whatever reason, she loved it. That will always stick out in my mind."

Stephanie shifts in her seat, and it seems to signal an approaching change in the conversation. "Talk to me about your dad. So many people believe he was somehow involved with the disappearances, both of Eve, and your mother years ago. Do you ever feel afraid, now that you're back in town? Do you ever worry that you might be next?"

I hold her gaze and let the storm that's been gathering in my heart spread to my face. Let it cloud up the room a bit. She notices but doesn't rephrase her question. "No," I say sharply. "My father had nothing to do with it, either time."

"You sound so certain. How can you be sure, when even police haven't officially ruled out his involvement?"

"Because I know him better than anyone. He's easy prey for the local rumour mill. And I love my sister. If I had a reason to suspect my father, I wouldn't keep that a secret. He is just as in the dark about this as I am. As you are, clearly."

Her lips twitch at my little dig but she seems otherwise undaunted by it. "Then if it isn't him, what do you have to say to anyone who might have taken her, if in fact she was kidnapped, or ran away?"

The question throws me a little. I've spent an extraordinary amount of time imagining what I would say to Eve if she turned up again one day, but I've never thought about what I would say to a kidnapper. I suppose, really, I never thought she was kidnapped. It just never seemed to fit the picture.

When the words finally come to me, I speak them low, and clear. "I would say, if you have her, I will do whatever it takes to get her back. And I would hate for anyone to find out exactly how far I would go."

I shiver a little at the words, but I know every one of them is true. I would do anything, go anywhere, suffer whatever came my way to get her back.

Stephanie blinks a few times, then nods. "Well, all of us here in the studio, here in Maine, and I suspect beyond, all wish her a safe and speedy return. And for you and . . . your father, we wish comfort, and if need be, closure."

Closure. The one thing I have never wanted for a second, because closure would mean she was gone, and if she was gone . . .

"Thank you for having me."

I can hear the TV playing downstairs as I lie in my bed, staring up at the ceiling. The edges of the words I spoke earlier fill the house, indistinctly. Dad is watching the programme, and I have no desire to see it played. No desire to see the twists of pain on his face when Stephanie asks me about my father's role in the disappearances.

A trail of thoughts I do not usually entertain find their way in, and for a moment I let them have their way. *What if he really did play a role? What if I live under the same roof as a murderer?*

But it is absurd. My dad watched the same thing I did. Watched as Eve orbited around the Moss for years, growing closer and closer like binary stars that spin and spin until they finally collide, ruining everything around them. That collision happened a year ago. I can feel it in my bones. My marrow. The depths of my soul.

After a few more minutes, the sounds of the TV cut off, and the house goes quiet. I wait to see if he will come up, but there are no sounds of footsteps on the stairs. So instead, I roll off the bed and head down to the living room, finding Dad standing by the screen door and staring out. The TV is off, a black surface that only shows distorted reflections.

"I'm sorry," I say when a minute or two has slipped by. He turns and looks at me, that sadness I was hoping not to see writhing across his face.

"It isn't your fault," he tells me, but I still feel responsible. Perhaps I should have been more direct with Stephanie or done more to shut down that line of questioning altogether.

"I don't think anyone will look at me the same again," he says. There's that shakiness to his voice that so often comes before tears. "And to a degree, I don't even care. I don't care what people think about me. All I want is to get her back. That's the beginning and the end of it. All I can think about. But when the phone stops ringing and people stop coming around, and everyone looks at you in the grocery store like you might be the last person they see while they're alive, it grates away at you. And you . . . you shouldn't have to answer those questions, Emma. No one should corner you like that. Sometimes, I think about leaving. Going to Vermont or Massachusetts, or even California. Staying with family for a while. Starting something new."

He turns to look outside again. Maybe I should cross the room to give him a hug, but my feet stay rooted to the spot. I can't stomach the thought of leaving. Of setting the Moss and the memories behind us and driving away with all of this unfinished business still rotting away.

"But I can't leave," he continues. "Not before she's come back. Not before we know what happened. I want to be standing right here, and see her coming back to the house, and I want her to know that we never gave up."

My own throat tightens, and I swallow hard.

"I won't leave," I say. "Ever. I want to wait."

The smile he offers me is a sad one, but it's a smile all the same. "Then we will wait," he replies, and this time, I do hug him.

twelve

Before Mom

IT IS THE SUMMER, *the year I turn thirteen, and a hot one. The mornings come early, and the days linger late, and in between, the sun bakes us like an oven set to grill. Dad bought us a splash pool to cool off in outside, but even that warms up quickly, and our house is on a well. We cannot refill it every day.*

It's the heat that wakes me up, sweat soaking into the bedding and making it impossible to get comfortable. The only air conditioner we have upstairs is in the hallway in an attempt to reach all three bedrooms, but it does very little unless you stand directly in front of it.

The clock on my bedside table reads 5.15 a.m., and the sun is just coming up outside. Already, a chorus of birds chimes in the trees outside, and I know I won't be getting back to sleep. Not between the heat and the noise and the general sense of annoyance that has settled in and found a home. I kick off the thin blanket and slide on the little slippers that sit next to my bed. Before I can leave the room to go downstairs in search of food, something outside catches my attention. I have to blink a few times to clear my vision after sleeping and sweating, but when I do, it's a person. My mom, I think, slowly making her way from the house towards the Moss.

There is something unhurried and dreamlike about the way she walks, still in her pyjamas and with her eyes trained on the bog, paying little attention to where she's walking. Maybe sleepwalking, although I don't know much about it. If the heat woke me up, it could have woken her up, and being out in the morning air sounds better to me than being inside this stuffy house, so I can't blame her.

I slip down the stairs and out the door quietly, careful not to let it slap against the house and wake anyone else up. By the time I get outside, she is only a tiny and distant form in white, and suddenly the reality of where she's going sets in.

I am not meant to go to the Moss. Ever. But if I can't, then why is she?

Glancing back into the house, I steal off the porch and into the garden, climbing over the fence and making my way down after her. I don't have to enter the Moss, but if it's as dangerous as my dad makes it sound, then she shouldn't be down there alone. So I follow her, as quickly as I can despite my slippers and the damp ground. The going is slow, but up ahead I can see that she has stopped. It gives me more time to catch up to her.

She stands just on the edge of where the Moss begins, even though the transition is hard to tell. There is a point where there is suddenly less ground than before, more water, and the plants all change a little. More reedy and shrubby.

The morning light is still grey and dim, the sun not having crested the horizon yet, and mist still holds fast to the ground. Ahead, my mother reaches out a hand to something, palm out, her fingers upright – and before her, I see a yellowish light dancing around. Not a flashlight or anything of that kind. It isn't attached, as far as I can tell. It's just free-floating, moving and waving, almost like it's excited to see her. Like it's inviting her in.

I've seen that light before, out my bedroom window when my mother was watching it, but I thought little of it. Fireflies, maybe, or someone out trespassing in the bog. But up close, there is something haunted and strange about it. Something that feels very much apart from the world and everything in it.

The movement carries on, like it is pulling her inside, urging her to follow, but she stays still with her hand outstretched. This could all be a dream. So little of it feels real, except for the morning air and the scent of the bog and the call of the birds nearby. But what's happening before me feels dreamlike, maybe born from the hot night air and bad sleep.

I am about to step forward again, to find out if she can hear me and see me, but a hand on my shoulder makes me start.

It's my dad, although I didn't hear him approach.

"Don't," he says quietly, barely above a whisper. "Go back to the house." There is an order in his voice. I do not have a choice.

With a final look at my mother, whose hand has returned to her side, I cross my arms over myself and climb the garden to the house again. They are too far away to see clearly by the time I reach the porch, so I head back inside and go back up to my bed, where I lie and stare at the ceiling until the morning finishes taking hold of the world.

thirteen

MORNING IS A STRANGE, lurching thing that arrives in fits and starts. I fell asleep early, and it made my night's sleep uneven. For hours, as the sun haunts the edges of the sky, pewter and then blue and then peach, I lie in a state of both wakefulness and sleep, neither one nor the other. Then the sound of the screen door closing downstairs brings me round fully and I open my eyes.

I am not alone in the room, although I can't place why. I can see no one else, and there is not a fibre out of place, but a distinct presence sits – or perhaps stands – beside me. As with the girl, when I saw her on the plane, he's there just to my right if I don't look too hard, although this time I can't see him so much as just make out a shape. An outline, haunting my periphery. A man, I think. Black clothing, not of this era. Not of any recent era. But the details aren't there.

My heart is thunder in my ears, and I don't dare to move. Don't dare to breathe. I just lie still, staring up, frozen in place in my bed. And it's then that I realise my pounding heart is not the only sound in the room. That steady *drip drip drip* of water is back, and out of the corner of my eye, I can see it falling from the ceiling and onto the desk.

I can't look at it because then I would have to look at the man in black, and his presence is too awful, too suffocating and dark, to try for a better look. Even though I know he will just fade to invisibility if I tried. No part of me wants to risk seeing him better. This impression of him is enough. Too much.

Sweat soaks into my bedding.

Emma.

My name comes to me, but I don't hear it so much as feel it, like hot breath on my neck. The stench of rot drifts in behind it – the same rotten smell that always haunts the bog. Swallowing hard and trembling like a candle flame in the wind, I snap my head towards him, though he instantly vanishes into the ether.

"*What?*" I say, harshly. Bitingly. I feel safest when my words have sharp edges. "What do you want?"

There is no answer, of course, but I can feel something like a departure, and an instant later I am alone again. The strangest relief floods in, and with it the faint and distant scent of bog laurel. I close my eyes against the memories it brings back, my sister holding armfuls of it and wandering around in the warm sunshine, humming a tune and stuck – always stuck – in her own little world.

Memories, memories, memories, everywhere. I climb out of bed, kicking off the covers, and leave the room before any more can find their way back.

There is no one else in the kitchen, but it is full of the evidence of my dad having started his morning. A coffee cup in the sink. A ring of it spilt on the counter and never noticed, or never wiped up. The chairs that sit at the island are askew, and I hate all of it. It's not the way Mom used to leave the kitchen. She loved it too much, loved everything about cooking and just sitting in here to sip tea and stare out the window and drink in the heart of the home.

I pass everything and move to the fridge, where a magnet holds a small scrap of paper that has only a name and a phone number written on it. Jordan's new number. He left it in case I needed anything, and today, I need a friend. Even a friend with awkward baggage, who I still worry is waiting for the answer I never gave him, but is too polite to ask.

I punch the number into my phone and open up a new text.

Are you free after school?

He responds almost immediately.

Is this the police? Because if so, no.

I laugh aloud.

It's Emma.

Emma! Yes, I'll be free.

Pick me up then?

I'll be there.

I leave it at that.

A sea of eyes watch as I enter the school for the first time in over a year. Or perhaps I'm just imagining it. But I do meet the eyes of curious students, some who seem surprised to see me, and others who don't. I suppose word has travelled fast that I am home.

The halls feel strange and unfamiliar, despite how long I spent here. Despite all the classes, the games, the homecomings. All the things I did to try to feel like everyone else, before going home to the Moss. It never quite worked. I never quite felt like I belonged –

even less so now, as I hug my books tight to my chest and search for my first classroom.

I am joining partway through the school year. I'll be behind everyone else, but the school understood. No one minds, given the circumstances. There are faces I know, and some I don't, but everyone seems to know me. Everyone in Scarrow knows our family.

English is my first class. I sit way at the back of the room. Jordan and I share one class, at the end of the day. But I wish he was here now. Wish for a comforting, warm face to anchor me to this cold, lonely place.

There is someone I know at the front of the room, and he turns once to give me a long, unreadable look. Theo, the only boy I know that Eve ever fell for. But not even he was enough to keep her attention here, on the world in which she lived, instead of the shadows of the Moss. I still don't know if he blames me for telling the police his name. For implicating him in her disappearance. Could he blame me, really? Would anyone have done anything differently?

I step outside for a break after a hasty lunch. The walls feel so close, the air too thick, and my soul longs for blue sky and birdsong. I lean against the wall, drinking in gulps of the afternoon air with my eyes closed, when voices shatter my calm.

Amelia, a classmate I have never once managed to get along with, and two of her friends watch me from a few paces away, their faces caught somewhere between fearful and annoyed.

"What are you doing out here?" Amelia asks. She takes a small step back. When Eve disappeared, many of the rumours that spread like wildfire through the school could be traced back to her.

That she had run away to join a cult, that our father was a serial killer, that she was pregnant and ashamed.

The panic of a few moments ago lessens some, as annoyance and a touch of resentment take their place. The girls didn't need to pass me. Didn't need to talk to me. But by interacting with me, they'll have stories to tell later. Rumours to start. Walking away would only make it seem like they'd won something, so I decide instead to answer.

I can tell that *talking to dead people* or *summoning a coven of witches* is the sort of answer Amelia expects. "Trying to keep up the tan I got in California," I say instead.

She isn't impressed. Looks around to see if anyone is watching, but there is hardly anyone else outside.

"It's fine," I say, putting a little more distance between us. "I don't often bite, unless provoked."

The joke doesn't land. Amelia's eyes narrow, her head tilting.

"People disappear when they go near you," one of the other girls says. "We don't want to be next."

A laugh catches in my throat, but behind it is a deep, aching hurt. *Walk away,* common sense says. But I'm angry, and hurt, and I want to retaliate. "Then don't come near me," I tell them through my teeth, and yank the large doors open to go back inside.

fourteen

THE HOUSE RUMBLES AS Jordan's truck makes its way along the driveway an hour or two after school. He has an after-school study group for physics that I don't, or I would have left with him. I sit on a rocking chair on the front porch, resting my elbows on my knees and watching the bog as though if I look away for a moment it might sneak up on me. That presence that was with me in my room this morning still sits fresh and awful in my mind, and some small part of me worries that I might be losing my mind. Too much loss. Too much pain. Not enough places to stash it.

But a lightness fills me as Jordan drives closer. My spirits lifting, even just a little.

"You coming?" Jordan calls from the truck. I haul myself to my feet and hop down the porch steps, slipping into the seat beside him.

"Thanks for picking me up," I tell him.

He cranks the truck into reverse, a breeze wandering through the open windows. "It was this or play a video game, and one of those is objectively healthier."

"The video game?" I quip, because in no way am I healthy to be around.

He stops the truck at the end of the driveway and looks at me, but I don't notice at first because I'm turned away, looking out the window back towards the bog. I'm not even sure why.

"So . . ."

I turn back to face him. "Yes?"

"Where am I going?"

"Shit. Yeah. Um . . ." It takes me a minute. An idea had felt so fully formed in my head, but I'd never quite acknowledged it into a plan. "The town museum, I think. I have some . . . questions about the house. My mom probably knew more about it than my dad, but she's . . ." I trail off, unsure of how to continue, but Jordan jumps in.

"Right. The museum. Let's do it."

We pull out onto the road and the wind whisks through the truck, threatening to undo the tight ponytail I had pulled my hair into earlier. Neither of us speaks for a short while, as we just wind along the road, darting in and out of the shadows of the trees. The sun is in fine form today, casting a harsh light over everything, even glinting off the pavement.

"What are you looking to find out?" Jordan asks, after a minute.

Two of my fingers drum in quick succession by the window. Jordan has always been good, and nice, and the kind of person to whom you could tell anything, but the troubled goings-on of Lark House are hardly light conversation. I decide to dance around it, while still allowing for some honesty.

"I think there's something strange about it, which I know is *very* specific. But I want to know more."

"It's an old house. Old houses have long histories. I went into a house in England one time that was built in the 1600s. I wouldn't say I'm a sceptic, but I'm not exactly a ghost hunter, either. But there was definitely something about that old house that sticks with me to this day. Like with so much history, it just piles up and up until it's something you can feel."

A few heartbeats slip by. I know exactly, precisely, what he means. "Yeah, that . . . that might be it."

The town's historical society and museum take up the same small building. Just a couple of rooms put together. It was an old school from the nineteenth century that continued to be used as such right up until the eighties, when they at last moved into a bigger building across town. I only know that because the museum hosts a trick-or-treating event at Halloween that my mother always volunteered at, and the older woman who runs it told us the story every year of how she attended school in this exact building until she graduated.

"Might be a dead end," Jordan tells me, hopping out of the truck. "Most information is available online nowadays, but I assume you've already looked there."

I don't tell him that I spent a good portion of my time in California trying to learn about the house. "Yeah, not much luck."

Inside is small and cramped and filled with shelves of random items that have been found around the town over time. None of them are very interesting – no dinosaurs or mammoth tusks in this part of the world – but the locals still cherish them all the same. Old farming equipment, coins, sets of china, things of that nature. I heard someone in the forties dug up a skull very near to the bog, but that didn't make it into the town's display. It wasn't considered family-friendly, although I remember Eve saying she would have loved to see it.

The man behind the counter bids us a good day, but he watches me as if I'm going to steal something. It's a look I've seen before, of uncertainty or distrust because of the strangeness that follows my family. I just nod to him, while Jordan strikes up a conversation first about the weather – always the weather – and then about the house.

"You must know Emma here. Carver. Lives over on the edge of the Moss, in the old white house."

The man nods to me just once, without smiling. "Nathaniel's daughter, right?" Like he doesn't know.

"Right," I say.

"I'd heard you were in town again. What brought you back?" He leans his elbows on the counter, staring. Like my family is a running soap opera that the town can't get enough of but also wants to keep at arm's length.

"My dad," I tell him. "I missed him." *And I want to find my sister,* I don't say.

He says nothing for a time, then asks, "Good to be back?"

"Yeah. The town feels the same," I tell him, holding his gaze. "Just with fewer people in it."

He nods sombrely at the reference to my missing sister. "She may come back, you know."

I want nothing more than to believe it.

I take advantage of the natural breaking point and turn to inspect some old, chipped dishes that were found near one of the more historic homes in the town. Jordan steps forward again and leaps straight to the point.

"We were wondering what you can tell us about the house. Lark House, by the Moss. Or, if you can't tell us much, who might be able to."

I glance back subtly, and the man eyes Jordan over his glasses.

"I guess that depends on what you want to know. Tax records and deeds and whatnot are usually pretty easy to find online."

"Maybe we could start with the previous owners. Any of them. Any random facts. Deaths, major events. Things like that."

The man looks at me again, and I don't look away.

He stands up straighter. "Well, not much was written down back then. Anything we know about any of the older houses has been pieced together or passed down through the families. And you can never rely on word of mouth to hold much water. You know how people are."

"Did anyone die there?" I ask, because this feels like the sort of person you need to be direct with.

"Lots of people, I'm sure. People didn't go to hospitals to die in those days. But I presume you mean did anyone die under . . . unnatural circumstances?"

I let my silence be my reply.

He turns away and goes to a bookshelf behind the counter that holds some large, old books. When he brings one back and opens it, it looks like a register of some sort, a list of names with small details scrawled next to them. I send Jordan a quizzical look, but he just shrugs in a *We're just along for the ride* kind of way.

"Sorry, I couldn't recall the name." A pause. "Simon Lark. That's the one that comes to mind, but there's not much to tell. He built and lived in the house from 1705 until 1744, when he died. His daughter passed away at some point during that time, but some people said she went missing. Blamed it on the bog. Not a lot of details from that time, I'm afraid."

A chill seems to drift into the room. It's always the Moss. Somehow.

"How did he die?" I ask quietly.

"I wish I could say. The how and the why don't always linger on through the years. But he's likely buried somewhere on the property. I don't think there's any record of him in the town graveyards."

Jordan turns to me and cocks an eyebrow, perhaps unsure of what to ask next. I run my tongue along my teeth, thinking.

"Thanks for your time."

"It's what I do. And it's good to have you back. Tell your dad I said hello."

"Will do." I head for the door, with Jordan close behind me. He reaches to try to open the door for me, but I'm faster and push it open first. The cool air smacks us as soon as we exit.

"There you go," he says once we're in the truck, like he's proud of himself. "Your first lead."

"Lead to what?" I ask, pulling one foot up onto the seat of the truck and hugging it.

"To whatever it is you're trying to find."

Find. It's such an active word to describe my life, at least of late. If I could find anything, it would be Eve, but if all the local law enforcement officers have failed, then what business do I have thinking I could do better? But all the while I was in California, it felt like something was always just out of sight, whispering things to me that I couldn't quite understand. Calling me to something. Begging me. Pulling me. So I came back, expecting to just continue cruising in this holding pattern I've felt caught up in for the past year. Two. Three.

Then that *strangeness* grew, the same uncanny sense that had haunted the house and the bog even when Eve was still here.

Stay away from the Sedge Man. He won't stop, like a hunter, until there's nothing left of you.

So that was it, I guess. Why I came here. Why I'm out with a boy I tried to forget. To find whatever answers will take me out of this stagnant existence. To find answers that might point me towards Eve. I was younger when my mom vanished. Too young to really know how to help. But not this time. The year I spent away against my will has already set me back, but now I feel like it's finally my chance. To find Eve, before it's too late. If it's not too late already.

Who was the man my sister and I have seen? What – or who – took her away from me? If strangeness insists on following me around, then I at least deserve some answers. I deserve to find out what happened. I owe it to myself, to her, to Mom, to Dad.

Jordan's statement felt an awful lot like a question, but I'm not sure I'm ready to tell him the answer yet. To lay bare the details of the bizarre happenings at our home. Perhaps he wouldn't laugh, but instead listen and understand and even help. But these are early days yet, and I'm still learning to walk again, at least through this delicate new life back at home without Mom and Eve.

I lean my head and elbow out the window into the sunshine as we head back towards my house. I can feel Jordan's gaze on me, but leave him be until the drive is halfway over, just soaking in the autumn sun and the wind and letting myself get as close to forgetting as I've managed in a long while. The earthy bouquet of evergreen trees reaches for me from the forest. It plucks back memories of holidays or traipsing through the woods beyond the house with Eve, looking for ferns or mushrooms or just wandering because sometimes the house felt too small.

Then just like that, I'm wrenched back.

"So," Jordan says, as though sensing the shift in my thoughts. "What's next in your . . . scavenger hunt for the past?"

A smile twists at my mouth. That's just how it feels sometimes, like I'm on a scavenger hunt for the truth of what happened. To understand the pieces left behind by Mom and Eve. So much of our life felt like me standing on the other side of a foggy window, face pressed up against the glass, and trying to watch their every move, but only ever seeing smudges and shapes. No details. No answers.

Stay away from the Sedge Man.

The words were senseless, full of nothing. Sedge was a plant that grew around the bog. And who was this man? The presence that visits me sometimes, certainly, but who *is* he? Or what is he? And if I am meant to stay away from him, why not tell me more? Why keep secrets? But Eve loved her secrets. They were in the air she breathed and the reflections in her eyes and tucked behind her carefully chosen words.

"I don't know," I told him. "I suppose I have enough to start googling."

"You'd be surprised what you can find online. And you could always try to find previous owners, if you're really interested in the history of the house."

"There's an idea," I reply absently.

That weight in the pit of my stomach slips back the moment the tyres turn into the driveway. Since I've been back, I've realised it was always there, lurking through the long summers of childhood and the cold winters of my teen years. That sinking, creeping, rotting feeling like the moments before throwing up. So much time spent here made me grow used to it, even learning to barely notice it, but my time away has stripped me of whatever resilience I'd built up.

Jordan shifts in his seat, and I wonder if he can feel it, too.

I start to climb out as soon as the truck stops, but he puts a hand suddenly – gently – on my elbow.

"Hey, Emma," he says, and I almost startle at how softly he says my name. My eyes find his and stay there, trying to ascertain what he'll say next. Warmth flutters in my chest, like a butterfly's wings. Then I stop – grit my teeth. *Calm down.* "You don't have to tell me what's going on. Really. It's none of my business. But I am always happy to help, even without asking any questions. I know being back is a lot, and being alone might be painful. So if you just need someone around, but you don't want to fill them in on the details, just call me. OK? I mean it."

Suddenly, I want to cry, or laugh, or hug him, or – Jesus Christ, kiss him – but I don't do any of those things. "Thanks, Jordan," I reply, and I hope he can feel the sincerity. I really am grateful, and I really, truly do not like being alone. "I'll call you."

I climb out, choking on a lump in my throat, and head back towards the house.

fifteen

Before Mom

I HAVE NO MEMORY of seeing ghosts when I was young. None before eleven or twelve. At fifteen, I have my first experience with a ghost that rattles my core.

I am seated on the floor with my homework spread out around me, trying to make sense of it all and finish it before my mom calls us down for dinner, when, very slowly, my bedroom door closes with a long, drawn-out groan. No breeze. No hand. No other body in the room to make it move. I cannot think to do anything but stare at it, mind tripping and stumbling as it tries to fill in the blanks of what just happened. How it could be possible. I settle on the most likely thing.

"Not funny, Eve," I call, turning my attention back to the papers on the floor. But a heavy, dreadful feeling in my stomach keeps me from being able to focus on it. The numbers on the papers all blend together into chaos, and I keep blinking like it will put them all back into order. When there is no answer, after a long moment, I call out again. "Eve, open the door."

Nothing.

Caught between annoyed and afraid, I start to climb to my feet so I can open it again, but something makes me freeze. Soft thuds, like the sound of shoes on the floor. Walking from my door and coming to stand just behind me. Slowly. Deliberately. One awful step at a time.

My breath is short and ragged, and I think there is something behind me out of the corner of my eye, but it is little more than a shadow. It could just be the edge of my mascara and the light coming through the window – but the shadow stands just where the footsteps stopped.

I turn my eyes back to the ground, collecting myself, then whisper, "Is someone there?"

No voice answers me, which is only a small relief and very short-lived. Then, another footstep, with the awful creaking, stretching sound of leather boots as something bends towards me. The shadow is closer now, but only a flutter on the outskirts of my vision. I cannot angle it into any more of a thing than that, but now, at least, I am certain that there is something there.

"Who are you?" I whisper, because my voice has fled the room.

I am the end, comes the reply, but the voice is distant and intangible. It fills my veins with shards of ice that sting and set me to trembling.

"Who are you?" I ask again, but the voice does not return. Instead, the boots creak again, and more footsteps sound on the floor, and the door opens to just where it was before. The papers before me flutter with the breeze it creates on opening and there is the sense of someone departing, and a minute later, it is as if nothing ever happened.

Except something did happen. I can still hear the voice in my head. Feel the breath on my neck. Catch the echoes of the leather's awful creak as the ghost bent down towards me. They are sounds that will linger, impressed upon my mind for years to come, inescapable in their awfulness.

I later find out that Eve wasn't even home, shattering what little hope I had that it was a joke, even if it was exactly the type that she would play.

sixteen

JORDAN HAS LEFT, BUT I don't feel alone. I should, because no one else is home, and I'm sitting by myself on the front porch rocking chair, but the sense of another presence is thick and overwhelming.

I scan the bog, but there is nothing out of order. Just brown and green and water and secrets. Secrets are everywhere, so deep you could drown in them, and sometimes I worry that I have. That whatever I am doing now isn't living, but slowly dying, and worse, that there is very little difference.

To my left, a shape moves, but when I turn to look, there's nothing there. I eye the garden and the nearby trees, thinking about Simon Lark and where he might be buried. Where would a body have been buried in the 1700s? Where would *I* bury a body? It's a wicked thought, but it springs to mind as I stand and slip down the porch steps. I'm not even certain what I'm hoping to find. As if answers will just be etched like a name into the gravestone.

Indecision creeps in, so before it can take too strong a hold, I let my feet go where they will, and just follow along quietly. Tall grasses reach for me, and I pluck the tips of them off as I walk, rolling them between my fingers before tossing them away again.

Pieces of hair that have fallen from my ponytail tickle my

face in the light breeze. I am headed for the far corner of the garden, opposite the porch and by a dense line of trees, close to the bog. A tumbledown fence tries to cordon off this area of the Moss, because it hosts a small but very deep pool that my father once fell into. He claims to have plunged several feet down and still not been able to reach the bottom, so he extended the fence that keeps us out of the Moss, though it is slowly being reclaimed by nature.

I climb over the beams and carry on, the dark, hungry water shivering lightly as I approach. A dank chill skitters over me, coiling and reaching. Something forces me to stop, even though I want to press on right to the water's edge. Then a breeze whips in, suddenly and fiercely, and is gone in the space of a heartbeat.

The land goes very still. The leaves stop whispering. The water stops rippling. Even my breathing slows, fear sparking to life.

Something urges me to turn around. Movement draws my attention, and that spark of fear cascades into something hot and dangerous. My heart skips and thunders, unleashed like a violent summer storm.

A girl makes her way across the garden towards me, from the house, walking through the fence as though it was never there at all. Her hands are folded in front of her, and her eyes are on the Moss. I have seen this girl before – most recently on the plane, then in the field on the way home from the airport – but this time I am able to watch her without her disappearing. So I know, real though she looks, she can't be.

When I look at her, she doesn't vanish. Doesn't slip away into my periphery, like she's always done before. Perhaps this close to the Moss, she doesn't need to.

With slow, careful steps, she moves closer and closer, then stops and lowers herself to sit on the ground, where it drops down into the deep, swampy pool of water.

Silence surrounds her – the grass, trees and water seeming too afraid to move. She hasn't noticed me, although I can't imagine how. She sits only steps from where I stand, watching. Her clothes are simple and dated, a white nightgown with ruffles at the neck.

She is not my sister, but something about her reminds me of Eve. A curious energy. A longing for something out of reach.

"Who are you?" I finally whisper. She doesn't turn my way. Ghosts seem willing to speak, but never to listen, I have found. Her gaze is trained on the Moss, unmoving, and after a moment, her eyes close. She sucks in a long, slow breath, drinking in something unseen. Almost as if she's feeling, communicating.

I want to take a step closer to get her attention, but before I can find the will to do so, something shifts in the air around us. Another presence – one that is familiar and wretched – sinks in. Instead of moving closer, I shrink backwards, towards another part of the fence as if I can hide behind the lichen-rich wood altogether.

A man in a black coat and boots walks towards us from the house. His face is swallowed by shadows, although I can't tell what is casting them. He moves slowly but deliberately, giving the sense of having purpose but being in no rush to see it through. His gaze does not fall on me, and the longer I watch him the more something strange begins to happen. With every other footstep, he shifts, morphing into something else entirely. A man still, but his clothes ragged, his face longer as his mouth hangs open, with grass and moss and mushrooms growing from his skin. Through his skin. Popping out of his skull. Like the fence, he has been consumed by the nature around him.

But then he seamlessly shifts back into the man in the black coat, moving ever closer to the girl that sits quietly on the bank of the Moss, like she's waiting.

He stops when he is only a few steps away from her, staring down at her.

She says something, though I can't hear the faint, distant words, and I take a step closer. He replies, but again I hear nothing, much like how she couldn't hear me only a few moments ago. Like watching a silent movie, while starting to suspect that the ending is going to change me for ever.

The words from earlier, about the man whose daughter died here, come back to me. Simon Lark, he had said.

He takes another step closer, and she stands, turning to face him. There is fear in her face, but also a deep, resounding sadness and resignation. She knows why he has come, and somehow, I know too. I reach out towards her, but neither of them can see me and my limbs begin to shake.

The man in the black coat is fast. He snatches at her shoulders quickly and forcefully, and even though she claws back at him, he sends her over the edge of the grass and into the deep pool before she has the chance to find her footing again . . .

But not before her eyes dart to me for the briefest of moments. So fleeting that I can't even be certain it happened at all.

She cannot swim, and he knows this. While she kicks and flounders and opens her mouth as if calling for help, he calmly kneels down and reaches out to where she is. He takes the neck of her nightgown and shoves her back beneath the surface. Her hands fly out from the water, clawing at his arm, reaching for the ground around her, but he holds her there, steady and unwavering, his face all shadows and covered in plant life.

That is how they stay for several long, aching minutes, my heart thundering so loudly it seems impossible that he can't hear it.

That wicked stillness lingers, the girl's body limp and invisible under the water. The man holds her for longer than he needs to, ensuring the job is done, before he at last lets her go and rises. She floats just beneath the surface, lifeless, and he stares for a long while. There is no sympathy in his eyes, nothing to show how he feels about what he's just done. Only a resonant, echoing emptiness.

"Simon," I whisper, my voice barely audible, even to me.

He looks up in my direction – looks *at* me, I'm very nearly certain, but without being able to see his eyes, I'm unsure. His face is still shrouded by moss and sedge grass and shadows. He just stands there, facing me, motionless, then he turns and climbs back up the garden towards the house, vanishing behind it.

Then I am alone again. As if nothing happened. I am nearly positive that at any moment I'll wake up to find I fell asleep on the front porch, or went for a nap in my room without remembering, but the seconds tick away as I stand unmoving in the grass, and I do not wake up. A breeze returns to the leaves, and they set to whispering about what's just happened.

I suspect that it happened long ago, that either I am dreaming it or I have somehow become caught in a memory of it. A vision, the ground here by this pool being so rich and haunted that the events couldn't help but spill out.

The pool. I cast my eyes down to where the girl's body had been floating only moments ago, but only find it empty.

Sucking in a wild breath, I let my knees buckle and collapse on to the grass.

They aren't real. They *are not* real. *But were they once?*

Shaking takes hold of me like I'm outside in the dead of winter, frozen and shivering. I fight through it and crawl towards the pool again, leaning over to peer in as far as I can without tumbling over the edge.

There is no body inside. Or, if there is, she is long out of sight. Back in the direction of the house, there is no sign of the man. Only the rocking chair exactly as I left it, moving back and forth gently in the breeze. Though it puts me in mind of someone invisible rocking lightly on the creaking porch.

Minutes slip by. I don't rush to collect my thoughts and stand, because whatever's just happened has sapped every last drop of life, energy and willpower from my bones, leaching even the marrow.

Two minutes. Five minutes. Ten.

Twenty.

Tyres on gravel. The thud of a car door. I look towards the driveway, more loose hair falling over my face, and see my dad making his way into the house. He hasn't seen me, because why would he think to look here? But lest I worry him more than I should, I force myself to my feet and make my way with unsteady steps back up to the porch.

"I thought maybe you weren't home," Dad says when I step inside. He's just coming back downstairs.

"I was taking a walk." My shoulder brushes against his as I head for the stairs myself, in desperate need of a nap, or a shower, or maybe just to lie down and stare up at the ceiling for an hour.

seventeen

DAD IS SITTING IN the living room alone when I come down later. Just sitting on the couch, staring straight ahead, and I can feel the weight of his thoughts like another presence in the room. Thick and inescapable.

He turns when the stairs squeak, pursing his lips into a thin line of greeting that isn't quite a smile, and isn't quite a frown.

"Did you sleep?" he asks, shuffling down the sofa to make room for me, but instead I move to the wingback chair across from him. Evening is gathering outside, and something is simmering on the stove. For just a moment, it feels like home.

"Yeah." I lean back and let the chair swallow me, remembering how large it seemed when I was young. I want to feel small and invisible, like I did then, but I know those days are gone.

Dad leans forward and puts his elbows on his knees, jumping in without mincing words. "I'm worried about you, Emma. Really, really worried."

I eye him from deep in the chair, his worry dark and unwelcome. But I also feel bad for him; he's done enough worrying for two lifetimes.

"I'm fine," I assure him, but I'm not even certain if it's true. Whatever happened out by the bog earlier has left me wondering if I hallucinated the whole thing, or if it was just a dream. I keep wishing it was a dream.

"I know you aren't fine." The words are quick and sharp. Not unkind so much as firm. I pluck at some loose threads on the chair and watch him.

"I think you came back too soon. I wanted to see you, of course, but I don't think you took enough time away. You needed to really put down roots. Build a life. Find distractions until all of this was ... further behind you." He motions to the house around us, shaking his head, then he looks at the floor. "I know you blame yourself for what happened. I know you feel like you could have stopped her. That because she left the note for you, you should have found something in it that led us to her."

My throat tightens, but I don't look away.

"I think coming back here just keeps cutting at you, and you grow smaller every day. And I don't want to watch you wither like ... like your mom did. Like Eve did." He shakes his head again and looks towards the door – towards the Moss.

"What was it?" I whisper, letting a single tear run down to the corner of my mouth.

His gaze meets mine again, and there is so much pain and pressure and torment in them that I haven't seen before. A man forcing himself to carry on with his life while a hundred thousand questions remain unanswered.

"What was what?" he asks quietly.

I let myself take in a deep breath, trying to keep any more tears from falling. "What came over them? Mom, and Eve."

He knows what I mean. Remembers how it became all they could speak of. How they would sit outside and stare at it for hours on end, even forgetting about meals sometimes. Remembers how Eve would come home with armfuls of bog laurel and place it in vases around her room. Remembers the long nights when she or my mom would go missing, and Dad and I would sit on the porch and wait.

There are a lot of memories that we share, and none of them are good.

"I wish I knew," he breathes suddenly, choking up. "I wish I could have stopped it. But the next best thing I can do is to keep it from happening to you."

Now would be the right time to tell him. About the girl I've seen so many times now. The presence I sometimes feel in my room, the dripping water, the vision I had out in the garden. If I can even call it a vision. I know opening up to him would be the right thing to do, because he's all I have left, and his love for me is as real as the chair enclosing me, or the ground beneath me.

Tell him the truth.

But instead, I stay quiet, because while I do worry that whatever is happening to me is also what happened to my sister, some small, distant part of me hopes that perhaps it's what might lead me back to her, or her back to me.

"I want to keep you safe," my father says finally. "And if I have to send you away again, I will. I'll do whatever it takes."

"I won't leave again." I'm hardly in the mood for a fight, but I know I'd rather run away and disappear like my sister did than be sent 3,000 miles away again. Better to let him know now.

He just watches me, his hands twitching nervously. "I'll do whatever it takes."

I pull myself from the chair and lean forward, closer to him.

"I'm not going to end up like Eve," I say, with as much strength as I can muster. I am saying it for him, to reassure him, but also for me.

"It might not be your choice," he says, barely above a whisper. His eyes are full of tears, ready to fall, and it yanks at my heart, suddenly and violently. "It might take you anyway."

The way he says it catches me off guard. "What do you mean?"

He stares at me, shaking his head softly. "Stay away from the Moss, Emma. Promise me."

A few heartbeats slip by. "Why? Because I'll drown?"

"Only if you're lucky."

The words slither into the room on muck and mire. I feel I can smell it, the dank scent of rotting earth and dead things. Coldness reaches out with bony fingers, leaving ice down my spine and frost in my lungs.

"What is it?" I whisper. Fear is everywhere, in everything. Filling my lungs, my head, the air around me. "What is the Moss?"

He shakes his head again, and one tears finally escapes his eyes. "A predator," he says eventually. "A hunter. Neither here, nor there. Neither land, nor sea. Liminal. In Europe, they used to tell stories of things that lurk beneath the surface and pull you to your death. That's the bog, Emma, as far as I can tell. Always waiting. Always watching. Looking for its chance. You *can't* give it that chance."

My legs and hands tremble, so hard I shift and wrap my arms around myself.

"I would leave," he adds softly, "but what if . . . what if they come back?"

My trembling suddenly stops. "You think they're in the Moss?"

He tenses, staring at me. The whites of his eyes flash, and he nods quickly. "I hope they aren't." He shifts uncomfortably.

"Do you believe in ghosts?" I whisper. I wasn't intending to, but the moment felt right.

"Ghosts don't care if we believe in them or not. They'll haunt you all the same."

I swallow, coldness settling in.

Then the sudden rattling of a lid on the stove jerks our attention away. The conversation is over, and even though the words were dark, and the world suddenly feels far more wicked than it did before, I feel better, somehow. Like this conversation had been clawing to escape and we finally set it free.

eighteen

After Mom

IT IS SIX MONTHS *before she disappears. The end of summer is nearing, and while Abby – my mom's friend who still comes to visit and help clean the house even though Mom has been gone for a while – and her daughter take up space in the house with their chatter and laughter, I sit under a tree in the garden outside, drinking in the afternoon. There is so much winter in Maine that it always shoulders out all the good memories of summer. Smothering it in snow and ice and dreary grey clouds.*

Close by, velveteen rose petals dance a little in the breeze where they grow by the house. Very little else grows here, but the roses have learnt how to thrive. Now and then when the air moves just right, I am caught in the face with a rush of floral air that I wish I could bottle and keep for always. Hanging amongst the bushes are a few gangly spiders, resting on elaborate webs that attach to the house.

Eve is somewhere in the house right now, probably in her room, hiding from our guests. My eyes climb up the outside of the house and to the window of her room, where shadowy movement inside tells me I'm right. Maybe playing guitar, or reading Seamus Heaney, or organising all the Polaroids she's taken over the years. She keeps them in binders, with locations and dates carefully scrawled on the back.

The scabby bark of the tree behind me presses into my back, so I shift a little and close my eyes, letting the heavy afternoon sun beat against my face. My mind starts to drift towards what could be a light sleep, but then suddenly Eve is here, standing close to me, and telling me to wake up.

"Come on. Elise wants to play hide-and-seek." Elise is Abby's daughter.

"You do it," I say, closing my eyes again.

"Come on," she tells me. "Now."

We have always been close, but I've also always hated that bossy cut to her voice. The way she can tell me what to do and I'm meant to do it because she's a year and a half older than me, and also just because there's something about her that makes people do her bidding. She wields it delicately, but she wields it nonetheless.

Still, I'm sure to groan in protest as I climb up from my place on the ground, making her roll her eyes. It's somewhat satisfying.

Elise, who is eight – or maybe nine, but possibly seven – meets us on the front porch. Her hair is in two braids, and she jumps excitedly from foot to foot.

"I'll count first," Eve says. "Outside only this round. No going further than the fence. Especially that fence." She points to the fence that separates our garden from the Moss, and Elise nods. She's been told this before and doesn't really care. Eve turns to face the wall of the house, closes her eyes, and begins to count.

Elise and I hurry off the porch to start finding our hiding places, both heading in opposite directions. She moves to hide behind the old stone well cover that sits between our house and the road, and I slip into the trees behind the house. There's a large, old trunk with a semi-hollow area that you can shrink up against if you try hard enough. It hides you from view when someone approaches the tree, and they would have to walk all the way around it to find you. Eve and I used to hide here when we were little, and I'm hoping she's forgotten.

Back by the house, I can hear her call out, "Ready or not, here I come." Then faintly, a giggle from Elise finds its way to me. If the laugh has given away her location, Eve won't let on. She'll take her time finding her, or come for me first, letting her think she found the best hiding spot in the garden.

Footsteps reach me, Eve entering the line of trees. Of course she would look here first. Ridiculous to think she would have forgotten in the few years since we stopped playing hide-and-seek ourselves. I vaguely regret not picking a better spot, but at least Elise will feel like she won. That's something.

They draw closer and closer, and, annoyed with myself, I say, "I thought you forgot about it."

The footsteps instantly stop. Not wanting to drag it out any longer, I climb out from behind the tree and turn to face her.

But Eve isn't there. Someone else is, or the shape of them, and I can see where their shoes leave impressions in the leaves below. When I look away, the edges of my vision catch the outline of a man, just like the man in my room with the creaking boots.

A familiar fear wriggles its way back in.

"Who are you?" I ask, just like I did back then. The fear is there again, but I am better at keeping it tame. I have seen Eve practise over the years, even when she thinks I don't know. Speaking to things that aren't there, staring at something in the dark that seems to have revealed itself only to her.

I am what you are afraid of, *he answers, his voice water and stone. But there are worse things in the world than me.*

I work to find my voice before I speak. "I don't think there are."

He laughs then, a slippery, harsh sound that sends me back a step. Behind him and up in the garden, Eve rounds the house and stops when she sees me. She stands there for a minute, and then in my periphery, the man turns to look at her, too.

You two are of the same cloth. The same darkness. And you will meet the same end. I have learnt to be patient.

Leaves crunch on the forest floor again as he departs, deeper into the trees, and away. My eyes meet Eve's from across the distance, and we hold each other's gaze. Somehow, I can feel that she knows what just happened. Or at least knows that he was here. I wonder if she will come over to ask me about it, but instead she just turns and walks towards the well, where she finds an ecstatic Elise hiding.

I look into the trees in the direction the man went, but there are no signs of him. No signs of life at all, other than me. Just a coldness he left behind, and the scent of rotting, damp earth creeping over everything.

nineteen

NIGHT HOLDS ON WITH grey, ashen claws. If the sun has come up, it's buried somewhere behind a mantle of unforgiving clouds. I stare out towards the bog, my forehead pressed against the window in my room. The smell of coffee is growing fainter and fainter downstairs, my father having already left for work, but I haven't yet found the will to make my way down. My dreams were murky and thick, continually pulling me from sleep before plunging me back again.

Somewhere out in the storm, lightning illuminates the sky. Rain hasn't yet begun to fall, but it won't be long. The clouds press down so low I feel I could touch them if I opened the window and reached out with one hand.

But I'm afraid of what might reach back.

On a whim, I slide up the creaking window and push my face against the tattered screen, drinking in the musty, damp scent of the approaching storm.

Eve used to love thunderstorms. Still does, probably, wherever she is now. I wonder why that is my only thought, when I, too, have always loved a roiling, angry storm. I feel like whatever made up me as a person has been slowly sifted away, until all that's left are thoughts of Eve, Mom, and the life that used to be.

For some reason, the memory of Eve and the smell of the summer storm activates something in me that makes me stand and cross the room. I open the old wardrobe and reach under a pile of my jeans where I tucked her note for safekeeping. I haven't touched it since I returned, but holding it feels like a hug from her. Keeping her close.

The words are as clear as ever, and reading them still gives me that pang in my chest like it did the first time I found it, folded neatly on my pillow.

I cannot take it any more, Emma. I've tried for so long, but I miss her too much. I can still feel her, sometimes, but it isn't enough. I want to be with her. I know how to find her, I think. Don't follow me. I mean it. It will break Dad if you do. I love you, Em.

P.S. Stay far away from the Sedge Man. He won't stop, like a hunter, until there's nothing left of you.

The words were messy, either written hastily or while crying. Or both. Some read it as a final note before her death. Some read it as the words of a runaway who didn't want to be found. But I know it's neither, because Eve and I were close, even when she felt miles away.

Refolding the paper gently, lovingly, I tuck it into my pocket just to feel like she's closer than she is. Like the Moss didn't swallow her whole and leave nothing behind. Like holding on to the note might somehow make her materialise from the mist and dank of the bog, like she'd never left at all, and her absence was just a dream.

Thunder rattles the house.

Back by the window, large raindrops begin to splat against the glass, some finding their way in and on to the ledge after I opened it. I stand before it and watch in awe as the slate clouds unleash lashes of rain, torrents pounding against the roof. Sheets of it hang in the air, and water pools into the lower points of the ground in seconds. I haven't seen rain like this in a long time, especially not in California. I remember Jordan saying how much we needed rain, though I suspect it would take days of rain like this to make up for what we've lost.

Lightning splits apart the ebony sky, thunder crashing directly behind it. The glass of the window rattles again, the old house showing its age.

Something prickles at the back of my neck, like a spider falling on me from the ceiling. I swipe a hand across my neck, but there's nothing there.

Lightning strikes again. *Boom.*

Water splashes in through the screen, landing on my legs.

Emma.

I spin violently, wondering in the back of my mind if the storm might have masked the sound of my father coming home, but I'm alone.

Mostly alone.

Like when the girl was beside me on the plane, I can feel someone with me, but when I try to avert my gaze to see them better, I only get faint traces. No details. No real form.

My heart thunders like the storm outside, my vision blurring with fear.

Stay away from the Sedge Man.

The image of him drowning his daughter, his face empty

and hollow, fills my mind as I move until my back is against the window.

To my right, I hear it again.

Emma.

I turn, but catch only the faintest of movements before it vanishes. Somewhere else in the room – or maybe far, far away – a laugh reaches me. Then movement to my left, but this one different somehow. Slower.

Water drips from the windowsill and onto my floor. It soaks into my socks, but I can't turn my back to close the window. Fear keeps me rooted to the spot.

Leave.

I can't hear the voice so much as feel it. I sense it tracing along my senses like a finger over my skin. There's another laugh, closer this time, and cold. Unfeeling. Then movement to my right, but it's gone when I spin around to face it.

"Leave me alone," I say. "Leave me. Leave me alone."

Leave, the voice comes back. Confusion makes me falter, wondering vaguely if my own words are echoing through the large house. It sounds like it could be my voice, but it isn't. I'm sure of that. It isn't my voice.

I am patience. I am for ever.

Never.

A conversation, I think, but one I'm not a part of. Two presences? Or perhaps I've gone mad. I think quickly to things Eve used to say before she vanished. Musings of a madwoman that had Dad calling a doctor more than once. Talk of people in the house no one else could see – except sometimes for me. But they weren't people so much as feelings, or impressions, or subtle movements that I worked tirelessly to ignore. I felt like if I pushed them away then they wouldn't consume me in the way they had consumed Eve. Like I might escape whatever fate awaited her.

Like the fate of disappearing.

And now I've become her.

Behind me, the rain stops in all but an instant. The torrents cease, pulling back to a gentle drizzle. Water stops gathering on my floor and, as the deluge departs, so do the ghosts. I can feel them leaving the room like sleep leaving your body, and in the next instant, I am completely alone.

It takes minutes for me to move. I keep my head still, eyes wandering, checking my periphery for movement. Listening for voices. Sensing voices. Afraid if I turn away for even a moment, something might patter up behind me on silent, grassy feet and slip slender fingers around my throat.

I'm not certain how I'll ever sleep again.

Raindrops coat the window, making it nearly impossible to see anything other than mottled grey and twisted, refracted shapes. I suck in a breath of the cool, rain-washed air and let my eyes wander to the bog. What I can see of it, through the droplets.

Movement arrests my attention and I freeze, waiting to see if it happens again. Thinking perhaps it was only water shifting on the glass, bending images into something they aren't. As I stare for longer and the movement doesn't return, I worry that must have been it.

Although not all of me believes it. I've seen enough in my seventeen years to know that ghosts like to hide behind things that have other explanations, and whatever extra sense I have that makes me aware of their presence is almost never wrong.

twenty

THE SHARP SUNLIGHT THE next day makes it hard to believe in yesterday's rain, that there were ever clouds at all. The air is cooler now, not cold, but with that toothy edge to it that comes with autumn.

My dad's car rattles and shakes as we make our way down the road in silence. That's how it's been since our conversation the other night. Silent. Good morning. Goodnight. Little else. But today I asked him to drop me off at the library after school. I told him I would find my own way home, either by walking the two miles or calling Jordan. Probably walking, though, because I worry Jordan is one strange sentence away from thinking I've misplaced my sanity. He wouldn't be wrong either.

The car is mostly quiet while I read an article on my phone. It's about bogs, of course, and it leads me to another article about will-o'-the-wisps, or lights sometimes seen in bogs back in the day that were said to lead people to their death. Others said they led you to what you wanted the most, and being blinded by hope often meant people drowned in the bogs.

I have seen lights in the bog before, but they were so strange and otherworldly that I kept them only on the edges of my thoughts. Giving them too much room might mean trying to understand them, and they were frightening. Bizarre and unnatural. Best left alone.

"What's it like being back in school?" Dad asks. I think he's been wanting to ask it for a while but hasn't got up the nerve.

I close the article and lock my phone, remembering the faces of Amelia and her friends. The fear they carried, even being close to me. "I wish I didn't have to go," I tell him honestly, but I don't quite feel up to explaining why, so I add, "but it's fine."

"That's good. That's good." He pauses, then shifts the conversation. "I think the library is a great idea. Reading's good for the brain."

"That's what the experts say," I reply.

"What are you into?"

I stretch out my arms a bit, and one elbow cracks. "I'm not sure, exactly. Maybe crime novels. Thrillers. Something like that." Then, after his prolonged silence, "Or maybe something romantic."

"Great." That clearly makes him feel better.

I did used to enjoy reading, in the years before life began to unravel like a hole in jeans and the emotional blood loss became too much to bear. Mom used to take me and Eve to the library once a week, every Thursday after school, and we would spend the weekend reading in the grass. Eve always went for the ghost stories or tales of haunted houses and cemeteries. I read fantasy, because nothing intrigued me more than the thought of escaping from the ghosts entirely into a brand-new world.

"Thanks," I say, climbing out and shutting the door a little too quickly. The fear from yesterday lingers, plucking at me if I let my mind rest for a second too long. I worry if I spend too much time around my dad, I'll end up blurting out what happened, and nothing will have me on a West-Coast-bound flight faster than telling him I'm seeing apparitions in the house, just like my sister did.

I will go into the library, eventually, but as soon as he's out of sight, I dart across the street to the police station. My steps are quick at first, but slower and slower until they stop altogether, halfway across the parking lot. I haven't been here in a year, but in those few weeks around when Eve went missing, I felt like I lived here. Giving statements, giving them again, interview after interview, coming in just to check and see if anything had changed. If there were any leads.

There never were.

And that's where we are to this day. Without any leads, other than the note she left for me, and without Eve. They kept regurgitating the same thing a hundred different ways until all I could feel was the urge to scream.

We're still doing everything we can, but sometimes people just don't want to be found.

There's no evidence of foul play, but we are leaving no stone unturned.

Don't worry. When we have something, we'll call you.

Now it's been a year without a call, which might as well be a year without air or food. She is still missing, which is a strange word for it when we are the ones missing her. The ones left behind.

The door handle of the station feels all too familiar as I yank it open. A bell rings overhead, one I heard in my sleep for months afterwards, and I grit my teeth against the clang of it. The woman behind the counter – Therese – looks up at me with a bored expression that quickly bleeds into recognition.

"Oh. Hi, Emma." She catches the eye of Officer Burnside at his desk. "I didn't know you were back."

"Just," I say, rubbing my sweaty palms together. "Too much sun in California. Not enough inconsistent weather. Had to come back."

She smiles, a faint, forced thing that only makes my palms grow sweatier. I'm not even certain exactly why I came. It just felt like the right place to go, thinking of Eve so much.

"I just wanted an update. I could have called, but now that I'm back I figured I'd come in person. I don't know if there's much to say, but it's been a year, so . . ." I stop talking before my words can tumble out any faster.

"Emma. How you doing?" Officer Burnside holds out a hand and I shake it, even though I'm ashamed of the sweat.

"Fine. Good. OK, I guess. I just wanted – I was hoping maybe there was something new. Any leads. I mean, I know you said you'd call if you had anything, but anything at all, even if it's small. I'm back now, and I can help in any way."

"Come over here." He rolls his arm a few times, motioning for me to follow him to his desk. The station is busy around us, phone calls and conversations and general humdrum. I like the steady noise of it all. It's enough to drown out my nerves.

Why are you nervous? The question pricks at the back of my mind, shy, but growing stronger. I came here a hundred times before, to the point where I know almost everyone by name. I think, if I focus on the feeling for more than a minute, it's that I'm afraid because they're the ones who can tell me she isn't coming back. They can tell me there's nothing to go on, no sign of her, no hint of her whereabouts. That they're only looking for a body, at this point.

"I could have saved you a trip in, if you'd called. I'm afraid that we're pretty much where we were last year. Nothing new has come in, even though the tip line is still active. The note she left you is the biggest piece of evidence that we have, but even that hasn't given us very much."

I play with a loose piece of plastic edging on his desk. In a way, it feels like no time has passed at all, and I'm still sitting at this very desk, waiting for news that isn't coming.

"What about the bog?" The question is small when it comes out. I think I'm afraid to even ask it, because if she is in there, then we might never find her.

He shrugs and leans back in his chair. "That might be where she went. But if so, as far as we know, she never came back out. And we did search it, as much as we could, but there wasn't any sign of her in there. So, we wouldn't be looking for . . . I mean, at that point, we would be . . ."

"Looking for a body." I save him from clumsily trying to avoid the words. He nods, sadly, like it hurts him to say it just as much as it hurts me to hear it.

"Look, we'll keep working on it. We are always looking out for more information. For any new details. And, of course, we're always here if something new comes up that you can share with us. But as of right now, not much has changed."

I chew on my lip. "Leave my dad alone."

He hesitates. "What do you mean?"

"I mean that he knows as little as I do. As you do. He played no part in her disappearance. So let it be."

He studies my face. "We owe it to your sister to leave no stone unturned."

"And you owe it to my dad to not ruin his life. It's a small town. People talk. And people aren't good at separating fact from fiction."

With a sigh, he says, "We have no reason as of yet to believe that your father had anything to do with the disappearances."

"Then perhaps you could tell people that." After a pause, I add, "Thanks for your time." I scrape my chair back and stand quickly. I want to be anywhere but here, as fast as I can.

Therese calls a goodbye to me as I make for the door, but I just push it open and exit back out into the parking lot, drinking in the cool air as it pours over me. I don't know what I was expecting. If there had been any new leads, they would have called, and they hadn't called. But I think the longer I stayed away from the station, it kept the hope alive that something would change. That something would happen. And now I *know* that it hasn't.

The disappointment stings like a bee, and I crouch down on the pavement to rest my head on my knees.

"I know you're still out there, Eve," I whisper into my jeans. My hair falls around me, shielding me from the world. "I'm back now. Just show me where to look, and I will find you."

The words are foolish, whispered in a police station parking lot like the breeze might whisk them away to her ears, but saying them makes me feel better. When I stand up again, I feel more whole.

The dry, dusty smell of the library punches my senses when the door shuts behind me. A librarian eyes me over her glasses, but says nothing, so I play with my father's library card in my jacket pocket and turn right to head for the stairs.

On the next floor, a group of students are studying together quietly, poring over thick textbooks on the table before them. My eyes graze over them at first, before landing on one familiar form.

Jordan stands, nearly knocking over his chair in surprise. "Hey!" he says, his voice a little too loud, before he remembers we're in a library. Then, in a whisper, "Hey."

I take in a breath, trying to rid myself of the anxieties that followed me from the police station. "Jordan. Why are you here?"

"I come here every week with a few friends and we . . ." He looks around shyly. "And we do advanced math practice. For fun."

My mouth falls open. "That's your idea of a good time?"

"One," he says quickly. "Just one idea."

We start to wander around without much of a destination.

"What are you here for?" he asks, glancing through a rack of DVDs.

"Books, I guess," I tell him. I don't mean for it to be sarcastic, but the way it slips out in a flat tone lands harder than I wanted it to.

"I mean, yeah," Jordan says. "I figured."

I laugh a little, lightening the mood. "It depends on the day. Today . . ." The truth is that I don't quite know why I came here. Libraries always seem to have answers to questions you haven't realised you need to ask. I stop and look around, maybe waiting for a book to whisper my name. To tell me what it is I came here for. "Today, I'm not sure."

The section on history is closest to me, making up a series of shelves to my right, and even though I still don't know what to look for, I make my way over.

"Maybe they have a book on the bog," I muse, half because I'm genuinely curious, and half to see his reaction. He just nods a few times.

"*The* bog? As in, the Moss? I don't know if there are any books on it, except maybe mentions by local writers, but I'm not sure if their books are here," he tells me.

"*A* bog, then." Rows and rows of books all sit sleeping, waiting for someone to wake them up and take them home. Books on the medieval period, on the First and Second World Wars, on the time of the Romans, and Cleopatra, and the Celts. Books on the wives of Henry VIII, and on death and rituals in the Bronze age.

None of them jump out at me, so I move to round the corner and go down the next aisle, but then I take a step back. A book on death and rituals sticks out slightly further than the others, and the cover makes me pull it off the shelf. The cover shows the face of a man that I've seen before around the internet, perfectly preserved in a bog in Denmark. He only looks asleep, like at any moment his eyes might open and watch me.

"It's funny – I thought maybe you liked fantasy, or science fiction. Bronze Age death rituals didn't really cross my mind." Jordan laughs, then stops when a librarian passes by and glances at us.

"It depends on the day," I tell him. "I do like fantasy." But I'm intrigued enough by the book to give it a chance, so I find an empty armchair in the corner of the library and sit down with it, using the index to flip to the sections of interest. Jordan stands by my shoulder, the smell of a spicy cologne washing over me.

The title is apt. Pages and pages on deaths throughout the Bronze Age and into the Iron Age. Murder, punishment and sacrifice. Examples being made, criminals dealt with, warnings and threats. But it's the sacrifice part that I can't look away from. Stories of men and women sacrificed to the European bogs, out of fear or hope or merely a lack of understanding for how a place could be both land and sea. People nearly murdered with ropes, knives and rocks but kept alive long enough to be drowned.

The image of the Sedge Man drowning his daughter bleeds across my mind again, and I look away from the book to clear my head.

"They sound like nice folk," Jordan says dryly.

I flip the page, scanning as I go.

"What was that?" Jordan asks, turning back one page. Then he reads aloud, softly, by my ear. "Some historians argue it was the bog's miasmic effects that drove people mad. Noxious fumes and gases are known hallucinogens. Some argued it was a place of the gods. Others thought there was a presence in the bog, something that called to them, and so they sent in body after body to sate it, though it was never enough."

Miasma. The word clings to me, making me feel uneasy. A small worry sparks that the ghosts I've seen, the wild visions that have plagued me and my sister, are nothing more than phantoms born from a toxic bog. But I quietly lay those fears to rest. The ghosts are real enough to me. Real enough to cause fear, anxiety, sleeplessness.

Another page talks about the peat beneath the bogs, how people would use it as fuel for fires to keep warm. How well it burns, despite its home in a wetland. How today, people fight to protect it.

"It makes you wonder what's hiding in your bog," Jordan says. "In the Moss."

"Yes," I tell him. "It does."

An image of another bog body takes up the entirety of one page, the skin leathery and smooth. My gaze lingers for ten seconds. Twenty. Thirty. Then I close the book with a sudden *snap* and return it to the shelf where I found it.

There is only one place in town that does pizzas and, thankfully, they do them well. Dad picks up two on his way home, both pepperoni, and we opt to eat them on the front porch. With winters as cold as they are, you have to make the most of the good weather while it lasts.

The sunflower golden sky washes everything in warmth as the sun slowly dies away. The trees and grass are still, in that way that makes it feel as if the world is drawing in a breath, waiting for something.

I bite into my second slice of pizza. Neither of us have spoken since we came outside, and I'm happy to not be the first. The silence is peaceful. Needed.

"It'll be Eve's birthday next week," my dad says eventually. My chest clenches like a fist at the words, but I cover it with another bite. Like I could forget. It will be the second of her birthdays since she went missing, and I spent the last one crying so hard my head throbbed for three days.

"I'll pick her some flowers," I say through the pizza. "Bog laurel. Put it in her room."

My dad nods. "There'll be the vigil. Don't forget."

"I haven't."

A tiny breeze bends the tallest grass, then settles again. "It's funny, having you back," he says. "Sometimes I think it's Eve moving around up there. Coming down the stairs in the morning. You two look so alike."

I can't take it as anything but a compliment. Eve's long dark hair and perfect smattering of freckles had stirred more feelings of jealousy growing up than I had ever admitted to her. The boys in school all fawned over her, and I could hardly blame them. There was something about her that was intoxicating. When she spoke to you, you felt important. Relevant. Special. She did everything she could to make you feel heard, and I think that was what hurt the most in the time since she vanished. Not being able to tell her how it felt. The pain it caused. How much I missed her.

The things I want to say to her form constellations on my ceiling every night.

I miss you. I love you. I would give anything to have you back. To tell you about my day. About my week. My month. My year. Years. Sometimes the pain is a deluge running in rivulets down my face, my room, my mind. And sometimes it slows to a trickle, and then I worry that I'm recovering, and if I recover from the pain then it means you're truly gone.

Sometimes I write it down and then I burn it, because I've always heard fire is cleansing. I have yet to feel better, but I also have yet to feel worse.

"I could have done more to stop her," I tell him, giving voice to the feelings that have haunted me for a year. "I should have done more."

He watches me, sadness coming to rest on his face. He polishes off the crust of his pizza and reaches over for another, ten thousand thoughts racking his face. The only sound is the creaking of my rocking chair as it moves back and forth, back and forth. "There wasn't anything you could have done, Emma. Anything. Believe me. And the truth is, no one could have done anything. Eve was just . . . she just wasn't the same after your mom disappeared. Something changed in her. You saw it. I saw it. It's like half of her went with Mom, and the part that stayed behind couldn't carry on. I blamed myself for a year. I still do, sometimes. I wish I could have seen the signs. Caught a hint. Realised. I don't know." He stops eating. "But there's nothing you could have done, and I would hate myself even more if I thought that you ever blamed yourself."

He looks at me now, earnestly, and I know I have to respond, but it feels like a tree has fallen on my chest and pressed the air from my lungs.

"I do. I did. Blame myself, I mean." The words are hard to get out, but each one gets a little easier. "We were best friends. Sisters. I should have known, and I didn't."

He shakes his head, over and over again. "You couldn't have known."

My gaze moves to the Moss again. Its tooth-like trees and blackened water sit perilously still, unseen eyes trained on me.

"I'm glad you're still here," he says, in a tone significantly lighter than the one from before. "I am. And I'm glad to have you back, even if I don't think it was the right time. I missed you."

I smile, pulling another slice of pizza from the box.

"Now, tell me about Jordan," he says.

My eyes dart up to his, questioningly. There's a smile there, and my jaw tightens. "What about him?"

"I don't know. You tell me. He mentioned you've been spending some time together."

"It isn't like that." I bite into the pizza harder than necessary. "If anything, I'm just using him for his truck." It's mostly true, although in the quiet of my own mind, I admit he has a calming presence.

"Uh-huh. If you say so."

The impulse to roll my eyes or push back rises, but the moment feels light and sweet in a way I don't want to minimise, so I just let it be. Instead, I let my gaze wander again, back to the waiting Moss. Always waiting. Watching. Listening. Starving. Aching.

Emma.

My head twitches towards my dad at the word, but he's looking away from me, eyeing some bird sitting high up in a tree. If anyone said my name, it wasn't him.

A shadow moves on the edge of my vision, but man or girl, I cannot tell. It is gone quickly, leaving behind only a coldness that creeps deep under my skin.

twenty-one

LIKE THE SKY KNOWS it's Eve's birthday, it burns orange, red and purple in the dying light of the sun. The road ahead is bathed in a salmon pink as Dad drives us towards town. We've been silent since we left the house, but it's an uncomfortable kind of silence that deserves to be broken.

Dad beats me to it.

"Heard quite a few people are planning to show up."

"More than last year," I add. Even people that barely knew her or never knew her will attend tonight's candlelight vigil in honour of her birthday. Everyone feels as if she were a part of their family – her posters still haunting the town and her face plastered on the evening news. She has more friends now than she ever had in real life, and there's something about it that makes me sad.

Dad's hands twist around the steering wheel, a nervous response I've seen before. There's little point in asking him why. I know being around so many townsfolk would be enough to make me sweat, if the town thought I had something to do with my wife and daughter's disappearance.

"It'll be OK," I tell him. He looks over at me thankfully, a glassiness to his eyes that makes my heart ache. "We can leave, if we need to."

He nods a few times, his hands still twisting.

The small bit of park in town is brimful of people when we pull up across the street. Candles are being passed around, and a few people hold up her missing poster. After a minute to breathe, readying, I pull the large collage of pictures I made out of the back seat of the car. Some are Polaroids she took, some I printed off my phone, and some were Mom's, taken when we were much younger. Seeing them feels like a razor grazing against my skin, but I wanted her to be present tonight in more than just the missing poster. She's more than one picture with a few words printed beneath it. So, so much more.

More and more cars park along the street as we make our way across to join the gathering crowd. Curious gazes find us before our feet have even touched the grass, a few whispers darting around: *'I didn't know she was back in town.' 'You know they say the dad had something to do with it, right?'*

Their words don't matter. There is a truth in every situation, and I can't judge them for being ignorant to the truth. Anyone who could think to blame my dad must not know him very well, and that's their loss.

I send a sweet smile to anyone who catches my eye. I'm not here to make enemies, or friends. Just to survive the night, remember Eve, and go home to my ghosts.

Not far from me is Theo.

Jordan approaches from the road, hands in his pockets. I watch him, and he watches me, but neither of us speaks.

A woman I recognise from the local Baptist church hands us both candles, wordlessly, and someone else follows with a lighter. It's as my candle is being lit that I realise everyone gathered is facing me and my dad, almost expectantly, as if one of us was supposed to speak. I lower my eyes, focusing instead on the flickering candle flame. I haven't come prepared to speak, and I'm confident my dad hasn't either.

"She would have been nineteen today."

The voice is mine, and my face burns suddenly, as I realise everyone is looking at me. I can't even recall wanting to speak, but here we are.

"She never liked birthday parties, but she would have liked to know everyone was here. I felt like the world got a bit darker when she went away. It's nice to see some light left in her wake."

A few heads nod, but no one speaks. My ears still burn, but I keep my eyes on the candle. I'm glad I spoke, because it was for Eve's sake, if no one else's, but the aching silence now makes my stomach turn.

"Losing Bethany and then Eve . . ." The voice is my father's, and all eyes turn to him as he puts a comforting hand on my shoulder. "It took a part of me away that I will never find again. Carved out a part of my soul I'm still learning how to live without. I loved them both like I love Emma: more than myself. More than anything. The world is not the same without Eve in it. The candle that went out with her left a darkness I don't think anyone can light again."

I wrap him in a hug, partly to hide the sudden heaving in my chest.

"I guess you should have thought of that." I let go of my dad to see who spoke. It's a man I don't know, at least not well, and his face is filled to the brim with anger.

"Who are you talking to?" Jordan asks.

"Nathaniel Carver. His wife went missing. Then his daughter went missing. And he's still standing here like a free man."

"He *is* a free man," I whisper, just loud enough to be heard.

"For now," the man says. He holds his chin higher, like a challenge.

"Come on, man," Jordan says. Beside me, I can feel my father tensed like a guitar string, quiet. What can he say?

"Acting like that man has no idea where they went. Like they aren't probably buried in his back garden, and like she isn't going to be next." He throws a hand towards me, and for a split second, I want to snap that arm right off his body. My teeth grind together with a sharp, crunching sound.

"It isn't like that," my dad breathes.

Jordan's mom takes a step forward. "Sam, this is inappropriate." Her tone firms up, a warning this time. "There's never been any evidence to suggest Nathaniel had anything to do with any of this."

"Well, you know what they say about absence of evidence, Sherry."

"Hey, Mr Shipp, that's . . ." Jordan looks around to see if anyone else might chime in. "That's not what we're here to do. We're here for Eve."

I've forgotten what it's like to feel embarrassed, because the anger has taken over. Whatever writhing, raging thing has awoken is in full control of my words. Before anyone can say anything else, I walk over to him and snatch the candle out of his hands. He starts to protest, but his surprise silences him.

"Get out of the park," I tell him, pointing towards the street.

"W-what?"

"Get out of the park."

"Emma, it's OK—" my dad starts, but I say it again.

"Get out of the park. Get *out* of the *park*."

The man just stares at me, his eyes narrowing in a way that might suggest I've lost my senses, but after a moment, he leaves, swearing under his breath.

Beside me, my dad wrings his hands, sweat glistening on his palms.

I turn my attention back to my candle, the flame bobbing around as my hand shakes with rage. I should look up again, try to read Jordan's face to see if I went too far, but I don't. I just keep my gaze down, until my dad slips an arm around my shoulder. He's sniffling a little, and the sounds breaks open a part of me, but I don't want Mr Shipp or anyone else to see me cry, so I bite it back and close my eyes.

twenty-two

Before Mom

I CAN BE FOUND up a tree on nearly any given summer day. There's something about the bark pressing into my skin and the rustling of leaves and the bird's-eye view of the ground that floods me with something like peace. And, occasionally, it proves useful.

Like one July morning when the birdsong is so loud it draws me outside and I climb my favourite tree near the house to lounge on a branch in the dappled sunlight – and voices suddenly catch my attention. A giggle, and a husky laugh, and I cling to the branch and scan the ground below.

Eve sits in the leaves, in the shade of the trees between the house and the road, and she isn't alone. That boy from school, Theo, sits with her, an arm wrapped around her shoulder, and both of them are caught in laughter about something I can't quite hear. Our parents don't know about them, so this little tryst under the trees is almost certainly meant to be a secret. I won't tell anyone, at least not unless I have to. But I am curious about what sort of boy Eve would allow into her life. She is such a wild mixture of self-assurance and the acknowledgement that there is something unusual about her. She is more comfortable in her own skin than I think I'll ever be, but she knows, too, that there is something *about her others can never know. The ghosts. The Moss. All of it. The secrets she and I share together, that will only ever be ours.*

Theo says something again, and she giggles louder this time, then claps a hand over her mouth in case Dad can hear her from the house. Theo runs a hand through her hair, smiling while she laughs, and I feel suddenly like I should look away. Like these moments are meant only for her, and I should at least announce my presence.

But Eve's laughter stops suddenly, and she looks off through the trees. I feel it at the same time she does, a cloud of cold that rushes in around the trunks and branches. Theo doesn't seem to notice, but he goes quiet at her sudden change. At the way she sits up straight, eyes wide.

Turning to follow her gaze, I see snatches of his form through the leaves. The boots. The dark coat. And little else. Theo sees nothing. He just looks around, trying to see what she sees, but his eyes do not find the Sedge Man. Eve stares for a long while, silent. Then the man's gaze must flick up to me, because Eve looks up and finds me in the tree. Her face doesn't give away her thoughts. She just watches me for a few seconds, before standing and heading back towards the house.

I slip down from the tree, startling Theo, and follow my sister. He wasn't mine, and these weren't my stolen moments under the canopy of leaves, but nevertheless, it serves as a reminder for me, too. That the man is always there, watching and waiting. That the Moss will never leave, and whatever part of us that it calls to will never stop listening.

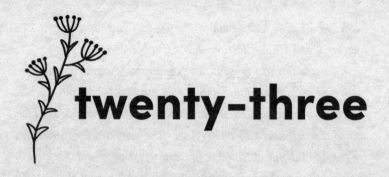

twenty-three

THE HOUSE HAS ALWAYS felt like a part of the Moss. Connected by some gossamer thread I cannot see but can feel. I have never heard of anyone being drawn into the Moss in the same way that my mom and Eve were. People have drowned because, like any bog, the Moss is dangerous in that way. But that same hunger, that same burning desperation, seems unique only to those that live here. And a house with that kind of history must have secrets in its bones.

Jordan came over to apologise for what happened at the vigil, even though it wasn't his fault. I'm thankful for the effort though, and for not having to be alone.

"Come on," I tell him, climbing the stairs. "Let's have a look around."

He's seen the house before, but as part of my efforts to understand the house – and the Moss, and Eve – I want to scrape along its bones a bit. See what's tucked away out of sight. If there's anything at all. As kids, Eve and I explored what felt like every inch of it: crawl spaces, closets, attics and basements. But back then, we were just exploring. Not looking for anything in particular. Now I am after secrets, wherever they may be.

"I love that," Jordan tells me, putting his weight on a creaky stair a few times so it groans. "I love a house with something to say."

"This one doesn't shut up."

He laughs. "That's when you have to show it who's boss."

There is a comfort in his presence now, with more time spent together. It's still there, but the awkwardness is calming, replaced by a gentle sort of affection that I am too tired and distracted to focus on now. But it is welcome nonetheless.

So often I walk through this house without looking too hard in any direction. Keeping my attention only on the matter at hand, on the thing before me. Afraid of what I might see if I look too long in the edges. But not today. Today, I want to know.

At the top of the stairs, my eyes wander up to the attic.

"You ever been up there?" I ask.

He shakes his head. "I feel like your dad would have frowned upon me climbing around his attic without much of a reason."

It is accessed by pulling down a ladder from a door in the ceiling of the upstairs landing. It's where Mom used to store all of our Christmas decorations, and I suspect they're still up there. We haven't decorated beyond putting up a simple tree in recent years.

The ladder screeches in protest as I pull it down, the joints grinding with disuse. It gets stuck halfway down, and Jordan has to pull it free. The steps have always been rickety, but more so now as I climb unsteadily up through the door in the ceiling. Cobwebs criss-cross everything, drenching the attic in a filmy grey. The imposing brick of the chimney takes up much of the central space, and the Christmas boxes still lurk in a pile close to the ladder. Dust coats everything. It feels like a time capsule of a life that's gone for ever, so I don't dare to touch them. Maybe one day, but not now.

"So," Jordan says when he has crawled up behind me and sat down. "You come here often?"

"Not as often as I should. I love little spots like this, hidden away. Where no one will think to look."

"True. Except for the ladder in the middle of the landing."

I giggle softly, though I was thinking more about ghosts than people.

The boards bend and creak below me when I pull myself to my feet. There are signs of mice everywhere. A thread-like mouse skeleton in one corner. Nests tucked into the shadows. Mom had talked once upon a time about finishing the attic into a small bedroom, or a library, but it feels like a dead space. A space that should be left alone.

Jordan checks out the Christmas boxes as my feet take me in a wide circle around the attic, cobwebs catching on my face and my eyelashes. I pluck them off and they stick to my hands, and it feels too much like the sickness that is the Moss. Sticking to you once and never leaving. Sometimes it feels like this house has sat here for so long, steeping in all the strange malice creeping up through the land, that it is just as evil as the Moss now. They are one and the same, inextricably linked. The Moss hungers for those that live here – or some of those that live here, while others escape unscathed, like my dad. The house is a dish left too long in the oven, blackened and unsalvageable. Best left to rot in peace.

"I think you have a pest problem," Jordan muses, pointing to the tiny skeleton. The sight of it makes me shiver.

"You can hear them in the walls sometimes," I tell him. "Scraping and clawing."

Jordan shudders. "Spiders? Love them. Snakes? Sign me up. But mice? Absolutely the hell not." He brushes off his arms like he can feel little feet climbing up them.

I turn away, staring through the space. There's such an emptiness up here. A forgotten place that feels best left forgotten.

But a small scrap of a mark on a board on the far wall snags at my attention. On hands and knees, I crawl across the boards to it, not looking away in case I lose sight of it.

"Where you going?" Jordan asks from behind me.

When I reach the far side, I stop, tilting my head. Scratched into the wood by something sharp, like a nail, are the words *Run away*.

The handwriting, if words scratched on to a board can be considered handwriting, looks strange and crooked. Not like the writing from Eve's note, but it could still so easily be hers. Or someone from long ago.

A shuffling behind me soon brings Jordan to my side. "I think we'll want to shower for a good six or so hours after this," he's saying, but he trails off when he sees the writing. "Huh."

We linger a few minutes longer, staring in silence at the scrawled words, before returning to the ladder.

But there is a building sense on the edge of my mind. A feeling that I am getting closer to something. I only hope it is answers and not more questions, so I press on in the hunt.

There is only one other place that calls for my attention once the ladder has been folded away. A small crawl space between the bathroom and my parents' room. It is big enough to climb into on hands and knees, and my sister and I sometimes used it for hide-and-seek when we were younger, but it otherwise serves no purpose. Just a hollow between two walls.

It has a small door, painted white, with an ancient latch that sticks when I try to pull it open. The handle is old and black, and when the opening yawns before me, my soul gives a small shiver. It was likely meant to be used as storage, to give every square foot of the house a job to do, but now it just looks like a place that should be boarded up and left alone.

When I open the door, Jordan says, "This feels like where they would find a body."

"What body?"

"I don't know. Any body. Like in a horror movie." He seems to regret commenting on it, like perhaps we might have found my sister's body here, but I know he meant no harm.

I crawl part of the way inside, using the light on my phone to see. The lath and plaster walls are visible in here, built sometime in the 1700s and left exactly the same until now. There may be other things hiding in here, like lead paint or asbestos, but I'm careful to keep from touching too much as I make my way further inside. It feels a bit like climbing into a box, barely big enough for two people, and I rock back to sit down on the boards, hugging my knees to my chest.

A coffin, almost.

"We talked about mice," Jordan says, climbing in behind me. We have to sit close together to both fit. "But confined spaces are my other no-thank-you."

"You don't have to be in here."

"I'm not about to be outdone by you, thanks." He hugs his knees, looking around uncertainly.

Being in here takes me back to a time a few years ago, when I found it unlatched. Empty, but unlatched. Eve was home, and I suspected she had come here for reasons that were a mystery at the time. But now I think I understand, crawling around on hands and knees, searching for what secrets this house might hold.

But there is little in here to suggest any answers. Old lath boards, crumbling plaster, loose flooring I don't think I should spend too long on or I might go crashing through to the bottom floor of the house.

"Well, whatever you were searching for doesn't seem to be in here," Jordan muses. "But it's cool to see the horsehair. Don't get to see that very often."

"My parents never wanted to demolish it. Not unless the walls started crumbling. Mom always said it was nice to hold on to history in old houses."

I am about to tell him to crawl back out when a final glance around the small space turns up something that catches my attention. What looks like a scrap of paper, stuck between some plaster and lath, barely visible. Paper is often found as insulation, sometimes newspaper or the pages of old books, but this one sticks out on its own. A single scrap in a wall.

With gentle fingers, I pluck it free and turn it over. It's yellowed with age and feels ready to crumble in my hands, folded over a few times to hide whatever is written or drawn inside. I adjust the light on my phone to see better, Jordan craning his neck to see as well, and unfold it to reveal words scrawled in what can only be quill and ink. The hand is slanted and seems to have been written quickly, uneven in places and riddled with blotches.

There is a sickness here. It bleeds out from the Moss,
infecting even the house and the air I breathe. I hate it,
yet it calls to me, and I feel powerless to resist it.
My father's eyes never leave me. He knows, I think
He knows, and he waits for just the right moment.
If anyone is to find this after I am gone, know that
there is nothing left for you to do but leave.
Leave, and do not ever, ever come back

My temples throb as I finish, then read it a second time. Many of these words I've heard before, in one form or another. From Eve, whispering from time to time about how it called to her. How she could not ignore it any longer. How it slipped into her blood and called her home.

There is a sickness here.

I know. I know because I feel it. See it. Smell it. Hear it. Taste it. It is everywhere, in everything, and like whoever wrote this note, I feel unable to escape it. More so now because I cannot leave before Eve has been found. Cannot pack a bag and return to the West Coast and forget about everything that has happened. There is sickness here, and I must either wait for it to run its course, or let it claim me, like it has claimed others.

Did Eve ever find this note? I can't imagine that she didn't, the way she prowled around this house and its grounds like an investigator at a crime scene. Turning over every rock, leaf and board. But if she did find it, she left it behind. Maybe for me. Maybe just because it's part of the house now. Maybe so she could come back to it later.

Across from me, Jordan's brows are furrowed, his face pale.

"Who knows?" I whisper, in response to nothing but the

unasked questions lingering in the air. "It's from a long time ago."

He says nothing, but my words don't seem to make him feel better.

The sickness. I heard the voices on the beach in California. Saw the dead girl on the plane when I came home. That sickness is a part of me now, and the ghosts and wretched call of the Moss will follow me wherever I go. Just as it followed Eve and would have continued to follow her to the ends of the Earth. There is no escape, after so long spent by the Moss.

It calls to me, and I feel powerless to resist it.

The words bend a bit before me, and I come back to them again and again.

What if Eve stopped trying to resist it? Gave in and followed the call? Went in after Mom, and just never came back out? Drowned or slipped or tripped or starved to death?

The words in this note ring with the same pressure, the same lurking desperation as the note Eve left for me. There is familiarity all around it, and that settles into the pit of my stomach.

"Hey," Jordan says softly. He takes the note from my hand and refolds it gently "It's old. It doesn't mean anything today."

I nod, repeatedly. "You're right." I tuck it back where we found it. If Eve left it behind, then so will I. Let it be a warning for anyone who might come after us.

I follow him back out of the crawl space, latching the door behind us.

twenty-four

A HANDFUL OF DAYS drag by.

The signs for the town's harvest party began sneaking up over the past week, all leading to tonight. I hadn't planned to go because despite growing up here I know precious few people in the town, and it's only September, so not late enough in the year to entice me with thoughts of Halloween.

But when Jordan messaged me the night before – *You going tomorrow night?* – and I couldn't think of an excuse not to go other than standing in my window staring out at the bog, I agreed. Even though standing in my window and staring out at the bog *is* apparently my favourite pastime.

He picks me up at six p.m., with my dad saying he will meet us there later, smiling like an idiot. This time I do roll my eyes, because Jordan is there.

"I don't usually go to these things," Jordan explains in the car. The windows are down, and there's a distinct chill in the air that wasn't there before. This morning, there were a few small patches of web-like frost on my window, although it's early for it.

"I haven't gone in years," I say. I actually haven't gone since the year before Eve went missing. It was a yearly ritual for our family,

Mom and Dad dragging us out of the house whether we wanted to go or not.

Jordan nods, his eyes still on the road. "Back in the day, I'd rather have been just about anywhere else," he says, "but today I could really use a cider donut. Maybe it was the frost this morning. It woke up my inner autumn."

I watch him subtly while he drives, his thumb tapping over and over again on the steering wheel. "How's your family?"

He glances at me, and our eyes meet for a brief instant. I breathe through the discomfort – embarrassment, really – and look forward again.

"They're good. Great, even. Dad's business is booming, which keeps him away from home a lot, but he likes his work. So, no complaints. He makes up for it on his days off."

"He's a carpenter, right?"

"Right."

"And your mom?"

"You know how she is. She's always happy. I think it's where I got my optimism from. She's still working down at the hospital, but she's nursing in the outpatient surgery department, so she's on the day shift now. She likes that much better than working nights."

"I imagine so." I have a few good memories of his family, from birthday parties, school gatherings and sports nights. Optimistic is right. They radiate light like the sun and it's impossible to be in the same room with them without smiling at least once. It makes me wonder what my family radiates, but perhaps that's one stone best left unturned.

The conversation dies down for a short time, and the

awkwardness seeps back in. I wonder if it will always be this way, our quiet moments punctuated by burning cheeks and rambling thoughts. Sticking my chin up a little higher, I'm about to start a whole new subject in a daring effort to push back the quiet, but Jordan beats me to it.

"I wish I hadn't . . ." he starts, but then stops quickly, looking out the window with intense focus. He flexes his hands on the steering wheel a few times, and now whatever awkwardness was there earlier has blown up like a balloon. "I should never have . . ."

The words he isn't saying crowd into the truck like a fog. I shift uncomfortably, plucking at some loose threads in my jeans, then decide that waiting for him to finish is only prolonging our misery.

"It's OK," I say, without looking at him. I see his head turn out of the corner of my eye and he looks at me, but I can't bring myself to meet his gaze. Everything I never said on the porch is suffocating me.

Thankfully, the conversation dies away again, and this time I don't try to resurrect it. At least, not until the crowded parking lot by the big harvest party field comes into view.

"I hate crowds," Jordan says, when he's put the truck into park and heaved a huge sigh. Now I do let myself look at him, smiling.

"So do I. We can both be miserable together." His face lights up a bit, even in the failing daylight, and I climb out of the truck after clapping him twice on the back. It was meant as an *it'll be OK* gesture, but after our truncated conversation earlier, it just winds up feeling weirdly over-familiar. I allow myself a few seconds on the far side of the truck to double over, hold my knees and collect my thoughts.

You're haunted, I remind myself. *A teenage boy should be the least of your worries.*

And yet . . .

"Shall we?" Jordan comes around to my side, tossing the keys back and forth between each hand. "We can try to stick to the less busy spots, if it helps."

The party feels bigger this year than I remember it. There's a bouncy castle and a ball pit for the children, rows and rows of food trucks serving every street food in the known universe, and about a hundred picnic tables. Cauldrons of non-alcoholic apple cider and hot chocolate, donuts cooked to order, a corn maze, displays of unnaturally large pumpkins, and more. We make our way to one of the cider sellers first, keeping a little bit of distance between us as that awkwardness lingers, and clink our paper cups together like they're filled with fine wine. Near the centre of the field is a giant bonfire that fills the air with the scent of warm smoke and marshmallows. We wander towards it, slowly, sharing our favourite memories from when we came here as kids.

"One time," Jordan says, "I got lost in the corn maze for so long that my parents and their friends all had to come in after me. It took over an hour for us all to find each other again. My mom was so stressed she made us go home."

I laugh, skirting past a woman walking two miniature horses. "See, Eve and I were the ones *trying* to get lost in the maze. Hiding in the corn and telling ghost stories to each other to see who could scare the other the most."

Jordan sends me a look like I'm crazy, and it's fair. Eve and I were always unusual, and denying it feels like stating that the sky is green.

The memory of her, of us, crouched in a cornfield and whispering ghost stories to each other, awakens an ache in the pit of my stomach. A sadness that even the harvest party can't chase away. If anything, I feel like I see her everywhere, or almost see her. Those memories touching the edges of everything, but only the edges. Never becoming something stronger. Never turning into her.

The bonfire draws us in, warm and bright enough to chase away the growing chill of the evening. For a few long minutes we just sip our drinks and stare, sparks cascading into the darkening sky and voices humming in all directions. Right now, I don't mind the crowds so much. The steady hum and murmur helping me to feel smaller. To be a face in a crowd, instead of feeling alone in a room with ghosts watching my every move. There is a sense of safety in numbers that our lonely house does not allow.

Sparks and firelight dance in Jordan's eyes, and it isn't until he looks over and notices that I realise I've been staring. But there's something about the warm tangerine flicker of a fire that paints everything in a romantic light. Makes the ordinary seem extraordinary, and Jordan is far from ordinary.

His mouth curves in a subtle smile, his eyes catching more and more flames. "Something on your mind, Emma?"

I look away finally, back to the bonfire. "A lot of things," I answer, stifling my own small smile. And maybe I imagine it, but it seems like he shuffles ever so slightly closer to me, our shoulders nearly brushing.

"Jordan!" His name ripples to us on a high, excited voice. Behind us, a small group of others from our school make their way over, their eyes darting nervously to me. I only smile. Not much has changed. If they were nervous around me and my sister back in the day, things have only grown worse since.

"Hey, Amelia." The way Jordan greets them makes me think he'd rather get lost in the corn maze all over again than get stuck in conversation, but it's too late now. I, on the other hand, do not need to talk to Amelia. So I take advantage of the distraction and start to slip away, taking one step back, then two, three, until I'm nearly on the other side of the bonfire. He turns to find me, throwing me a desperate look that only makes me laugh, and I spin away.

Emma.

The sound of my name makes me stop suddenly, throwing me off balance, and I whip around, cider sloshing on to the ground. For a fraction of a second, it felt like there was someone standing right behind me, our bodies nearly colliding when I turned around – but there's nothing. Only me, the cider spilt all over my hand, and a few uncertain eyes watching me as if wondering whether or not it's only apple cider in my cup.

A couple takes hold of their kids' shoulders and guide them away, and it stings a bit. Like the man at the museum, there are reminders everywhere of how little the town trusts us. If the rumours of our haunted house weren't enough to make people look sideways, two disappearances in the family certainly did it.

My chest heaves with either a shuddering breath or a sob, and I make my way from the warm glow of the fire and further into the field. I have to step around large wooden cutouts where people poke their faces through giant, painted pumpkins for pictures, and a small ring where a rowdy relay race is taking place. Excited screams and squeals split the evening air, and suddenly it's all so much louder than before.

Then a familiar face is there, eyeing me uncertainly. It's Theo, standing next to his new girlfriend, looking like he's not sure if he should speak to me or not. There's a bolt of pain at seeing him, and seeing him with someone who isn't my sister, but like everyone, he is allowed to move on. Although that is where most of the pain lies: seeing the world carrying on, while Eve recedes further and further into memory.

"You OK?" he asks. The girl beside him just watches us, silently. She looks nothing like my sister – curly blonde hair and freckles and one of those tiny diamond nose rings.

"Yeah," I tell him. "It's good to be back."

He nods. "I don't know if I ever got the chance to tell you, but I'm sorry about Eve."

My teeth grind when he mentions her name. "Hasn't been easy."

"I really did like her." Theo glances nervously at the girl next to him. "She was so curious about things. She didn't seem very afraid, so it was easy to get swept along by her."

But Eve was afraid, just not of the obvious things. She was afraid of the Sedge Man, and the house, and sometimes of the Moss. It made all the other things in life seem so insignificant. It's part of what gave her that veneer of confidence, I think, seemingly fearless to the outside world.

"I wished I could have helped the police more, but I'd hardly seen her in the weeks before she vanished. She got really reclusive. Would hardly talk to me any more."

Some small part of me feels vaguely guilty for pushing his name at the police now, but not much. She's still missing, and he's here.

"She might turn up," I tell him, glancing around. Wanting to be away. "I'm hopeful."

He nods, a little sadly. "That's good."

Without waiting for a goodbye, I turn and walk away, trying to catch my breath. Seeing him makes me think of her – everything makes me think of her.

Then, between two food trucks to the right, I catch sight of a girl, disappearing into some shadows. It isn't her, *of course,* but something in the clothes and the movement makes me think of Eve, so I head in that direction. It's stupid, and I make sure to tell myself that again and again, but with Jordan otherwise occupied and my sanity hanging on by an ever-fraying thread, I have nowhere else to go.

Following the girl's steps between the two food trucks takes me to the far edge of the field, where a small cluster of trees grows. They remind me of the lanky trees that grow in the Moss and, with no one else in sight, I turn away again. A dead end.

Emma.

I freeze, then spin back to the trees. "What?" The word slices out of me, razor sharp. A challenge. But, of course, there is no answer. The trees sit sullenly in the twilight, as lifeless as bleached bones. Anger, or maybe just frustration, washes over me and I scrub both hands over my face.

"Emma?"

This time it's different. A real, solid voice, calling to me from across the field. The sound warms me and I move closer to it, back between the food trucks and away from the trees, where Jordan turns in a slow circle, searching.

"Oh, hey. I lost you." He smiles and polishes off the last of his cider, tossing his cup into a nearby trash can. "Or, rather, you abandoned me at the first sign of danger."

"I can't get too close to them," I say, smiling so he'll think it's a joke, even though there is some truth to it. One of the girls in that group – Amelia – told me once that being around me gave her nightmares. I'll never forget it. "I'm like the town vampire. Better kept at arm's length."

He lets out a breathy sound that I think is meant to be a laugh but isn't matched with a smile. Instead, he eyes me with what looks perilously close to pity, and I hate pity.

"I need more cider," I say quickly, turning to inspect the field for the next closest cider stall. "I need my blood type to be apple by the end of the night."

We find one by a large makeshift pit filled with dried corn kernels, full of children and younger teens all pretending to swim around in it. The gravelly, grating sound slips under my skin and raises all the hairs along my arms, but at least I have cider now.

"I bet you I know where we can get the best view of this shindig," Jordan says, staring across the field to where a hill starts to rise up, punctuated here and there with a few large boulders protruding from the ground.

"It's a bit of a hike," I tell him, but even as I'm saying it, the group of other kids from our school comes back into view. "But I'm probably in better shape than you." I strike off towards the hill, balancing my paper cup so the apple cider doesn't spill out the top again, and Jordan trails a few steps behind me. My legs burn as we ascend the rise in the ground, but all those walks up and down the boardwalks and beaches of California keep me from getting too out of breath.

When at last we collapse in a heap on one of the large rocks, Jordan wheezing like a car on its last legs, the expanse of the harvest party opens up before us. From up here, the crowds don't seem so big and the space seems smaller. Even the giant bonfire glows like a match flame far below. Behind us, acres and acres of short wild blueberry bushes stretch into the growing darkness. They're all owned by the town, and in July my mother used to bring us here to pick as many bowls full as we could possibly carry.

Memories. They're everywhere.

"I think I see your dad," Jordan muses, leaning forward like the few extra inches will give him a much better view over so much distance.

I follow his gaze to a man chatting with a group of others near the entrance. Even from here, I recognise the orange cable-knit sweater my mom made for him shortly after they got married. He has worn it to the harvest party every year since, and then again on Halloween. It spends the rest of its life buried in the drawer of his dresser.

"Look who has owl-eyed vision," I say, sipping the cider again, which is now, thankfully, cooler.

"I'm pretty sure it's eagle-eyed."

"Whatever-bird-eyed. Owls have the best night vision. I'm about eighty-five per cent sure about that."

"I would google it, but I don't have any signal."

"This place never has good signal."

He leans back until he's propped up on his elbows, setting his drink aside. I watch his profile for a moment, half considering shifting closer to him. I bask in the warmth that his presence brings, when my soul so often feels cold.

"Anyway," he says. "How are you liking being back at school?"

I hike in a breath. "I don't, very much. But if you could take away the math and the science and pretty much just leave the poetry or the writing, it would be better."

"See, for me it's the other way around. If I could just have physics and math, I'd actually enjoy school."

"It's always one or the other."

"I've been working with my dad a lot and he wants me to come on full-time after school, but I don't know. I took a trip to an observatory with some friends over the summer, and it really got me thinking about astrophysics."

It makes me glance up at the darkening sky, where a few shy stars are just easing into view. "Stars are great," I say quietly, pulling in a long breath. "Steady, you know? No matter how much changes down here, they're still there. Every night."

He smiles at me, then looks up at the stars as well. "My parents got me a telescope a couple of years ago. We should drag it out one night, especially now that it's getting darker earlier."

An evening with Jordan, alone, under the stars. Nothing could possibly feel more awkward than that – although I would do it in a heartbeat.

"There are some meteor showers coming up, too. I forget when, exactly," Jordan continues.

"I always found meteor showers to be very relatable."

He looks over at me, confused. "You what?"

"I don't know. It feels like the sky is crying."

"I think you read a lot of poetry."

"I do read a lot of poetry. And I keep thinking—" but my words choke in my throat. Down the hill a little way, back by the cluster of trees from earlier, a pair of eyes is watching me. They glow softly in the twilight, too high off the ground to be a cat. A coldness catches me in the face, the kind of chill that only follows the inhuman.

"Emma?" Jordan looks over at me, confused by my sudden silence.

"Jordan," I whisper, keeping my gaze locked on the eyes, "do you see that?"

He turns to inspect where I'm looking but shakes his head. "See what?"

The coldness grows, and as I watch, the eyes move deeper into the trees and disappear. I can't wait any longer. The girl, the voice, the eyes – it's like a magnet pulling me in, irresistible and intoxicating. I have to know. *I have to know.*

"Where are you going?" Jordan asks, when I stand and strike off down the hill again. The sound of him shuffling to his feet rises behind me, but I keep my eyes on the trees. There is no sign of the eyes.

As I get closer, the ground levels off some, growing stodgy and sodden in places. It reminds me of the bog, even though the bog is far away. The whitish bark of the birch trees glows like bones in the dim light, made worse by the distant glow from the bonfire. There are no signs of a person. Or a ghost.

"Emma, what are you doing?" Jordan catches up to me, out of breath again, and reaches for my hand. I pull away and step into the trees, the smell of damp earth and peeling bark smacking me in the face.

Something in the air shifts, like I walked through a door and into another part of the world. I've felt this before, when I stepped into the bog. Outside the trees, I can no longer make out the light from the bonfire. There is only pale moonlight from a moon I can't see.

Emma.

My name comes from everywhere and nowhere. Soft – a girl's voice, I think. It's in the trees, in my head, rising up from the ground. It's in my blood and dripping from the leaves.

"What?" I whisper, then try it again, louder. "What? I'm here."

A branch snaps to my left and I turn, expecting it to be Jordan, but he's nowhere in sight. There's no time to worry about that now. Further into the little wood, something darts between two trees. Everything inside me screams to turn away, but instead I press forward, faster. My foot sinks into soft, wet ground, nearly pulling my shoe off with its clinging, hungry grip, but I yank it back out and carry on.

"Who are you?" I call, loud enough to be heard throughout the wood.

She is waiting.

The words are in the air around me, in the crunch of leaves underfoot. I can't follow a sound that is everywhere. Then again to my right, movement.

"For what?" I ask. I'm only vaguely aware that outside the wood, all sounds of the party have ceased. There are no fires or bouncy castles or corn mazes. There is only me, and this wood, and whoever is in here with me.

I reach the point where I last saw movement, but there is nothing. Only a puddle of water left over from the recent rain, mucky and filled with mosquito larvae. My own reflection on the surface is little more than a vague outline, but something about it catches me off guard. It is me, but it is not. My face, but not my face. Like a mirror reflecting someone else.

"Who are you?" I whisper. I can just make out the face looking back at me. The girl I've seen before, on the plane, and in the garden. Her mouth is open like she's screaming, but the details are lost to the darkness. "What do you want?" I ask. "Tell me."

It will soon be too late, that voice says. In the air. In my bones. Then the water ripples and a hand protrudes from the surface, pale and stretched like that of a corpse. Slowly, one finger bends, beckoning me in.

In the next second, she is gone. No reflection. No movement. Nothing to signal that there is anything or anyone else in these trees but me. And suddenly, I feel very alone.

twenty-five

JORDAN GRABS MY SHOULDERS when I emerge from the trees. This time, it's me who's breathless.

"What the hell happened?" he asks, far too loudly. I lower myself until I'm sitting in the grass, shaking. I am no stranger to ghosts or the wild and weird, but something about the events in the woods has sent cracks through my soul. There is *something* I cannot quite place, something I am missing, but hovering just on the brink of. So close, so close, so close.

"Emma, what happened?"

If I don't answer him soon, he might call my father, and the last thing I need is to explain this to more than one person. "I thought I saw someone," I tell him softly. "Someone in the trees."

"I'm sure there are people in there. There are people everywhere. But you didn't seem like yourself, Emma. You seemed . . . frantic. I don't know." He wrings his hands nervously, looking out over the field – likely searching for my father.

Frantic. The word slips on like a glove. That's how it felt. Frantic. Like whoever was in there was always just out of reach. One inch too far away. Just barely out of sight. If I moved a little faster, I might catch them. See them. Feel them.

"I thought I knew them," I lie, trying to make my actions

make sense. At least, I think it's a lie. Why did I go in at all? Why did I not just write the eyes and the movement up to some kids from the party? I can hardly recall what I was thinking. Or maybe I didn't think. I just ran. It was that kind of recklessness that ruined Eve.

Eve. Slowly, I look back into the trees, something pulling my head like a thread. The girl I saw by the food trucks. The voice. Something about it all reminded me of her, but I was afraid to think of it until now. To give it space in my mind.

"Let's just go back to the party," I say. Suddenly, I want the noise again. The crowds, lights and movement, to ground me in the world. To take me away from that dark, dank little wood with the voice and the shadows.

"Are you sure?"

"I'm positive."

He pulls me back to my feet, still watching me with furrowed brows and worry written in every line around his mouth. "Here. You left this behind." He hands me my paper cup, now much cooler.

"Thanks."

My dad finds us after a few minutes, trailed by a handful of his friends. "You two having a nice time?" I can't even bring myself to feel embarrassed by the twinkle in his eye. I just tell him we are, make my excuses, and then ask Jordan to drive me home. I don't think even the sight and noise of the party can keep me grounded tonight.

The silence in the truck is loud, but I have nothing to say. Nothing that will quell his worries. The truth will only make matters worse. Add flames to the fire, because things are so much worse than even he can suspect. So it feels best to say nothing at all.

Why did I think of Eve?

The question fills up the windshield in front of me, burning white-hot in the dark. That sense that I'd felt in the woods – the one that I couldn't quite put my finger on – the more I think on it, the more I can convince myself that it was familiarity. Of recognising something as normal to me as myself.

The longer I think about it, the more I worry that my father was right. I should have stayed in California. At least there, I could mostly escape the general weirdness that has always plagued me. A few odd dreams, a few moments of worrying I saw something but managing to convince myself I didn't. That was nothing compared to this.

Everything I've been locking up and holding in, pressing back and pushing under, bursts at the seams, and I think I might cry. My chest heaves a few times – *breathe, breathe* – and my throat clenches – *easy, easy* – and I manage to keep the tears from coming. But I can't take one more second of this god-awful silence or I might scream loud enough to break all the windows in the truck.

"I thought I saw my sister," I tell him again, solidly. I don't want to hide it. "That was the first time I've thought that, so I didn't realise what was happening at first. But I thought I saw her so I followed her, but I'm sure it was just someone else. I think being back at the harvest party where I used to go with her just brought back a lot of memories. And they're good memories, so I'm glad I went, but I think it made me lose my balance. You know, mentally."

I can hear him take a deep breath and let out a relieved sigh.

The air in the cab instantly grows lighter, easier to breathe. I've only told him a fraction of the truth, but sometimes the best way to conceal the big things is to concede the small things. For the moment, I feel safer.

"I'm sorry that happened," he tells me, and looks me in the eye when he says it. Just briefly, before looking back at the road. The words are true, his sorrow thick and dense between us, and I'm thankful for it.

There is only one light on in the house when we pull into the driveway: the one in my room. It leaves the rest of the house shrouded in darkness.

"I'm here if you need anything," Jordan says, when I open the door to climb out. "If I don't hear from you, I'll come check on you in a few days. Fair?"

I offer him a small smile. "Fair."

Inside, the floorboards creak their welcome and the shadows flutter at my sudden presence. I stand still in the living room for a long stretch, just letting the darkness wash over me. The only light comes from the faint glow of the clock on the microwave and the soft light spilling down the stairs from my room. Slowly, I let my feet take me up the groaning stairs and to the hallway at the top. My own room greets me, everything just how I left it, the lamp on the desk spilling an amber wash across the room.

But I do not enter. Something about it feels strange and unwelcoming, even though it's the only bedroom I've ever really known. The only one I can remember. It's as much a part of me as my own skin and bones. Instead, I turn and step into Eve's room, the scents of dust and disuse – and bog laurel – all catching in my nose.

On the dresser beside the door, in the small vase she found at a vintage shop, is a small bouquet of bog laurel. The conversation with my dad comes back to me, how I mentioned I would pick some for her birthday – but I haven't done it yet. I haven't been near the bog at all.

Tiredness tugs at my mind, keeping my thoughts from gaining any clarity. Nothing makes any sense – this day, this week. It's all so clumsy and nonsensical, voices and shadows and girls who look like my sister but aren't my sister wandering around the edges of the harvest party. My thoughts feel frayed and unsteady, and sleep, I think, will be the only thing to help.

So, with a tight throat and burning eyes, I climb carefully into my sister's bed, wriggle underneath the quilt that has laid here since she left, and let all the things in the waiting dark come for me.

twenty-six

Before Mom

A **VIOLENT THUNDERSTORM IS** *sweeping in from the south, and although it is still the afternoon, the house is dark as midnight. Dad is working, Mom is getting groceries and only Eve and I are home. I watch from the kitchen as sheets of rain begin to pour down from the sky, starting rivulets in the grass within minutes. It beats against the roof of the porch, the sound loud through the open screen door.*

There is something dangerously enchanting about thunderstorms, commanding your attention in a way that can't be ignored.

Lightning cleaves the sky, searing hot and bright as the midday sun, before vanishing again. I blink at the suddenness of it, the lines still splintering through my vision as the thunder cracks behind it. The old bones of the house rattle and shiver; even the windows clamour gently. It brings a dark smile, the power of it all. Like there is something that is more powerful than the Moss, even if it is only ephemeral.

A creaking upstairs, followed by silence, draws my attention. Eve has always loved thunderstorms. She is the one to wander outside in the rain and stand there until the storm passes, soaked through and sometimes shivering but smiling like a kid on Christmas morning at the experience of it all.

It puts the idea in my head, and I turn and step out onto the porch. The rain roars against the roof with relentless fury, sheets and sheets of it tearing down from the sky. I can hardly see to the line of trees across the driveway when I step out into the deluge. My clothes are soaked in seconds, water running down into my eyes and ears and the back of my neck, but a sense of wild freedom seeps in along with it. Like I can do anything, be anything, conquer anything. Like the rules are only made to be shattered, and I am every bit a force of nature as the wind and rain and sky.

I know now why Eve likes to stand in the rain. Somehow old, shy parts of me wash away with the water, and the parts left behind feel new and bold and fearless.

Lightning ruptures the sky again and thunder claps a second later. I may love the rain but the lightning is enough to chase me back inside, so I run, dripping and laughing, into the safety of the house.

Grabbing a hand towel from the kitchen for my hair, I call upstairs to my sister. "Eve, the rain is amazing. You should come see it."

I keep towelling off my head, a puddle slowly gathering on the floor as my clothes drip incessantly, but there is no answer from above. She is probably in the shower, or taking a nap, but I climb the stairs to find out anyway. Usually during thunderstorms, Eve is like a fly you can't get rid of. Buzzing around and laughing and opening all the windows to let in the mist and the noise. Her silence feels especially loud now.

The door to her room is open, but she is nowhere in sight. The bathroom is similarly empty, as is my bedroom and our parents' room. A subtle worry starts to tickle my mind, because I know she was home, and I know she never came downstairs. An unannounced game of hide-and-seek would be out of character, especially at our age.

"Eve?" I call from the upstairs hallway. The attic is closed, the ladder still folded up inside, and there are few other places she could be. When there is no immediate answer, I try again, moving into her room this time. "Eve? Where'd you go?"

A few seconds later, I hear a shuffling and a soft whisper. "I'm in here," she says, but it takes me a minute to realise that her voice is coming from her wardrobe. A big, old, antique affair that takes up one whole corner. The door is slightly ajar, a fact I had failed to notice before.

When I pull it open, I find her curled up amongst her coats and shirts, hugging her knees.

"Eve?" I ask softly, fear creeping along my veins. "What are you doing?"

"Come in here," she says, and for a second I don't know what to say. But I know Eve, and I know that she is not someone who is easily afraid. So I pull out a pile of jeans and some boots and I climb in beside her, pulling the door as closed as I can.

It is silent in here. The driving rain is nothing but a distant hiss outside the windows, and the occasional thunder is soft and deadened by all the wood and the clothes.

"What's the matter?" I whisper. I can only see a sliver of her face in the light from the cracked door, and her expression is one that I can't read. One I haven't seen before.

She doesn't answer immediately, just watching me for a lingering moment as the house gently rumbles with thunder. It feels like we are children again, hiding around the house or jumping out to scare our parents.

"You believe in ghosts, don't you?" she asks, her voice so low I can barely catch the words.

The question catches me off guard. It's a conversation we've never directly shared, only ever dancing around it. Teasing it. Keeping it tucked away for later. I suck in a long breath, hugging my knees tighter. "Yes," I tell her. I know enough about this house and the Moss to be able to answer that question unequivocally.

She doesn't nod or respond at first, just letting her eyes wander from me and back to the crack of light coming through the partially open door of the wardrobe.

I can't wait any longer, so I ask, "Why?"

She shakes her head just once and I think I see a tear gathering in one eye, but it's hard to be certain. "There is something here," she whispers, "in this house. But there is also something out there, in the Moss. There are ghosts everywhere, and not all of them are good."

Her words don't lead anywhere. Don't make sense to me in the way that they do to her. But my mind goes back to that time in my room with the closing door, the creaking boots, the game of hide-and-seek in the woods. I know that there are things afoot, because I have seen them. Felt them. Heard them.

"I have seen him," I say softly, and she looks back at me. "The man. Whoever he is. Twice now. But once was too much."

She lets out a sudden breath that seems to say You have no idea, and shifts a little where she sits.

"What about her?" she asks, staring at me as she waits for an answer. Her hair is long, down her shoulders, and unbrushed, which feels unusual for her.

"Who?" I ask.

"The girl."

I shake my head a few times. This is the thing about Eve. Sometimes conversations with her are just dead end after dead end, and the moment you think you're getting anywhere, it's over. I try to latch on to what she's given me. See if I can steer the conversation in a direction that makes sense.

"What girl?"

She shakes her head. "You haven't seen her, then."

"What is she like? Is she like him?"

Eve looks at me with her eyes narrowed. "She is nothing like him."

Another dead end. I close my eyes, trying to collect my thoughts which are scattering slowly around the room. "Why are you hiding in here?"

Her gaze returns to the crack of light, which casts a beam of soft white across her face. It feels fitting, somehow, an illustration of the two halves of her. The vibrant, wild, fun girl so many people love, and the one who hides from ghosts in antique wardrobes.

"The rain," she says, as though it should make perfect sense to me. My fingernails dig into my jeans. Then something in her face changes. Her features freeze, her eyes going wide, and the beam of light across her face shifts ever so slightly, as if something out in the room is blocking the light.

At the same time that I notice it, the sound reaches me. The same awful, creaking, groaning sound of leather boots that has clung like burs to my thoughts every day for years now. No amount of time will let me forget, outrun, leave behind. I hear it in my dreams, even my daydreams when I am meant to be studying.

Eve says nothing. She doesn't move. Doesn't even breathe, I think, as she just stares at him out through the crack in the wardrobe. I don't dare to turn my head to look, lest he should hear the clothing rustle and come for us.

Outside, the soft hiss of the driving rain lessens some more. The storm is dying away, as quickly as it came. Then, the scratch of the boots recedes, the shadow vanishes, and we are again alone.

Eve sucks in a breath like she has just come up for air from deep below the surface. My own breath is uneven, shaking, but I want to be strong for her. Eve has always been the strong one. The loud one. The leader of the two of us. Seeing her frozen with fear, rooted to the spot, not even daring to breathe . . . I cannot let her feel alone.

"He's gone," I say. It's obvious, but I feel like someone should speak. "I'm here." I reach for her hand and squeeze it hard. She looks at me through glassy eyes, and suddenly I don't ever want her to be afraid again.

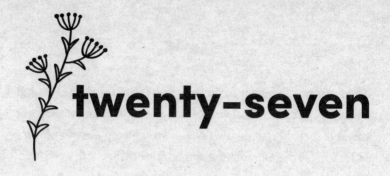

twenty-seven

THERE IS WATER EVERYWHERE. Under foot, above my head, bubbling at the tips of my fingers. Water, but also tree roots, mud, moss and rot. It's climbing up through my veins, inside my skull, spilling out the sockets of my eyes. I am not breathing, but I am not yet dead.

Silence. The heavy, throbbing kind that presses against your ears. No sense of time or place, or reason. *How am I here? Where? Why?*

Things unseen reach for me, but I can feel them morethan see them. Bony fingers, maybe vines, grasping at my hands and feet, but never quite finding their purchase. I am faster than them, if I am even moving at all. There is the sense that I am moving towards something, or searching for something. A way in, or a way out, but of what? How I am here?

Then a voice slices its way through the mire. A whisper, but strong as stone.

Emma. Emma. I am here. I am here. Stay away from him. Listen to me. I will guide you. I am here.

Nonsense. The words are nothing. Meaningless sounds in a meaningless, dank world.

Open your eyes.

So I do.

The sun is not up yet. I wake in Eve's bed, curled up on one side and shivering. The house is always cold in the autumn and winter, but this cold feels like something else. Like stepping out of a shower in January, or wading into the springtime ocean.

Several long minutes stretch away before I realise what it is. Water is dripping from the ceiling and onto the bed, soaking into everything. Steady. The kind of ceaseless *drip, drip, drip* that can drive one mad.

I sit up quickly, switching on the small bedside lamp.

The dripping ceases. The room falls terribly silent. Slowly, all the gathered water in the bed dries up like it was never there at all, and I'm left wondering if this is just another part of the dream. If the strange voice will come back to me and I'll find that I'm still floundering in water somewhere, unable to breathe.

Dad is still asleep when I steal down to the kitchen to make coffee. The floor is cold, even through my wool socks, wicking away all my warmth, and more webs of lacy frost line the windows. The coffee steams in the air, hot and rich. I drink it by a window in the kitchen, by the light of only one candle. There is something about the dance and flicker of candlelight that calms a shaken soul.

The dream is all around me, in every thought and every shadow. *Listen to me. I will guide you. I am here.*

It has haunted me for a year, even when I refused to believe it. When I imagined all the other things that could have happened to her that didn't end with her going into the Moss. But this was Eve, and she was drawn to it like a moth to a flame. The way she kept disappearing in the months leading up to it, just for hours or half a day, until she finally went and never came back. The way I would return home to find her coming back across the garden. Seeing her walk through the door with damp shoes, carrying fresh bog laurel. It wasn't much of a secret, and Dad found every excuse he could to keep her out of the house, and keep her safe, but the difference then was that she always came back.

Always.

Until she didn't.

But if she did go into the bog, why didn't she come back out again? Thoughts of the deep pools and snagging vines like in my dream come back to me. Dad had instilled fear into us over the whole course of our lives. I never much liked being alone, so the thought of dying alone was enough to keep me in the safety of home. But those fears didn't always work on Eve. She didn't seem to fear the same things that I did, or heed the same warnings.

There was something about the Moss that kept calling her back – perhaps not unlike how I can feel it calling to me now. The thought rises like the steam from my coffee: these same ghosts haunted her, as well. The man who drowned his daughter. The girl. Were they to blame for drawing her in? Perhaps she couldn't take it any more. If so, I cannot blame her.

First my mom, and then Eve. One by one, being lured in . . . How long will it be before it's my turn?

Bile bubbles up in my throat. It's a thought that's been simmering since I came back to Maine. That if I don't find Eve or, at the very least, learn what happened, then I'll be next.

My gaze scans along the bog, silhouetted against the paling

sky. Stars still shine stark overhead, but the edges of everything are softening, just a touch. Enough to make the trees and shape of the bog stand out. Enough to feel its gaze.

Would it really be so bad?

The question tumbles forth like it's been dying for escape. The memory of what happened the last time I went in comes back, but I was tired then and had only just returned to Maine. I can hardly count that as a true example of what happens in there. So again, the question bubbles up: *would it really be so bad?*

Before I can talk myself out of it, I have laid my coffee aside and I'm pulling on my boots by the door. Cold air slips in through the small gap underneath it, so I grab my dad's flannel coat off the coat rack and wrap it around myself before slipping from the house.

The grass is crunchy underfoot in the pre-dawn frost. My breath billows before me, and after only a moment my teeth start chattering. But none of it is enough to make me turn back.

My steps do not take me straight to the bog. Not without better clothing, and daylight to mark my way. Instead, there is another spot I want to visit. Somewhere I haven't let myself go since Eve disappeared. She always called it the Fort, although it was a naturally occurring bit of woodland that created an enclosed sort of room within a copse of trees, right on the very edge of the bog. It was one of the ways that we let ourselves stay just within our dad's rule of not going inside, while still feeling like it was just risky enough to satisfy our curiosity.

It's a five-minute trek from the house, buried down in the woodland that runs along the Moss. The trail is overgrown and wild, out of use since we stopped visiting it nearly every day. Every step kicks up memories like dust: packed picnic baskets and days spent hiding from visiting relatives, somewhere no one would think to look. I can very nearly make myself believe that Eve's walking just behind me, or up around a bend in the trail where I can't quite see her. It makes my chest grow tight and my eyes sting in the cold air, but I press on.

The sky is a deep, dark grey, the sun still hidden somewhere far away, giving the cold free rein.

Birds have begun their dawn chorus here and there, shyly. A song erupts to my right, then settles, then again to my left. It makes the woods feel less empty. Makes me feel less like I'm alone as I pick my way over rock and root.

It isn't long before the copse rises up before me like a cage of trees. Two of them grew with an odd bend that allowed us to climb inside. I gave it little thought as a child, but looking at it now, there is something vaguely cursed about it. Unnatural, although nature does not always seem to follow the rules.

I have to crouch a little to climb inside now, but as soon as I step in, it feels like walking through a door back in time. Because that's what the strongest memories do sometimes, I think. Let you pluck at points in time more vividly than others. There's an ache deep within my chest, but I stand in the copse, turning in a slow circle to take it all in. Everything is how I remember it, although this is my first time being here in the dark. Dad would never let us stay out after sunset, and we were never up early enough to see it before the sunrise.

I reach into my pocket for my phone – I need a torch to try and disperse the creeping shadows – but realise with an inner curse that it's Dad's coat I'm wearing, and my phone is on the kitchen table where I left it. Instead, I find Dad's lighter. He ostensibly quit smoking years ago, but the occasional whiff of smoke or sight of him popping in chewing gum when he comes back into the house has given away the truth.

I sit on the cold ground and flick the lighter on. It cuts through the shadows around me, only deepening the ones further afield. The ones beyond the Fort. It makes me feel suddenly exposed, like anything that's out there can see exactly where I am, so I let it go out again.

It takes a few moments for my eyes to readjust to the darkness, so I wait, enjoying the soft birdsong that pops out of random corners of the forest. It's pleasant and light, somehow jarring when compared with the sordid aura of the Moss. I remember the silence, though, when I went inside that time recently. The pressing quiet that felt like a pressure in my head. Nothing wants to live in the Moss, leaving it to rot and waste away in peace.

A sound makes me jump, close at hand. Maybe a squirrel or a chipmunk stirring for the morning, but nevertheless, hairs rise up on the back of my neck. My dreams have been dark of late, and they have made it far too easy to fill in the blanks when it comes to sounds like this. All manner of spirits and shadows spring to life in my imagination, each more terrifying than the last. And it's weird because there have always been ghosts here. Strange things that only Eve and I saw – and our mother, although that was only a suspicion on my part. She never breathed a word, one way or another.

Another soft snap nearby. The pressing need to see my surroundings overwhelms my fear of the lighter and I snap it to life once more.

A shape fills the space before me, so close and awful I fall backwards and lose my grip on the lighter. It tumbles, now flameless, into the leaves of the forest as I scramble backwards. The girl from the plane, I think, but different than I've seen her before. Dead and matted and rotted almost beyond recognition.

I feel around frantically in the leaves, searching with shaking hands for the lighter, and find it under a mat of twigs and branches. Holding it up in front of me, I strike it again, and this time it takes two tries before a flame kindles to life.

Nothing. No one. The forest is as empty as it was when I entered it. I leave the lighter shining for a time, holding it up in all directions – half expecting the girl to be behind me – but there is no sign of her. I'm struck by the sudden aloneness. The way even the birds have stopped singing, and it feels like I could be the only living soul in the world.

I pull my thumb away and let the lighter go out, wrapping my arms around my knees. My eyes take a moment to adjust to the darkness, but it's less complete this time. Sunrise is fighting for control of the sky, and a pinkish glow silhouettes the trees around me.

I'm here, Emma.

The voice slips in through the dark forest. Not from any particular direction. All directions. It isn't fear that floods me, but a burning, aching, hungry curiosity.

"Eve?" I say to the darkness. It feels foolish. Ridiculous. She's been gone a year. Why would the voice belong to her? Why wouldn't I recognise it? But I am alone in these woods, and my thoughts are free to roam to all the wild places they like. So I let them take me where they will. "Eve. Is that you?"

There is only silence – at least at first. But the voice comes back to me, softer than before.

I miss you.

The words trickle in like gently falling rain, but my body takes it like a punch to the chest. Everything tightens, air seems far away, and tears sting their way down from my eyes. *What if it isn't her?* I *know* it's her. *What if it's* him*?* I don't want to believe it.

"Eve?" It's barely my voice that says it, unrecognisable over the sobs. "Can you hear me?"

A long moment stretches away, and as the sky grows lighter and lighter, the voice grows fainter and fainter.

Yes.

My hands clench around leaves on the ground, and I try to stop the flow of tears. "Where are you?"

It's cold, Emma. It's cold, and it's dark.

Memories of the plane, the dead girl, the voice, the horror of it all wash back like cold water smacking me in the face. But the dead girl was not my sister, I am very nearly certain of that.

Be careful. He is after you, like he was after me.

"Where are you? Where are you, Eve?"

A long minute drags by, and when she finally answers, I can barely hear it at all.

You know where I am. You shouldn't come here.

And the sun is rising, and the birdsong starts up again, and I can feel her presence leave me like I watched her walk out of the room. I cannot even explain it. It is just a feeling that slips perfectly into place.

"I will find you," I tell her, although whether she can hear me, I cannot say.

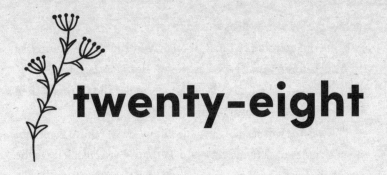

twenty-eight

I **STAY IN THE** copse of trees until the sky has shifted from pale pink to a soft yellow. Light floods all around me, and the racing feet of squirrels and chipmunks have joined the chorus of birds. I tried a few more times to speak to Eve, but I was only met with silence, like the rising sun chased her away.

You know where I am.

And I do, I know, though the police would struggle to believe me. What proof do I have? They looked everywhere for her, even in the bog – it made for a difficult search, what with all the uneven ground and pools of water, so they soon had to call it off. There was no telling where she could be in there, and the thing about bogs is that they do not like to give up their dead without a fight, keeping them well away from the surface. And anyway, according to them, the bog was a very unlikely place for her to be. Short of kidnapping – or murder – they said it was likely that she had just left. That she didn't want to be found.

But I have always known that couldn't be true. They didn't know Eve like I did. They didn't know of our friendship, how she would tell me almost anything, and how she would never just leave me like that. It hurt when she started keeping her own secrets – visiting the bog, wandering off on her own, spending time in her room – but we were still as close as ever.

If she did go into the Moss, though, why didn't she return like she had before? What kept her there? *Death*, a dark part of my heart whispers, but I push it aside. If she did die in there, then finding her would be nearly impossible.

The way the world changed and shifted the last time I went into the bog comes back to me yet again. Perhaps Eve *couldn't* leave the bog. Perhaps she has been there all this time, waiting for me.

Or perhaps she did die in there, and all that is speaking to me now is her ghost. This house, this land, it loves its ghosts. They have been here longer than us, and they will be here long after we are gone. But that thought makes the tears want to flow all over again, so I push it away.

There is a thread somewhere within me that plucks like a guitar string. One I feel has been there all along, but I have made sure not to hear it. Feel it. Acknowledge it in any way. But now it is strong and urgent, desperate for my attention.

It's the feeling that Eve is still alive. Some invisible thread that connects me to her as a sister, that tells me I would know if she had died, that something within me would change. But I've never let it breathe, because I worry I'm just telling myself that to cover up the pain. Embracing the denial, instead of the truth.

But there is a spark somewhere inside me that has stayed alive all this time, one that I feel certain would have burnt out if she were truly gone. Feeling that spark, and hearing her voice, and everything that has happened since I returned home . . . Some things are shifting into clarity, while leaving a thousand broken questions behind.

Eve is alive, somewhere. Somewhere in the Moss. I can find her, maybe, and bring her home, if whatever trapped her there doesn't trap me as well. But there is someone else after me, someone that Eve warned me about. The Sedge Man, Simon Lake, if I had to guess. The man who drowned his daughter. I don't quite know what he wants with me, or what he wanted with her, but bringing Eve home will only happen if I keep far away from him. Of that, I am certain.

The twinkly daffodil light of morning chases away the worst of the shadows, and I feel strangely calm off the back of my earlier fright. Like a muscle that suddenly tenses, then relaxes. All the strange happenings, everything up until now, slides softly into place and a sort of grim but determined resolve kindles deep within.

I can find Eve. I can bring Eve home.

I think.

I hope.

But that will mean going deep into the Moss. Further than I've ever gone before, which isn't very far at all. A bit like Hansel and Gretel, I can leave breadcrumbs to mark my way. Keep the Moss from swallowing me altogether, like it did Eve. I have to come back out because I cannot leave my father alone. Just the thought makes my head swim. Losing all three of us, one after the other. A breadcrumb trail of broken heart pieces.

Pain breaks like a wave in my chest, but I swallow it back.

I have to come back out.

Cheerful rosy light splashes through the house when I return. Dad is just leaving for work, pouring hot coffee into his travel mug and turning to me when I enter.

"Where did you go?" Worry highlights his features, the kind I've seen before.

"Just for a walk," I assure him with a fresh smile. A smile that says *good morning!* in a much more chipper tone than I feel. "I think I slept wrong. I needed to stretch my back."

"Wait until you hit fifty," Dad groans, taking his keys from the console table by the door. "See you tonight."

And once again, I am alone in the quiet house.

The brightest of the sunlight hasn't yet hit Eve's room on the west side of the house, but it is still brighter and warmer than when I left it earlier. There are no traces of water on the bed. Nothing to indicate that the strange, incessant dripping from last night was anything other than a dream.

Slipping back into my room, I reach underneath the jeans in my old wardrobe again and pull out the note Eve left behind. Unfold it, desperate to feel closer to her. Because that's how it felt in the trees. Like I could reach out and touch her. Like her voice was so close at hand I might see her face if I turned around.

I cannot take it any more, Emma. I've tried for so long, but I miss her too much. I can still feel her, sometimes, but it isn't enough. I want to be with her. I know how to find her, I think. Don't follow me. I mean it. It will break Dad if you do. I love you, Em.

P.S. Stay far away from the Sedge Man. He won't stop, like a hunter, until there's nothing left of you.

The words *I know how to find her* highlight themselves on the page, rippling and shivering.

I can remember the day Dad told us, as vividly as if it was yesterday, that Mom had disappeared. Then without warning she slipped quietly into the past tense and never came back out of it. There is no preparing for that. Nothing to make the blow any easier, so the pain just grows and grows and runs wild without restraint. I can feel the echoes of it now, the raw and grating monster that haunted me for months and months. That still haunts me to this day, if I think on it long enough.

I know how to find her, I think.

Why do the words strike such a strange chord in me? Like with Eve, there was never any proof that Mom went into the Moss. The police went over all the possibilities. Kidnapping, murder, even the beginnings of a serial killer – although that one came more from the locals than the police.

But if Eve knew how to find her, why did she keep it to herself?

A voice starts up, almost in a whisper, and somehow both in my room and far away.

> 'Tis the last rose of summer,
> Left blooming alone;
> All her lovely companions
> Are faded and gone;

Goosebumps slither along my skin. A hundred memories boil up, of my mother singing it to us on the porch, in the bath as children, while cooking dinner downstairs. Her mother was Irish, she said, and taught it to her when she was barely ten. She stitched a few of the verses into a towel that hung by the door, but it's gone now. I haven't seen it in years.

A sudden calmness comes over me. Refolding the paper, I tuck it back into its spot under my jeans then turn and head for the bathroom.

Questions. More questions than I could ever ask. They all collide in my head, breaking apart and forming nonsense. I let the hot water run and run and run, steam growing to fill the room, thinking of all the things I will ask my father this evening. I have half a mind to ask Jordan to drive me to his job, but I need time to think. Time to clear my head, after school, of course.

I wait on the front porch for my father to finish mowing the grass, rocking softly in the late afternoon light. My dad waves at me from across the garden, and some distant part of me feels bad for not waving back. How happy he must be to have one of his daughters, any family member at all, waiting for him at home.

But today, I am made of questions. Fuelled by confusion. Unrest. Hurt.

Determination.

He approaches me presently, lingering at the bottom of the steps.

"Nice evening, isn't it? But you can tell it's going to get cold tonight. The air has a bite to it. Maybe we should put on a fire!" His voice rises in excitement, and a bit of a question.

"A fire would be nice," I tell him. There's something about wood smoke that's good for the soul. "I need to ask you something."

Clouds drift across his face. He watches me, then climbs the porch steps and stands awkwardly, waiting. "What is it?"

I've had all day to think about it, but I choke as the words come out. "Do you know what happened to Mom?"

All traces of levity drain from his face. He stares at me for a few seconds. A few long seconds. Then he lowers himself into the other rocking chair and stares out at the Moss.

Somehow, it already feels like an answer.

"Why are you asking me that?"

I have always hated questions that are answered with questions.

"Because Eve thought she went into the Moss. But we've never really talked about it."

Now Dad looks down at his shoes, and I can see the corner of his eyes glistening. A breeze gently blows, and the song of the evening birds hums steadily in the background, and I just wait.

"I know we talked before," I say, softly. "But I . . . I still don't understand. What are you not telling me?"

It feels like the sun has at last crumbled from the sky before he speaks again.

"There's so much, Emma. So much that it would take me days to get through it all . . ."

"I have days," I tell him.

He sighs and looks at me, blinking away the tears. Small flecks of grey shine through his blonde hair and I can't believe I never noticed them before. "I don't know what it was, Emma. And I sound mad for even saying it. I think about it every single day, and it has yet to make any sense. When we came to see this house, you girls were just tiny. Toddlers. And your mom, she connected with it right away. In a way I just didn't quite get, like it was meant to be. So we bought it, and things were good. Great. You girls loved it . . ."

His voice trails off in that way it does when someone is wandering in their own memories, happily. I let him be for a time.

"It took a while for me to suspect anything was off. Years. She started to mention that she thought the house was haunted. That she saw things or heard things, from time to time. Sometimes, I would wake up and find her standing down by the Moss, just staring at it, without any shoes, or underdressed for the weather. She couldn't always remember how she ended up there, or why. I figured it was all because she wasn't sleeping well, because she wasn't. She kept having bad dreams, or waking up thinking she was drowning. We took her to a doctor, but they said she was fine."

My own gaze travels to the Moss, and for a moment I think one of the trees in the distance is a girl watching me.

"She kept saying 'he' wouldn't leave her alone. That 'he' wanted her to go there. She never said who. I searched the property for anyone I could find, but there was no one."

"Did you go into the Moss?" The question comes out scalpel-sharp and quick.

"A little, but you know it's not easy to get around in there. I checked the woods, the garden, the house, everywhere that I could think of. I even set up a security camera. Nothing. And it just carried on growing worse, but slowly. She barely slept. She grew afraid of baths or showers, and even the rain. It didn't make any sense. When I tried to get her to explain it, she couldn't. Or wouldn't."

Slowly, I let my gaze wander back to his face. *She grew afraid of baths or showers, and even the rain.* My mind traces back along the past few weeks, shakily. The bath, the thunderstorm, the water dripping from above the bed. The soggy ground in the wood by the harvest party. Water. Water, everywhere. And I don't know what *it* is, but immediately, I wonder if that's how it communicates. The Moss, or the things within it. The Sedge Man. Eve. The dead girl on the plane, with the raindrops slanting against the windows. That's its medium. Its conduit.

"One morning at sunrise, I heard shuffling downstairs by the door. I came down just in time to see her wandering into the Moss. When I ran after her, she was gone, like she'd walked through a door I couldn't see and it had swallowed her. I went in and looked everywhere, for hours and hours, getting lost over and over again. But that . . ." I can see his throat tighten, his jaw clench. "That was the last time I saw her. She never came back out again."

My heart beats in my ears, nearly drowning out the birds. The image of my mother entering the Moss is as vivid in my mind as if I had seen it myself.

"And Eve went in after her," I whisper.

His eyes wander over to the Moss again, flickering with hate. "I guess I've always . . . thought so, too. But I also figured she could have drowned. Your mother, I mean. Because there was nothing else that could have happened. It's not so large that you could get lost for ever. You'd eventually find your way back out again. But I can never stop thinking about . . . about the things she said. The things she saw. You know I've always been a sceptic. But there's just something about the Moss, Emma. Like it was plucked from the blackness between stars and left here to rot. Like it's a hollow in the world. A tear in the seam. I don't know. I'm not making any sense."

But to me, everything is finally making sense. All the weirdness, the darkness, the hunger and the hauntings . . . It has always been the Moss, because the Moss has always been there. Watching and waiting and luring and plotting.

"It doesn't make sense," he says again. "But all I can say is that I think there are parts of the world we don't understand. Things no one can explain. My first thought when she disappeared was to pack up and leave, but then, what if she comes home? I want to be here, waiting for her. Then Eve vanished, and I knew I couldn't leave, but I couldn't lose you either."

"So you sent me away."

"What else could I do?"

My chest tightens, but I don't cry. "I don't blame you," I tell him. "I did, for ages. But not any more. Not after knowing all of this."

"I only wanted to protect you, like I couldn't protect them. I have to keep you out of that place, however I can." He takes a shuddering breath. "The end finds us all. Don't go looking for it too soon. Like they did."

I wipe a few tears from my eyes, then onto my jeans. "I miss who I was before they went away. The rest of your life seems so much longer after you've lost someone."

Silence seeps in and lingers, thick and heavy. The day stretches away, the shadows growing longer, the birdsong softer, and the porch creaks under the slow rocking of our chairs.

"Every day," my dad says, finally, "I look out there and think they're coming back. I think I see movement, or a face, but it only ever ends up being a bush or a tree." Sadness weighs down his voice. "But I keep waiting. Maybe one day, I'll leave. When I've waited so long that there's no chance they'll come back. I don't know. Maybe one day."

I pull in a breath and hold it, just to keep from crying. "I never got to say goodbye to either of them," I tell him. "And that's the knife that keeps on cutting."

His lips twitch a bit, eyes shining.

I speak to fill the silence. "I think Eve's still alive."

His head turns to me. "Why?"

I shrug. "I just feel it. The part of me that would have died with her is still alive. And I know *that* doesn't make sense, but it's true." I can't tell him about hearing her voice, because then he will almost certainly send me away again.

He smiles sadly at me, like he forgot how to hope for such things, but that's OK. He can be content to wait, but I am going to find Eve, and I am going to bring her back home. He just doesn't know it yet.

twenty-nine

MY MIND IS A mess of distractions the next day, but I must try to focus nevertheless.

English has always been my favourite class, but there is an unease to the room from the moment I walk in. No one else seems to notice it, but it's everywhere I look. A steady but soft dripping sound reaches my ears, and it takes me a minute, standing just inside the door, to notice that there is a bucket in one corner, near the teacher's desk. It catches drips of water falling from the ceiling every few seconds.

My eyes meet the teacher's, and I can tell that he has had to explain this to everyone who has walked into the room.

"There's a water leak in the room above us. They're already working on it."

Nodding, I slide into my seat, only a row in front of Jordan. He gives me a smile before I turn away to face forward again, and there's a steady kind of calmness whenever he's in the room. I always felt like he had the ceaselessly optimistic personality of a golden retriever.

"All right," Mr Berry says, standing and clapping his hands together. "Speaking of water, let's take a hop across the pond to eighteenth-century Paris. Right? *A Tale of Two Cities.* How did you feel on reading these next three chapters?"

The conversation starts up, and usually I have something to offer but the dripping coming from the corner is the only thing I can think about. It rings loud and harsh, splitting my ears with every drop. My eyes can't look away from the bucket, slowly, slowly filling up with water.

Around me, the lights dim, then go out altogether. No one else seems to notice and Mr Berry carries on talking as if this is just another day, but my bones know it isn't. Something feels wildly, absolutely, chaotically out of place.

The only light in the room comes from the one window, but even that feels shadowy and grey, like something is blocking the sun. Without making it obvious, I turn to glance quickly at Jordan, sending him what I hope isn't a nervous smile, and I find him watching me.

From somewhere in the room, a whispering starts up, but the words are muffled and unclear. It takes some time for them to sort themselves into something intelligible. Something I can just barely make out.

I am patience. I will wait. And you will come. I know you have always wanted to.

My fingers clutch the edges of my desk to stop them from shaking, and as the last word rings out, the lights come back on. Daylight streams in again, pure and bright and beautiful. In the corner, the water has all but ceased dripping into the bucket, only a drop or two a minute. Whatever leak had happened above us must be nearly fixed, but I can think of none of that. There is only the voice, and the words that seem to have found a home in some secluded part of me.

"Emma," Jordan whispers from behind me. "Are you OK?"

I turn, my hands still trembling, jaw clenched tight, and nod once. "I'm fine. Thanks."

The rest of the class passes in a disorienting blur while I stare only at the book and papers sitting on my desk, afraid that if I look around again I might find a man in a black coat and boots watching me from the windows, the corner, a crack in the door.

thirty

After Eve

SCHOOL HAS ONLY JUST started. Autumn teases us with a shock of colour here, a chill wind there, signs for pumpkin patches and the harvest festival in two months' time. Mornings are cooler, and I wake up earlier and earlier only to climb back under my blankets for warmth.

It's upsetting, being awake before the rest of the house, so I pull the blankets up to my nose and shut my eyes against the pressing dark.

There is something wrong about today, even though it has barely begun. A subtle but unmistakable pressure that I can't ignore. There are no ghosts or boots or voices in the room with me, but it doesn't make me feel any less afraid. In fact, the house feels especially empty in a way that my still-sleepy mind cannot fully understand. I lie with it for a while, staring at the ceiling, nestled under a quilt while the sky grows light outside.

When the sun is high enough to send beams of light through my window, I finally sit up and kick off the covers. A crunching as my head leaves my pillow makes me start, and I reach for a small, folded piece of paper I hadn't noticed before. It looks torn from a notebook, the kind Eve uses for her homework, and was hastily and unevenly folded.

When I pull it open, hurried handwriting greets me.

I cannot take it any more, Emma. I've tried for so long, but I miss her too much. I can still feel her, sometimes, but it isn't enough. I want to be with her. I know how to find her, I think. Don't follow me. I mean it. It will break Dad if you do. I love you, Em.

P.S. Stay far away from the Sedge Man. He won't stop, like a hunter, until there's nothing left of you.

I quickly lose count of how many times I read it, because my mind can't force it all to make sense on the first read. Three times. Five times. Twenty. Then I let it fall to the floor and run, slipping in my socks, from my room to Eve's.

Her bed is empty. The room is empty, and I even check the wardrobe, just to be sure. Her backpack, which she usually leaves hanging on the back of the door, is also gone. Cold dread fills up my stomach, my throat, threatens to cut off my air. I run from the room and down the stairs, stumbling down the last few steps and crashing to the floor, but if I'm injured, I don't notice.

"Eve?" I call to the empty house, just in case I can catch her. "Eve? Where are you?"

There is no answer, of course. Our dad is already at work, Mom has been gone for two years now, and the only living soul in the house is me. No signs of life in the kitchen. The living room. I even check the laundry room and the pantry.

Eve is gone.

Yanking the front door open, I stagger out on to the porch and grip one of the posts by the steps. "Eve!" I scream into the garden. My voice just bounces off the trees, breaking apart and coming back *to me at an odd pitch.*

Don't follow me. I mean it.

My heart, soul and mind all know that there is only one place she would go that she shouldn't, and my eyes move slowly to the Moss. Perhaps I imagine it, but there is an air about it this morning that I haven't felt before. Like it won something it has been working for, for years. A smugness. A satisfaction.

"Eve." *A whisper this time. Barefoot, I jump down the steps and tear down the garden towards the fence as fast as I can, gravel slicing into my feet as I cross the driveway, but when I reach the fence, I stop. Like Eve's words reach out with invisible hands and force me to listen.*

Don't follow me.

I can hear the words this time in her voice, or maybe I can feel them. They press in on the sunlight and the crisp air, grabbing at me with slender, desperate fingers.

Don't follow me.

I lean over the fence, tears falling from my face to the damp ground. It is only a bog. One of many around the world. But I know this one, and I know that the last time someone I love went in, they never came back out.

"Come back," *I whisper, but only the birds can hear me. I am otherwise completely, utterly alone.*

My eyes are so full of tears that it takes three tries to dial 911. They send officers out, but they don't immediately launch into a search for her like I imagined. She hasn't been missing for more than a full day, and the note could be anything. The random musings of a teenager. Or something I wrote myself. They tell me to calm down, they call my dad home, and they say that they will follow up tomorrow, when it has been twenty-four hours.

She might not have twenty-four hours, but they don't listen to me. With no signs of foul play, no body, and nothing to go on, they just climb back into their car and leave, and once again, I am alone.

"Did you see which way she went?"

"When was the last time you saw her?"

"What was the last thing she said to you?"

"You didn't hear her come into your room to leave the note?"

"Did she say anything strange last night?"

My dad's questions pour out, his eyes white and wild, and I can see the same fear, the same horror, in them that was there when Mom disappeared. We are cursed, surely, for history to repeat itself so soon. He keeps leaving the house and going down to the bog, wandering around until he is soaked from the waist down, and then coming back to shower off and change. I've searched everywhere I can think of. The woods, our little secret copse of trees, the attic, but there are no signs of her anywhere.

My answers for him offer nothing of substance. No, I didn't see which way she went. I saw her last night, before I went to bed. She poked her head in to say goodnight, like she sometimes does, but I was already half asleep.

I work backwards and try to piece together the past few days, knowing I should be able to pull out some sort of detail that will make all of this make sense, but there is nothing. I think she worked hard to make it that way. To make her impending disappearance unobvious. That's her way. Just like Mom. Here one minute and gone the next, and that's just it. That's the end of it. No sightings of her, no traces left behind.

When Dad has grilled me enough and collapsed on to the couch to make some phone calls, I climb the stairs on unsteady legs, the house wobbling all around me and the daylight cracking and shaking and stinging my eyes. When I reach the top, I face my room, a sort of numbness working its way through me from my feet to my head. I don't know where the pain has gone, or the confusion, but in its place is just a yawning chasm. I remember vaguely feeling this before, when my mom disappeared, but I forgot just how deep it runs. How empty a person can feel.

Turning away from my room, I slip instead into Eve's, stopping just inside the door when a vase filled with bog laurel draws my attention. I don't remember it being there yesterday. I don't even remember it being there when I checked her room this morning, but in the panic of her vanishing, I could have missed it.

I could have missed so much. I did miss so much. There must have been signs leading up to this, and I feel foolish for not noticing them.

Tears run swift and hot down my face. I push past the bog laurel and climb into her bed, lying my head back on her pillow. Where she must have been sometime during the night. Only a wall away.

All the memories I have with her play like a silent movie in the background of my mind, and I worry that those memories are the only ones with her I'll ever have. That, as with my mother, Eve's disappearance will reach forward in time and snip away all the things that could have been. The moments that could have happened, robbing us of new memories.

But in my head, I snatch at the future, holding on to it with all my might. Clutching and clawing, desperate. I have had enough of goodbyes for one lifetime.

I will not, cannot, say goodbye to Eve.

thirty-one

"**OK, BUT REMIND ME** why you need hiking boots on a random Thursday in October?" Jordan asks when he picks me up after school the next day. "I mean, as far as needs go, that's one of the more unusual ones."

"My dad and I are thinking about getting out more, and I want to show him that I'm excited about it." The lie is a little too easy to tell, but there is some small amount of truth to it. Dad has expressed interest in taking walks, especially up some of the nearby blueberry hills that are done producing for the season. That's just not why I need the hiking boots.

"That woodland trail near Adam's place is a nice one, if you're looking for more ideas. I had my first kiss out there, actually."

When I look over at him, surprised, he's blushing. The way he shifts uncomfortably makes me think that he regrets saying anything.

"Who was the lucky lady?" I ask lightly, hoping it makes him feel less awkward.

He clears his throat. Drums two fingers on the steering wheel. "Amelia."

I'm not sure what I was expecting, but that wasn't it. Amelia, the girl who isn't followed by ghosts and doesn't have a trail of missing family members behind her, or a house by a bog that collects strangeness like vintage figurines. I only have a few memories with her, but none of them are good.

That girl was always strange. Amelia to another friend, in the bathroom, regarding Eve's disappearance.

Eve had always made me feel better about our collective weirdness. *Life is so much more boring when you're only limited to seeing living people,* she had said. One of the only times she ever spoke of the ghosts out loud. A way to make light of something I knew bothered her, but that she could not control.

"I know you don't like her very much," Jordan says sheepishly. "It was a couple of years ago."

"It's not that I don't like her," I tell him. "It's just that she's afraid to be around me."

He looks over at me, looking me up and down as if there is something about me that he should be worrying about but might have missed. "You don't seem, I don't know, very scary to me."

"My sister and I were always a little weird. It's not much of a secret."

"I have heard that. It's not very nice, though."

"But it's true."

Another glance at me. I can tell that he's hoping for the truth. I'll give him a little of it.

"I think it's our house. It's really old, and really old houses pile up with history. I think sometimes that history spills over into our lives." I don't have any science to back that up, of course, but it's the way I always looked at it.

"Ghosts?" he queries. His tone is light, but deeply curious.

"I don't know what they are, really," I say. I'm quieter now, drawn back in time to those feelings of being left out in the cold. All those birthday parties we were never invited to. The groups of kids talking amongst themselves that dispersed when we tried to join. I never asked for any of it. And I never told anyone about our house or the things we saw there, but sometimes things have a way of setting themselves loose: a conversation overheard between me and Eve, a doodle on a page that another student saw, a book checked out from a library about communing with the dead. Secrets love to escape, like lost balloons love to climb into the sky.

"Sometimes you see or hear things that don't fit in with what we know," I say. "Things that don't follow reality."

"One time, I saw a robin that squawked like a crow."

I laugh at that because it is so unexpected. "Could you have just been looking at a robin and hearing a crow?"

"I don't think so. I remain convinced to this day that I saw a glitch in the simulation."

"I've seen a lot, Jordan, but I've never seen that."

"It's nice to feel unique. I even looked it up online, but no one else seems to have seen it."

"You must feel special."

"I do, actually."

We drive in a nice sort of silence for the rest of the way, and I feel lighter having said what I said. Like it was always in the room with us but never addressed.

The shop is quiet when we get there. I make my way to the back, where a rack of outdoor boots sits under a *Sale: 25% off* sign.

"Hey. It's your lucky day," Jordan says, flicking the cardboard sign with a nail.

"Good. I don't have a lot of those," I say, laughing a little.

It's just as well, too, because it turns out that boots are expensive, and I am nearly at the end of the last dregs of money my dad gave me before I left California.

Jordan wanders around the aisles, circling back every thirty seconds or so while I try on a pair of mid-calf hiking boots that boast water resistance. They're snug and heavy, but I think they'll do the job. Staring at myself in the tall mirror, wearing the boots but not a smile, I wonder what my mom and sister did to prepare. Did they just wander in one morning, one night, with nothing but the clothes on their backs? Did they take food, or drink? When I think back to Eve's last few days, I recall very little. Seeing her very little. Hearing her very little. If she was planning or packing, I have no way of knowing. It was like she had already left, even though she was often still in the house. Hiding away in her room like a silent cobweb.

"Earth to Emma."

My attention snaps back to the present and I glance over at Jordan, who stands a few steps away.

"Sorry. I'm tired today." Sitting back down on the stool, I pull off the boots and put them back into the box. "These will be perfect."

There is work to do, things to prepare, but I cannot rush.

If, like my mother and sister, I do not return, I want to know that I said my goodbyes. That I spent the time needed with each person I would leave behind.

There is a small ice cream shop by a pond that is about to close for the season, and Jordan begs me to let him go in. So we do. If my footsteps follow Eve's and Mom's, and the Moss refuses to give me up, then an afternoon eating ice cream with a boy will, at least, be one of my better final memories.

"How can you eat peppermint ice cream if it isn't Christmas?" Jordan asks me when we find a picnic table overlooking the water and take a seat.

"I don't tend to eat a lot of ice cream around Christmas time, what with all the snow."

"My mom always puts ice cream on our pumpkin pie."

I make a face as my spoon digs deep into the cup. "I hope it's not peppermint."

"Vanilla."

We eat quietly for a time, Jordan working his way through his pistachio, me my peppermint, and not far away, the pond lies glassy and bluish, reflecting the hills that rise up like teeth all around it. A large sign nearby, standing at an odd angle, announces that they will be closing for the season in two days.

"When I told you what I told you before you left," Jordan starts, and my hand stops scooping out another bite, "I was really nervous, as I'm sure you can imagine. I was embarrassed for weeks afterwards, and not because you didn't say anything. Just because it's hard putting yourself on the line like that. But right now, I'm not nervous, I'm not embarrassed. I just want to tell you something."

Very slowly, I pull another bite to my mouth, keeping my eyes fixed on his face. There's no redness, no darting of the eyes, nothing to signal the awkwardness that I've seen before.

"I've liked you for a long time, Emma. I think you know that. I didn't really know what it was for a while, but I figured it out just before your sister disappeared. I don't just like you, like I like this ice cream, or my favourite blue shirt. I *like* like you, and even if you never *like* like me back, I just need you to know that. I don't think of you as a vampire that needs to be kept at arm's length." A small laugh, and he looks down to scoop up another bite, but leaves it in the cup. "I like your strangeness, and your ghosts, and that weird house you live in. It's all part of you, and I like all of you."

He falls silent but meets my gaze, the edges of his mouth ever so slightly upturned. For some reason, it doesn't feel like he's waiting for an answer this time. He's just watching me because he wants to.

"Jordan," I say after a minute, and this time his name sounds different leaving my mouth. "You should never fall for a girl who's haunted. The ghosts are a package deal."

He laughs a little and takes another bite. "As long as they don't watch me sleep, I'll manage."

I look away from him to collect my thoughts, watching some ripples run along the surface of the pond. I hardly give them a second thought at first, but they get larger and larger, and small white caps seem to indicate something thrashing around. Nothing large. No bigger than a person. A girl, in a white nightgown, fighting something as she is shoved further and further beneath the surface.

After a moment, the ripples stop.

Water.

My gaze returns to Jordan. I cannot leave him unanswered, not for a second time. But I have hardly even let myself linger on thoughts of him for more than a few seconds, although why that is now feels painfully more obvious than it was before.

"I do like you, Jordan. I'm careful not to let myself think about it for too long, but I've probably liked you for a while. I remember one time shopping in LA and I thought I saw you in a coffee shop, and then I remembered that of course it wasn't you. But I wished it was. When Eve disappeared, I thought a few times about calling you, but really, I didn't want to talk to anyone. I think a chasm opened up before me when it happened, and I just let myself fall into it. I stopped thinking about anything else. Stopped caring about anyone. I just wanted her back, or I wanted my mom, or I wanted everything that I couldn't have. And no one could make that better."

Sorrow – for me – glasses over his eyes. "I'm so sorry, Emma."

"You know what they say. The only way out is through. And that's . . ." There's more, but I stop then, because I don't know how Jordan would take it. If it would all make sense, or send him running, and I'm afraid to lose anyone else.

He seems to sense the unspoken words and nods once, as if encouraging me on. "What is it?"

I take one more small bite, thinking. "That's something I think about a lot. About the only way out being through. Like for Eve, there was such a deep sadness after Mom disappeared. A thing that was always there, untouchable, always feeding and growing. A thing you never talked about or looked at directly. And I think for her, that was like the Moss. A thing that's always there. A thing you can feel, and sense, and see, but never touch. And I think going in, for her, was a way to manage the pain. To go through it, just to see if she could. If she could survive it. And, hopefully, find Mom along the way."

Jordan stares, and I meet his gaze unflinching, wondering what thoughts hide behind his eyes.

"And I think it's become that way for me. Grief makes a place in your mind that you cannot go. Cannot touch, because it hurts too badly. And the Moss is just that place in the world."

His shoulders rise slowly with a breath, then fall. "And what about your mom? Why did she have to go in?"

I shake my head, wishing I could pluck answers to questions like that the way one picks flowers. "I don't think I'll ever know."

I finish off the last of my ice cream, while Jordan just picks at his. Then I toss my cup in the nearby trash can and meet his gaze again. "Jordan, I just want you to know that if anything ever happens to me, I *like* like you too."

A smile, then a frown, then eyebrows furrowed in confusion as he unpacks what I just said. "Why would something happen to you?"

"My mom, my sister . . . Bad things follow us like our own shadows. And I think . . ." I catch myself about to tell him that I think I can find my sister. If I do, the risks of him telling someone, involving the police, my father sending me away – it's all too much. I want to tell him, more than anything, but I want to find Eve more. "I would just hate for something to happen without having told you first."

Confusion still twists his features, but he allows himself to smile. "So, you *like* me? I'll have to write it in my diary."

"I said what I said." Back out over the water, all is still. No trace of anything amiss. No drowning girls or murderous fathers. "But I don't know what I can do about that right now. Liking you, I mean. My life is still like a jigsaw puzzle box that's been shaken by a toddler."

He laughs a little. "I know. I'll be here. I haven't felt this way before, so I feel like it's worth waiting for. And I'm happy to keep

spending time with you. I promise I won't make it awkward."
Another smile.

His words strike a chord in my chest that resonates with
unfamiliar notes. I try to follow the reverberations, to understand
what it is, even though my emotions feel all out of tune and off-
key. It isn't sorrow, or pity, or any of the other feelings I've grown
used to giving and receiving. Instead, it feels more like . . . the
sense of being enough for someone. The weightlessness of being
loved for who you are, and all the faults and oddities that come
with you. Not having to hide them or stuff them into your pockets,
hoping no one will notice them.

"Thank you," I say, and it's all I can get out before my eyes
start to burn.

We chose to set up the telescope in our back garden, only because
the wide expanse of the Moss offers the best horizon, and I force
my gaze upwards while Jordan swears and fiddles with the go-to
feature on the telescope.

A pitch-dark sky watches from above, flecked with white-hot
specks of starlight. Somehow, that feathery blackness above feels
less frightening than the darkness that lives down here. On Earth.
All around me.

"They don't make these things like they used to."

I laugh a little, plucking at the petals of some pinkish flowers
growing up from the grass. "You sound like an old man."

"Sometimes I think I might be. I like to get an early bedtime,
and I'm pretty sure my knee hurts when it's about to rain." He

pauses. "But my mom thinks that's psychosomatic."

"I feel like she would know."

"Maybe."

He messes with the telescope again as I bring one of the flowers up to my nose and sniff. A light, sweet aroma floods my head.

"There. Finally." He points to the eyepiece like I should look through it, so I lean over and peer through. A furiously bright star waits for me, bright like the sun against the dark. "It's called Aldebaran. It might be my favourite star, but I'm privately partial to Betelgeuse, as well. This one is only sixty-five light years away, so that light has only been travelling for sixty-five years."

"*Only* sixty-five years?"

"Well, that's nothing when it comes to outer space. The *Pioneer 10* probe is headed that way, but it won't arrive for something like a couple of million years."

"It looks so close."

"That's because it's huge."

We go quiet while I keep staring at the dazzling star, the telescope whirring now and again as it tries to stay centred. Beside me, Jordan shifts a little bit closer.

"You want to look again?"

"Sure." His voice is lower. Deeper. I step aside so he can have a look, but he only glances through it briefly before looking up again with his own eyes.

I sit down on the grass so I can look up easier. Take in the full view of the wide, glistening sky, and a moment later he joins me. So close our shoulders lightly touch. I can't think about the stars, or the perfect, clear brilliance of the night. I can't really think about anything except for how close he's sitting, and how comfortable it would be to lean over and lay my head on his shoulder.

I won't, but I want to.

"It's your sign," he says softly, and my heart trips over itself.

My sign to what? To lay my head on his shoulder? To kiss him? What?

I clear my throat. "Sign to what?"

He seems confused. "No, I mean – you're a Taurus, aren't you? That's Taurus." He points to a collection of stars in the sky.

Thankfully, he can't see the searing red that burns across my face. "Oh, right. Yes. I am a Taurus. Well remembered."

He laughs a little. "I wouldn't forget something like that."

There it is again. That tingly feeling like I should do something now. Like he half expects me to, and like I half want to, but something in me tells me no. That there's no time for fraternising with boys when all I want is to find my sister.

But before I can stop myself, my head lulls to the left and my cheek rests on his shoulder, and I can feel his whole body tense.

I wait, wide-eyed, wondering if he'll pull away, but he doesn't. Instead, after a few desperately long seconds, he rests his own head against mine and we just sit like that, in silence.

thirty two

I CATCH JORDAN IN the hall before our first classes the next day. Brush his shoulder lightly, quickly, and say, "If you're free after school, will you come by?"

"Uh, sure. Want me to drive you home?"

"Please," I say. "Wear good shoes."

He looks down at his sneakers. "I mean, it is what it is."

Smiling, I dart into my classroom.

Then stop smiling, feeling guilty for why I asked him over. I've thought about it carefully, considered all the possibilities, but I need to know. I need to know what version of the Moss exists for Jordan and others, and what version of it I see. Eve saw. My mother.

Jordan will be safe, I think. But I have to know. I have to take him there.

When the end of school comes, a thick kind of anxiety prickles along the back of my neck, my arms, tightening the base of my throat. Intermittent clouds release patches of sun, now and again sending darkness across the garden. Birds sing, lifting the shadows into something brighter – lighter – as we bump along in his car until the tyres hit the gravel of my driveway.

I crack the knuckles in my hands and glance down the garden.

"I want to go on an adventure," I say, like I'm six. He wrinkles his forehead, confused but intrigued.

"Are we going to build a tree house, or pillow fort? I'm not sure why the good shoes were necessary for that, but—"

"Not today," I answer. Then, more gently, "Have you ever been into the Moss?"

His mouth falls open and he follows my gaze down towards it. Adjusts his shirt a little, maybe nervously. I hardly blame him. "No," he finally answers. "Not really. I've wandered into the edge of it, but I don't think that counts."

I cross the driveway to the garden, hoping he'll follow, but he doesn't. At least, not immediately. "It's beautiful, in its own way, and I think it meant something to my sister. I want to go in again. See what she saw. I just don't want to go alone." I have another reason for wanting to go in with him, but I leave it tucked away, a secret in the back of my mind. No need to scare him off just yet. When he still hasn't moved to follow me, I face him fully, letting my arms hang at my sides. "Will you come with me?"

The direct question seems to land with him, and he takes a few tentative steps towards me. "I know your dad doesn't like it when anyone goes in there. Especially you."

"He isn't home," I tell him. When his face immediately tells me that's little comfort, I add, "And he would feel better knowing I wasn't alone. We won't go in far, just a short way. To see what she saw, to appreciate it. Not enough people do, I think." I hate saying aloud how beautiful it is, as if the Moss might hear me, and no part of me wants it know that. But it is, whether I like it or not. It arrests the senses and holds your attention, making it hard to look away.

Jordan bites down on his lower lip, eyes scanning over the Moss.

"He doesn't have to know we went in," I say softly, unsure if it will help or hurt the situation.

But he nods, once at first, then a few more times. "All right. All right. Yeah. I guess I've always been curious. Bogs are an interesting part of the world."

Relief surges in like the tide, cool and refreshing. A smile consumes my face, and I lace my fingers together in a show of thanks. "Not far," I promise again. "Come on." That relief is very short lived, as a cold sort of dread settles in its place. Like I'm feeding someone I care about to something I fear, but I have to know. I *have* to know what he sees. What my father sees. What the Moss shows him, and what it shows me. I will keep him safe. As much as I am able, I will let no harm come to him.

As we make our way down the garden, crossing the fence as we go, a swath of clouds devours the sun, sending the world into shadow. Jordan glances up but says nothing, as we leave the sound of birdsong behind us.

"You know how to swim, right?" he asks, traces of a smile in his voice. But I can tell he means it.

"I do," I say, crossing into the edge of the Moss even as his own steps slow. Arms of mist wander about, barring patches of the bog from view. "Stay close. Sometimes the fog gets worse without notice."

He wordlessly closes the space between us, walking so close that our shoulders brush. In one of the pools to our right, ripples gently roll out from the centre, lapping towards the bank. They cease after only a short time, but the sight of it settles into my nerves, cold and clammy.

"This is the furthest in I've ever gone," Jordan announces after another few minutes. "I came in when Eve disappeared, just to help with the search, but it was raining and hard to get around."

The days surrounding her disappearance feel like a strange blotch in my head. Some parts of it I recall as clear as anything, sharp and well-defined, while other parts are missing entirely. Hours on end, plucked away like when you complete a puzzle but find two or three pieces are missing. I have no memory of Jordan helping to search for my sister, or even of him being here at all. I do remember the crying, and the look on my father's face, and the sound of the rain on the windows. "We shouldn't go far. It's so easy to get lost in here."

Jordan stops walking as I carry on, turning to look back towards the house, which is small and faint through the distance and the intermittent fog. "It really swallows you up, doesn't it?" he muses.

Something cold gathers around me. Looking down, tendrils of mist have swept closer, enveloping me until, for a time, all I can see is white. It tickles my skin, brushing against my shoulders and hair, and when I hold out a hand before me, it vanishes into the ivory wall. Thicker than the steam in a shower. Thicker, even, than the mist that sometimes rises from the sea. I spin slowly, looking in all directions, feeling a strange tugging as though the mist is encouraging me along somewhere – somewhere further into the Moss. I've crossed whatever border exists here. The one that allows this place to swallow me whole.

I plant my feet into the sodden ground, fighting the urge as the sensation of falling sweeps over me, of not knowing up from down. One wrong step might send me tumbling into a pool.

As it at last begins to thin, Jordan has turned back towards me, but his eyes graze right over me even as the air clears and I can see him fully again. Surprise twists across his face. "Emma?" he calls, much more loudly than is necessary given the short distance between us.

"What?" I ask, waving a hand in case the residual mist is thicker than I realise. His head twitches, like he's listening to something far away.

"I can hear you," he says, spinning to look around in all directions. "I can hear you, but I can't – I can't see you. Emma? Where'd you go?"

"I'm right here." Damp fear slithers up my body from below. *This* is why I brought him here. *This* is what I feared would happen but have never seen in such stark relief. Proof that the Moss is one thing for some, and something else entirely for others. That a few steps too far into this godforsaken piece of land and I am gone from the world as I know it, invisible to searching eyes. Whatever version of the bog exists for my father and Jordan and others around the town does not exist for me. Or for Eve. Or our mother. It swallows you, a maw riddled with tree-like teeth and rancid breath, dripping with moss to make the edges seem softer.

I take a few more long steps away, further in, hopping over a narrow pool of water. "Can you hear me?" I ask, trying to call out but my voice shaking itself into a loud whisper.

"Emma? I can't hear you any more. Where are you?" He looks down into the pools around him, in case I've fallen in. "Emma!" The word is desperate now, panic settling in.

"Jordan," I say, as firmly as I can. Beside me is the bony husk of a dead tree, branches angled like bizarre fingers. I take them and snap them off, one by one, dropping them into the water as if I can tear the Moss apart limb from limb for what it's done to my family.

Jordan turns towards me, still searching frantically, and for a moment I think he sees me, but then his gaze moves on.

I want to be afraid because I know I should be. Because I am balancing on a fence, and on one side is safety, and my life, and on the other side is whatever fate befell my sister. I *am* afraid – my hands are slick with sweat and my fingers twitch uncontrollably – but I am angry, too, and the anger is so ravenous that it is all I can feel.

I cannot keep this up any longer. I know if I go in much further, it will swallow me. The world I know will slip away, and all I'll know will be the Moss.

I pick my way across the distance between us, tugging against that incessant pull, moving closer and closer to the house. I'm just behind him now, and when I think the Moss has released me because I haven't gone in far enough to be swallowed, I try again. "Jordan," I say, and he spins around – finally locking my gaze.

"Oh my god!" he says, so loudly that his voice breaks. He leaps across a pool of water and grabs my shoulders. "What the hell happened?" His eyes shine, but I can't tell if it's from tears.

"I was here the whole time," I say, not sure how much to explain. Not even sure how much I know. "You couldn't see me, but I was. It's OK."

"You weren't there. You definitely weren't there. I looked everywhere."

I shrug, shaking a little, plucking off a large handful of moss from the stump of a tree and tossing it away. I hope it can feel it.

The bog. I hope it can feel pain like we can. Like Eve could. "You couldn't see me, but I was here. I'm sorry."

He shakes his head, like if he does it enough times it will make sense. "You weren't here, Emma."

I stop injuring the bog and look at him again, my own eyes stinging. "Welcome to the Moss," I tell him heavily. "Nothing makes sense in here."

thirty-three

MY DAD KEEPS WHAT he calls the "important papers" box up in his closet. Birth certificates, tax forms and paperwork from when he bought the house. I flick through it all carefully, searching for the name of the woman who sold it to us. I've heard it before, but not in years, and it's been lost to memory.

Halfway through the box, there's a countersigned letter with her name printed on the bottom. Sally Broussard. The name stares back at me, like it wonders why I care. Why I've dug it up out of a dusty old box all these years later. But when I pull out my phone to look her up, I find nothing. No social media accounts, no websites, no trace of her. Disappointed, I rock back on my heels and drop the letter back into the box.

The thought of speaking to anyone who used to live here, who might understand this house, had lifted my spirits more than anything else could. Sometimes it feels like this place is a curse that only my family can see or feel, like it's only for us.

I stick the lid back on to the box, then pull it off again. I'm not sure what I'm looking for, but I flip through the remaining stack of papers just in case. Hope rising again.

Near the bottom I find a letter, addressed to my parents at this house, from Sally. Her return address is written in messy handwriting in the top left corner of the envelope. Pulling it out, I read quickly.

Dear Carvers,
I hope you enjoy your new home. It holds much history gained over centuries, and that history demands respect. Keep an open heart, and a watchful eye, and I wish you all the best.
Sally

Thankfully, when she sold the house, she stayed in the area. Now she lives in a small neighborhood a town over. A phone call would save me a trip, but with the questions I want to ask, I feel like that leaves too much of a chance for her to hang up on me. I'd rather be face to face. Maybe she'll just slam the door, but at least I can see her reactions. See how she takes the questions before that happens.

Dad is working and Jordan is busy, and thankfully the taxi driver who picks me up stays quiet as he drives. I'm not feeling particularly chatty, trying to go over all the things I want to say. To know. To understand.

It's a small house, can't be more than two bedrooms, on the end of a street before the neighbourhood gives way to trees. The garden is bare, brownish grass with no flowers or bushes in sight. There are three or four stumps littered around the garden as well, where trees were chopped off and hauled away.

Simple. Bare. Unassuming. So different from the house I grew up in and that was once her home, surrounded by plants and trees, with character hanging from every nook and cranny.

I knock three times on the door and wait. There's no immediate answer, but a small car sits in the driveway so I suspect someone is home. A moment later, there is a shuffling sound inside, but the door stays closed. So I knock again.

This time, it cracks open. She has salt-and-peppered brown hair, cut short, and bright blue eyes that seem to glow even in the shadows.

"Hi. Are you Sally Broussard?" I ask.

Her eyes narrow. I'm right, then. "Can I help you?" she asks. It isn't gruff, but it isn't friendly either.

"My name is Emma. I think my parents bought Lark House from you when I was very young. I was wondering if we could talk." I memorised the introduction on the way over, but now I'm wondering if I shouldn't have led with a mention of the house.

Her eyebrows crease together, and she draws her head back. "I . . . talk about what?" Her voice is quieter now, almost a whisper.

I have to be very careful here. Something has already set her on edge, and I worry I'm one wrong syllable away from the door slamming shut and my answers staying on the other side. "It's an old house, as you know. It has a lot of history. I'm hoping to understand more of it, and I thought talking to previous owners would be a good way to start."

She stares at me for a long while, leaving the door only barely cracked. Then she looks up and down the street, and opens it just wide enough for me to step inside. "I don't have long," she says as I enter. "I'm sorry."

"Even just a few minutes would be fine." Inside, the house is very simple. Quiet furniture, monotoned rugs, a few lamps. No houseplants.

She points to the kitchen, where a kettle is working towards a boil on the stove. I climb on to a stool at the island while she takes out a teacup, then another. She holds it up towards me, as though asking me a question.

"Please," I say.

She pulls out a box of tea and places bags into each cup. "What is it you want to know?"

I take in a breath. It will be hard to tread carefully from now on. The only questions I have might immediately set her on edge. "It's a beautiful house, to start with. As I'm sure you remember. Very old. Lots of . . . lots of history, like I said."

She nods once.

"When you lived there, did you ever . . .?" Despite all my practicing in the taxi, I have to cast around for the right words. "Did you ever notice anything strange about it?"

She watches me for maybe half a minute, thinking hard. "Aren't you the sister of the girl who went missing?"

Carefully, I say, "Yes. I am."

"They still haven't found her, have they?"

"No. Not yet. Soon, I hope."

Her face tells me she doesn't think it's likely. "Did they ever find your mother?"

I shake my head.

"It was a strange house. Strange house, strange place, strange . . . everything." Her voice quivers when she says it. There's something all around her words, clawing for escape from her throat, but she is careful to keep it back. In the background, the kettle rumbles away.

"I'm young," I tell her, prodding, "and I was very young when we moved in, so I don't have a lot of memories from where we lived before. But I feel like most houses don't come with the baggage that ours has. I feel like there's something about it."

Sally turns and looks out the window, which doesn't offer much of a view. Just some trees on the other side of her bare yard. "It isn't the house, so much," she says after a minute. "At least, not as far as I reckoned. The house is part of it because it's been there for so long. It's been . . . steeping for so long."

The kettle suddenly lets out a shrill, piercing whistle, and she pulls it from the stove. Pours the water into both cups. Colour immediately starts to bleed out from the tea bags.

"It's that *bog*," she tells me, like the word tastes sour. "It poisons everything. Gets into everything. All that water and darkness, it's like an infection. One you can't cure." She pauses, then snatches a small sugar canister from a nearby shelf. "The house has been there the longest. It might as well be part of the Moss now. The ghosts, the sounds . . . all of it."

She holds up the sugar, again asking a question, but I shake my head.

"What about the people who live in the house?" I ask quietly.

She points down to the tea bags in the cups. "I don't know anything for certain, but I believe that the longer you live in the house, the worse it gets for you. The longer you steep, the more infection you take in. *If* the Moss calls to you. It doesn't call to everyone."

"Did it call to you?" I ask, though I suspect I know the answer.

She nods a few times, still staring into the cups. "And to my daughter."

I wait for her to go on.

"She went in, even though I begged her not to. She was gone for three days, and when she came back out it was like she'd left her soul behind. Not all of her came home, and she never found the missing parts. Even to this day."

The words send cold hands over my skin. "Where is she now?"

"She moved to Wales, to the middle of nowhere, to be far away from here. I never see her. She doesn't see anyone."

She hands me my cup of tea, although now I'm not so sure that I want it.

"It's like that man," she says. "The one who drowned his daughter. He's been there so long now; the infection has eaten away everything that might have once made him good. He is beyond humanity. Beyond anything recognisable, or redeemable. He hates the Moss, and yet he is inextricably a part of it. He uses that hate to bring people inside. To bring them to their death. To ruin anyone that the Moss might call to. He thought his daughter was a witch because it tried to pull her in. It started with her, but it didn't end there. He hated anyone it pulled at. You can call them witches, or you can call them gifted. It doesn't matter what they are. They hear something that no one else hears, and that's that. Once he knows you can hear it, he will never stop."

"Why didn't you tell anyone?" I don't know if it's sadness or anger that's making my heart race.

She looks at me with tears pooling. "Who would believe me? No one believed my daughter when she tried to tell them. When people start googling, they read that bogs can come with noxious gases, and that's all they needed to see. It's all in your head, they say." She smacks her temple a few times. "No one listens. No one cares."

I take a slow sip of the tea, but it sours my stomach.

"And the light . . . the light is always there. She talked about it at length, but mostly just musings. Unfinished, messy thoughts. She said it would show you what you wanted. Taking you deeper and deeper . . ." She stops, breathing to calm herself. "She said so much, and very little of it made sense."

I wait.

"But you can get away from it," she tells me, looking into my eyes like she can speak directly to my soul. "It will stay with you for a while, no matter how far you travel. Across the state, or around the world. You'll hear the voices, see the ghosts, feel the Moss trying to pull you back in. But the longer you spend away, the quieter it gets, until one day you'll realise you haven't seen or heard anything in months, and you'll know you escaped."

"Did you escape?" I ask, my voice breaking.

After a pause, she nods. "It took years, because I lived there for so long. A decade. For a while, I thought I had to leave the state, get as far away as I could and stay with family, before I realised it wasn't making a difference. I just had to wait it out. So I came back, and it's been years and years since I last heard anything, or saw anything. I feel as close to at peace now as I've ever been. And then I see pictures of the missing girl, and I know that nothing has changed. That it's still hunting, and killing, and nothing will ever stop it."

"Why didn't you warn us?"

She shrugs, holding up both hands. "I thought it was just us. I had no reason to believe it was happening to anyone else. I thought my family was cursed. But I do remember telling your mother that it was a strange house, and to keep a sharp eye out." She pauses. "I'm sorry about her, too."

"Thanks." I take another sip of my tea. Silence ticks by as a hundred questions bubble up and I push them down. There will only be more behind those, and more and more until I'm drowning in them, with no hope of answers.

"You have a choice," she tells me after some time has passed. "You can leave now, and start letting it all leave your body, your mind, your DNA. Or you can stay and hope your sister will come back out like my daughter did. But she's been in there a long time, and it gets harder to find your way back out again. So you might be waiting for ever."

The words slip into the air around me, sending another shiver along my spine. No part of me can fathom leaving Eve behind and putting the Moss and the house behind me for ever. I know Dad would feel the same. But imagining it growing stronger over the years, the infection getting worse and worse when I could leave instead and put it behind me, makes the tea bubble back up into my throat. Things were better in California. Not by much. I still heard the voices and saw shadows now and then, but much less often than I did here.

But Eve is a part of me, and even though I could be imagining it, some part of me still feels her presence. Still feels a thread of her life bound to mine. And because of that, I could never put this town into my rearview mirror again until I've found her.

I *have* to find her.

thirty-four

IT'S GAME NIGHT WITH Dad. I planned it myself, texting him
yesterday so he would be sure to get home at a reasonable time.
I cooked a lasagne from the freezer, set out some chips and dips
and a two-litre bottle of Pepsi, and got Scrabble ready to go. Now
I'm just waiting at the kitchen window, watching the Moss grow
darker as a thunderstorm rolls in, and listening for the crunch of
gravel in the driveway.

It's getting late in the year for thunderstorms, but then again, we
sometimes get thunder and lightning with our snowstorms. You
never really know about the weather here. Mostly, I'm watching
for the first signs of rain, because it's with rain that the Moss can
stretch its gnarled, hungry fingers around my throat.

I want to enjoy tonight. Damn the Moss. Damn the Sedge Man.
If it consumes me the way it did my mother and sister, I want to
leave my father with some well-deserved good memories.

"Stay away from me tonight," I say into the quiet house, eyes
trained on the distant bog.

I'm certain I imagine it, but my ears faintly pick up on what
sounds like a low, heavy laugh.

I shiver and turn away, just in time for the crunch of gravel to
signal my father's arrival home. Through another window, I see

him climb out of the car, glancing up at the angry sky, and hurry into the house.

"I think the sky is about to let loose," he says when he enters, eyes washing over the meal and snacks I have set up. "Hey, look at this! I don't even have to do anything!"

"You do plenty," I tell him, wrapping him in a quick hug. "And I thought I would soften the blow of beating you, when history inevitably repeats itself."

He tosses his coat and keys aside.

"I installed this word game on my phone that we all play at work. I think it's been training me to kick your ass."

"Impress me then," I say, when he sits down across the board from me. "You can go first."

After some thought, he starts with *TICK*. It's a decent start, and the game of Scrabble takes off from there. We eat as we play, taking our time, listening to the first few raindrops hitting the porch roof outside. I swallow back the tickling worry over the things that come with rain.

A few rounds in, I get lucky and play *TWITCH* off Dad's original word. I mark down my points and wait smugly for him to take his turn.

"Damn," he says. "I'm going to need more lasagne for this."

Outside the window, rain pours down in torrents, so thick I can hardly see the trees in the garden. I know Jordan said we were in a drought, but it's hard to believe watching so much water tumble down.

When I look back at the board, something has changed, but I can't immediately place it. I have to read each word in turn before finding the answer: the *T* in *TWITCH* is missing, leaving only the word *WITCH* behind.

A chill climbs up from my feet, sending waves of shivers along my bones.

"Did you move the board?" I ask Dad, my voice breaking. But he's only just returning with his plate.

"No. Why?"

I shake my head, over and over again. "Just wondering."

When I blink, the *T* is back and the board is exactly like it was a moment ago.

"Right," Dad says, taking his seat again. "Where were we?"

The game carries on but my mind wanders elsewhere, eyes glancing around, looking for whatever, or whoever, lurks nearby. My dad has to prompt me a few times to take my turn, and I'm apologetic but I cannot focus any more.

Then a shadow darkens the window to my left, and all thoughts of games and snacks and fun die quickly away. The form of a man passes by the window, moving towards the front garden. If I listen hard enough, I almost think I can hear – or feel – footsteps resonating against the ground. His black coat and face overgrown by grass and sedge and weeds are all grossly, sorely familiar.

"I'll be right back," I whisper, but my voice is so small I'm not certain if my dad can hear me. "Could you get me some more food?"

"Sure," he says, uncertainly.

I push myself up from the ground, watching out the windows as the man rounds the corner and I slowly push open the screen door. It creaks in protest as I step out on to the porch – and standing there, just at the bottom of the steps in the garden, is the Sedge Man. His face is still gone, overgrown by the greedy plants and lichen erupting from his body. His long black overcoat puts me in mind of the Puritans, or sometime in the 1700s. His hands, folded in front of him, are cracked and worked over with moss.

"What do you want?" I ask him. I am afraid of him, without doubt, but also angry. Violently so.

When he answers, his voice is the rain itself. Rich, crushing, thunderous, and packed together to form words.

It calls to you, like it did to her. To your sister. Your mother. Sybil. The rain stretches out the '*S's*, like a snake, but deep and frightful.

"Sybil. That was your daughter, wasn't it? The one you drowned."

Perhaps he is surprised that I know because he is silent for a time.

It calls to the wicked. The devils. The dark-hearted. And those to whom it calls must not be suffered to live.

I think of the Scrabble board. The word *witch*. "What is it that calls to us?"

Something far older than me. It rots and ruins. Hungers and craves.

My gaze wanders towards it, even though the rain is so complete that it shields the Moss from view. "That's why you're after me. Because you know it calls to me."

I know you wish to enter.

I look back at him, surprised.

I know everything, dear Emma. There are no secrets in my house.

My skin grows colder with every word he speaks, that awful, resonant voice splashing at me through the rain in all directions.

You will see her again if you come.

I suck in a long, deep breath. "You drowned your daughter. To trust you is to die."

Suit yourself.

He turns to walk away. "Wait," I say. "Do you know where to find her?"

A spider wheels down from one of the vines covering his face, eager to be out of the rain. The sight sends a shudder along my frame.

I told you. I know everything.

He walks away, down towards the tree line, and disappears into the deluge after just a few seconds.

I look after him, rainwater splashing up on to the porch from where it hits the grass and the walkway. Somewhere close by, thunder rattles the world, and I just keep staring after the dead man and his vine-ridden face and the sense of consuming cold that settles in his wake.

Stay far away from the Sedge Man.

My sister's warning haunts the forefront of my mind, but I know that he is right. I know that the bog is vast and dangerous, and that's to say nothing of whatever things lurk inside it. Like the deer that wasn't a deer that my sister and I saw when we were young, when we gave the almost-dead bird back to the Moss. The sight of it clung to my nightmares for years afterwards, and to this day my heart jams up in my chest when I see one dart across the road.

But he says that she's there. I thought as much myself, but if he comes from the Moss, he must know.

Tonight was meant to be about my dad, and only about my dad. So, with a shuddering sigh, I step back inside.

"You OK?' he asks. Worry pulls at his features, although he's doing his best to hide it.

"I'm fine. I just wanted to listen to the thunder."

"Didn't have much of it in LA, huh?"

"Not really."

I know where I have to go now. I know what I have to do.

We settle back into the game but my dad wins for the first time ever, because no matter how hard I try, I cannot wrangle my mind away from the Sedge Man, and the Moss, and the things that wait for me there.

thirty-five

I SLEEP IN EVE'S bed again, because some part of me hopes I might dream something that will give me a clue as to her whereabouts, but I hardly dream at all. I just fall in and out of a rich, black sleep, occasionally waking to what I am certain is the scent of bog laurel, though there is none in the room. The storm is long over and no rain drums on the roof, but from time to time I am still dragged from my sleep by something unheard or unseen.

Just before morning, I am caught in some in-between place that is neither dream nor wakefulness, but I am convinced that I see Sybil, the drowned girl, and she is trying to tell me something. But then my mind drifts away from her, and there is soft morning light in the window and a new day has come.

It is a Sunday, and the day my dad joins a few of his friends for breakfast at a diner across town. It's our only real sit-down restaurant, and the locals are terribly proud of it. I have planned for today just for that fact because I do not want him to have to watch another member of his family make the long crossing of the garden and down to the Moss. I simply won't be here when he gets back, and for a while, it won't matter. I might be out with Jordan, or napping, or walking, and it won't be until evening comes that he will begin to worry.

We have coffee together in the kitchen while he tells me that even though he always goes for an omelette, he is thinking about ordering a stack of pancakes instead. I tell him that he should be adventurous and try new things, and he says I sound like Eve. That makes me smile, and miss her. I look at the clock on the stove. 8.30 a.m. He'll be leaving in just a few minutes.

"You don't want to join us?" he asks, polishing off his coffee.

"Maybe next time," I answer, after I've waited long enough to make it seem like I'm giving it some thought. But I have other, riskier, plans for today. "I might meet up with Jordan. Go for a hike somewhere. I'm not sure yet."

"Got to get out there before it gets too cold."

"Exactly."

He pulls on a sweater and takes his keys from the table, then pats his pockets to make sure he has everything. "All right. Then I guess I'll see you later."

I cross the room to hug him. *Don't cry,* I order myself. *Do not cry.* I can't let on that this is anything other than a normal goodbye, or he might not leave – and if he doesn't leave, then he might not let *me* leave.

"I'll see you later!" I say, as lightly as I can. But I won't, because I have waited long enough. If my sister is in the bog, then I will search until it claims me too.

Relief nearly makes my knees buckle when at last he pulls out of the driveway and I am alone. I catch myself staring after him for a handful of seconds then turn quickly away. I cannot allow any dead time where I might start to second guess myself. If Eve is out there, then I will bring her home.

No. Eve *is* out there, and I will bring her home.

A smile finds me as I climb the stairs and pull the new boots out from underneath my bed. I lace them on and walk in circles around my room, trying to get used to the feeling of wearing them. From Eve's wardrobe, I take a rich green hand-knitted sweater that she used to wear almost every day in the winter. When I think of Eve, I think of green. And if I find her, I want her to feel at home from the moment she sees me.

In a small backpack, I stick a handful of cereal bars and juice boxes I've been collecting, plus some of the stash of beef jerky that Dad has tucked away around the kitchen. And a few other things I take from beside the hearth – things I hold on to for a few seconds, wondering. My plan not yet fully formed. But I know, whatever happens, that I will find Eve, and I will ruin the Moss. However I can.

Worries about how long I will be gone, how hard she will be to find, and if I will find her before something worse finds me, all start clamouring for attention as I carefully load up the bag. So I stop and run my hands up and down the arms of the green sweater, taking comfort in the rough-knit feel of it. In all the memories I have of Eve wearing it on Christmas morning. Her birthday. Nights at the cinema. A lifetime lies knitted into every stitch of this sweater, and that lifetime is worth saving. Worth bringing home.

I remind myself: if I am afraid of merely entering the Moss, then how much worse must it be for Eve, trapped in there for a year with no way out?

So I take the backpack and head for the door, but stop to take in the house one last time before leaving. All the crooked little familiar memories jump out at me, aching for me to stay. The uneven floors, the noisy floorboards, the old windowpanes that warp things on the other side of them. All the quirks of a house that has been my home for most of my life. All the things Eve must miss too.

"I promise I'll come back," I tell the house, and I imagine it groans softly in reply.

I'll be waiting.

A flint-grey morning greets me outside, heavy with fog and dew. No frost, though the air is cold through my coat. Sunlight struggles to pierce the pressing clouds above. My new boots crunch on the gravel as I cross the driveway and make for the garden, sloping down towards the Moss. I hold its gaze as I approach, lest it should think I'm afraid. What quiet fears sit in the corners of my heart are none of its business. It is a predator, and I am its prey. I cannot let it know that I'm afraid.

The post-and-rail fence is damp and slick as I climb over it, lingering for a minute atop it to look back towards the house. It is still and quiet and sleepy, and every fibre of my being longs to return to it. To climb into my bed and pull the covers up over my head and forget every memory I have of the Moss.

But Eve is out there. So I hop down from the fence, my feet sinking slightly into the soft earth, and I make my way slowly, carefully, into the Moss.

I keep my steps slow, even though the urge to run is overwhelming. I pick my way forward in the cloudy morning, working to move from one bit of solid ground to the next, trying to keep my eyes from the water below as though I might find a face staring back at me.

And for a moment, there *is*. Eyes and an open mouth and ghostly skin, barely submerged.

My heart lurches. The world spins. But when I look harder, what looked like hollow eye sockets was just a trick of the faint light, vanishing quickly.

My breath returns with a violent flood of relief, my heart quiets, and I carry on. Hop from one bit of ground to the next. Hold fast on to a scrawny tree when I momentarily lose my footing, then move forward again.

Distantly, a yellowish light flickers. My heart thunders to a stop, then a thumping start again. I peer through the fog, finding it hard to focus on any one point, and see it dance and bob about before disappearing again. Just like I've seen before.

I trip and pick my way over the rough land. Now and then, a foot slips and splashes into the water and I pull it back quickly, imagining rotted hands and bony fingers wrapping around it and pulling me under. Everything about this place makes me think it wants to drag me down, down, down. Below the surface. Below the ground. Below the world.

A twig snaps behind me and I whirl. Nothing. No hint of anything else about but me. Just shadows and mist. I stare for longer than I should, making certain nothing lurks in the fog that sways and drifts about, but there is only me, and the Moss.

Onwards.

There is a strange feeling in the air here, unlike anywhere else outside it. A charge. An energy that prickles against the skin. I feel somewhat like I'm walking through a fence or a wall, and over time, the sensation deadens some.

Over the sound of my footsteps, something like whispers begin to sound all around me. Like the fog itself has a voice – an ancient, dead voice that is entirely inescapable. The whispers rise up like curling mist from the ground, pressing in and smothering me. A thousand of them, thick and unintelligible.

My pace quickens, even as I try to keep my composure. Some sort of presence lurks at my back, my sides, all around me, in all directions. Above and below. The Moss itself, maybe, but I can't be sure.

How could Eve have ever come this far and carried on? I want nothing more than to turn around and flee back to the house, curl up under a blanket and stay there.

Blurred shapes try to take form around me in the mist, desperately hard to make out as I move further into the Moss. A large, ancient tree? A stone doorway? A man standing alarmingly still? They're impressions, like the painting in the house, intangible and without true form, but they still cause my heart to falter in my chest.

Then ahead, the mist moves and gathers itself into the form of antlers – large, dreadful antlers I've seen before – but they dissolve almost as quickly as they came. All the feelings of that long-ago day come charging back: the awful sound of the bird hitting the window, the sadness at knowing it would die, the horror at seeing the deer – or the thing that pretended to be a deer. I am a child again, standing beside my sister, sacrificing a bird to the Moss.

> *All her lovely companions*
> *Are faded and gone . . .*

The voice – a girl's, I think, although it's hard to be certain – wafts towards me from ahead. Pulling me along. The song again.

My song. Our song. The song that twists like a knife in my heart every time I hear it. It propels me forward, quicker than before, and I leap between the patches of solid ground, following the direction of the voice. Excited now, and less afraid.

"Eve," I say aloud, my first words since I entered. "Eve, can you hear me?"

There is no response. At least, not at first.

That familiar coldness bleeds back into my skin, and I stop running and turn in a full circle. Over the mist rises a cackling, guttural laugh.

"Where are you?" I whisper, letting my hand curl around the handle of a kitchen knife I tucked carefully into my belt. What good it will do me in here I can't say, but knowing I have it gives me a sense of security, even if it's false. "I know you're here, Simon Lark." I feel a power in using his real name, like it somehow makes him smaller. "You said my sister was here. So where is she?"

He taunts me, letting the mist gather into a form here, then there, then in a rush of coldness behind me. I keep twisting to follow him, waiting, until at last he materialises directly in front of me. But he is different this time, with a bloated face and pale, empty eyes, and I take a quick, unsteady step backwards, stumbling into a deep pool of water.

It cascades around me, over me, plunging into my ears, mouth and eyes. I reach upwards to find anything I can to pull myself back out, but all I find is slick grass and mire. The weight of the sodden boots lures me further and further under – and then a pressure at the top of my head pushes me down, down, down.

I can no longer reach anything above the surface. All I know is water, mud and darkness, and, just like in my dream, all my senses fail me.

Stay away from the Sedge Man. He won't stop, like a hunter, until there's nothing left of you.

thirty-six

MY LUNGS ACHE LIKE they could burst, and all around me my fingers only find oily, slippery surfaces. Nothing I can hold on to. I am well under the water, and with every second exhaustion grows heavier and heavier.

Out. I have to get out.

My fingertips claw into anything they can find, panic making them fast and unsteady. Vines. Reeds. Underwater grass roots. Anything. But they always come up empty, the roots just pulling away from the mud until my hands are full of clumps of them.

Air. I need it now. Need air *now, now, now.* Need to breathe. *Breathe.*

Then the downward pressure on my head shifts, and something grasps my wrists with a painfully tight grip. Water rushes around me as I move up, up, up, and a few seconds later, my head finally breaks the surface.

My body heaves, choking and gasping, mud clogging up my mouth and nose as I'm dragged all the way out and on to solid ground. I cannot see or hear yet, but there is *air*. Air flooding into my aching lungs, my chest rising and falling as I lie on the damp earth, and I can focus on nothing else besides how beautiful and sweet it is just to be able to breathe.

I claw my hands along my face, scraping off the mud and dirty water, and blink open my blurry eyes to see better.

Simon is gone. I catch snatches of the moss-ridden deer, but my vision is still too blurred to see details. There is a girl, I think, but she is not my sister. She stands paces away, beside the deer, very still, watching me.

I have seen this girl before. On the plane, in the field. In the garden, when Simon drowned her.

"Sybil," I cough out. My voice is gravelly and small, and not like my own.

She stands perfectly still, more of an outline than a person. I keep blinking to clear out my eyes, and they sting with all the dirt and water.

"She is here," Sybil says after a pause. She climbs on to the back of the deer, almost gliding up through the air without effort, her white dress rippling. "But you will be dead before you reach her. She is deep in the Moss, and either my father or the older things will get to you first."

And they are both gone in the next instant, vanishing into the mist like the smoke from a candle that is there one minute and gone the next.

I stare after them, panting, shaking, before rolling over to look all around me. I am thankfully alone. No signs of Simon. No other forms lurking nearby, watching. Just me, the water, the brown grass beneath me, and the air that I drink in like each breath might be my last.

It is several long minutes before I at last climb to my feet. My chest still throbs a little, and I sway as I stand, but the feel of solid ground beneath me instead of above me is a delicacy I do not take for granted. My clothes, boots, backpack are all sodden – but thankfully the food inside was all sealed. The wool sweater won't dry any time soon, but I can deal with that later. No real harm done.

At least, not yet.

My feet drag me forward, deeper and deeper into the Moss. The landscape shifts in subtle ways as I go, at first almost impossible to notice, but soon impossible to miss. Empty areas where nothing grows are suddenly overrun with bog laurel or lush grasses, bending in a breeze I can't feel. Now and then, when I glance up, I think the sky is about to clear, but it never does. But even when it seems like the clouds are about to depart, no real light seems to reach the bog. Around me is only ever grey and dull, as though caught in the in-between hours of the day.

I feel a presence nearby before I see it. Drawing to a stop, I glance to my right, where a figure stands, watching me in the faded light, unmoving. It's a man, I think, and one I've never seen before, standing deathly still. Dressed in clothing from a time I don't recognise, years upon years ago. His throat is slashed, but he's standing nevertheless. Staring. Arms hanging limply at his sides.

A scream wants to bubble up in my throat, but I've seen worse things today. Felt worse. And he makes no attempt to draw nearer. I would be foolish to think I am the only thing about in the Moss.

As I start to walk away, the man limply raises one hand out to me, beckoning to me, inviting me closer. I don't take my eyes off him as I stumble and traipse past, refusing to look away until the fog has swallowed him behind me.

It feels strangely like nighttime in the bog, or at least almost night. Maybe almost morning. Some time that feels like an *almost, but not quite,* and it creates a constant sense of waiting, watching the time. Expecting the sun to rise or set at any moment, but it never happens. I cannot imagine spending as long in here as Eve has without going mad from it all. The shadows, figures, voices, and the eternal sense of *almost*.

Part of me is certain I've only been in the Moss for an hour, but I am hungry like it's been days. I find the trunk of a large tree and sit with my back against it, pulling a cereal bar out of my bag. Even here, pressed up against a tree, I feel painfully exposed. Like everything else in the Moss can see me, even if I can't see them.

The cereal bar tastes hollow here, not like the one I ate yesterday. I go for a second one, just to be sure, and it's the same. Tasteless and mealy, like it's about to go rancid. I ball up the trash and stick it back in my bag, then pull out one of the coins I stashed in there last night. I prop it up against the tree as a marker for when we come back this way, and then press onwards.

Direction is hard to tell. All the half-dead grass, reeds, vines and twiggy trees mesh and melt together, a blur of brownish green that infects my vision until I'm convinced I'm walking in circles. There are no landmarks, nothing to give me a sense of direction, and a headache is setting in, the likes of which I've never felt before. I would kill for some ibuprofen, but it's the one thing I forgot to pack. So instead, I sip some water and try to take stock of my surroundings. Figure out which way to go, when the land is just an endless blob of brown-green and water and rot.

Then, a good distance from me, light flickers. That yellowish, dancing light I've seen before, when my mother stood on the edge of the Moss, reaching for it. It waves and undulates, like it's beckoning me onwards. Inviting me deeper and deeper into the bog. I don't like the feeling of an invitation, like I am wanted in the Moss. It makes me want to turn and run back home, leave this place behind for ever and remember it only as a dream. But I cannot.

So I follow the yellow light and press on.

As I walk, I wonder if the Sedge Man can see the light. Worry that perhaps it works like a beacon and he will always know where to find me.

Around me, though subtle at first, the landscape begins to change. The spindly, boggy trees are replaced by thick, ancient ones with trunks as wide as a car. They are leafless and twisted like the silhouettes of trees you sometimes see on Halloween cards – and drenched in vines. Their trunks are covered in a rich green film, like a thin moss, and there are more and more of them as I walk until, instead of the desolate and open Moss, I'm in a sparse woodland of contorted trees.

The flat land shifts too, rises and valleys leaving dark and shadowed places where the steely light doesn't reach. Like a world from a fairy tale, but with ink spilt all over the pages. The frequent pools of water meld together into larger ponds, with solid, grassy ground between them that makes walking much easier. I try to keep to the higher points, avoiding the shadowed valleys and rocky crevices that feel like nowhere I've ever seen in Maine. In America, even. It is a landscape pulled from somewhere else entirely and dropped here, incongruous with everything around it.

It is easier to just accept that nothing here makes sense than to stand, dumbfounded, and try to rationalise it all.

Neither here, nor there. Neither land, nor sea. My dad's words follow me as I walk, and I wonder how much he knows about this place. Whether it's only as much as he told me, or more than he let on. He is a good man, whose love for his family is boundless. If he had known what lay just beyond his house, he would never have moved us there. But once the disappearances started, he had no choice but to stay. To wait. To hope.

It never seemed to call to him like it did to Mom, and to Eve. To me too, I guess. Pulling us in, one after another. It feels like it doesn't matter that I am only here for Eve, because I am here, and it wanted me to be here, and taking my sister gave me a reason to come. So, in a way, the Moss got what it wanted. I hate that thought.

I am still following the light, which stops now and then to let me catch up, waiting until I am a few paces away before darting off again. The glow it casts on to the ground does not travel far, and when it begins to lead me through a rocky ravine, where the grey light does not reach, I stop.

"I don't want to go in there," I say, taking a step back. Rocky outcroppings wait like sharp teeth, and a thick mist spills out of the ravine and drifts towards my feet.

But the light is insistent. It darts back and forth, beckoning me to follow, *ordering* me to follow.

"Let's go another way," I say, fingers gripping tightly to the straps of my backpack. "Let's go around."

It does not obey. Instead, it starts off into the ravine without me, the soft glow slowly fading into something darker and darker. If I don't follow now, I might lose it for ever, and it's, so far, the only thing in here that hasn't seemed capable of killing me. So, with gritted teeth, I step forward and follow it.

The darkness presses in hungrily on all sides, eager to meet the newcomer. I keep my gaze forward, only on the yellow light far ahead, barely visible with the distance between us. I quicken my pace, trying to keep up with it. I can think of little worse than being trapped in the dark, and I suspect the light on my phone will not offer help. I pull it out as I walk to try it, just to be sure, but it won't turn on. I know it's charged, because I was careful to charge it overnight, but the screen is black and dead, and after repeated attempts, I slip it back into my backpack. Maybe the water got to it, even though it's meant to be waterproof, and the contents all seem dry.

I suspect it is this place. Apart from the world, in some way.

A soft hiss, like a breath or the scraping of a foot on the ground, comes from my right. It's enough for me to break my gaze on the light and turn to see what caused it, although the darkness is too complete to offer me any clues. There is just a wall of black on either side, formless. When silence reigns again, I let my eyes return to the light, a beacon guiding me through.

Suddenly, a *thud* sounds, almost like the sound of a horse's hoof on pavement. The noise is hollow and quick, and it pulls my feet to a stop, though the light does not wait. Again, I peer into the dark, searching for a hint. A clue. Anything to tell me what lurks just beyond the light.

As I'm stopped, mist coils up from the ground, thicker than before. Vine-like and twisting, consuming what little visibility I have. Ahead, the yellow light is almost completely gone, but even in the second or two it takes me to decide to carry on, it vanishes into the distance.

Shadows devour me, everywhere, above and below, damp mist

clinging to me from all directions. I want to wring it all off and shake away the darkness, but it holds fast with a firm, inescapable grip.

Away through the ravine, I think the light is coming back for me but I'm afraid to look away from the darkness long enough to find out. As it bobs through the mist, images flash around me, glimpses of things hiding in the dark. A horse, or maybe another deer, or something else altogether, crow-black and with long saber teeth hanging from its mouth, dripping with blood. There are antlers too, or perhaps they're horns. For the brief second I see them, I am reminded of a goat, or a ram. A horrid amalgamation of things that do not belong in our world.

Somewhere else in the ravine, I hear a laugh, or maybe a scream. The flapping of wings – large wings. I step back, but my foot lands on a rounded rock and I slip backwards on to the stony ground. A pained cry escapes me, loud in the near-darkness.

Before I can scramble back to my feet, the thing with the saber teeth and the horns steps forward, its hooves clicking dreadfully on the rocks, and comes to stand over me with its head only inches from my face. Blood drips from its fangs and on to the ground, then on to me. My coat. My jeans. It sniffs my neck and my hair, the scent of something long-dead invading my senses.

I do not breathe. Blink. Move. I have forgotten how, terror the only thing I know.

It sniffs and snorts, trying to understand me, then its mouth opens and those teeth come nearer, and I close my eyes because I cannot stand to see them come any closer.

And, as the fear overtakes me, I try to scramble away, clawing at the ground and scraping my knees against stone in my haste. A stinging pain starts up on my palms, but I can think little of it in my panic. *Get away. Get away. Get away.* A low roar rises from its throat, and as I look back, still clambering for escape, its horrid mouth opens wide, those saber teeth exposed in the dim light, reaching for me. Hungry. So close now. Closer every second. I can feel them sink in, even before they've reached me, my mind filling in the blanks. Body tensed, hoping it will be quick – and that this is not how my sister met her end.

I swing my head around to face forward again . . .

And it smacks into the rock wall.

Darkness.

A thick, syrup-like blackness surrounds me, but I sense light behind it. My eyes open, and there it is again. That warm yellow light that guided me here. I don't know how much time has passed, but there is no sign of the monster. No teeth, no hooves, no guttural roaring. I look for it in all directions, but there is no sign that it was ever here at all. Nothing to make me believe it was anything but a dream.

Save for the drying spots of blood on my clothes that fell from its teeth.

The yellow light bobs before me. It's lower to the ground, like I am, and seems to be encouraging me to stand up.

My legs protest with shaking, but I force myself up, watching the shadows again for a hint of teeth or blood. *Stay close to the light,* I think. No matter what, stay close to the light.

Onwards.

The ravine ends soon enough, opening up on to an entirely new landscape. It is still a bog, in a way, but there are gargantuan trees and roots protruding from the water, hung with giant ropey vines that cascade towards the ground so much that I have to push them aside to get through. Hanging from the vines are strange, awful flowers, not unlike the carnivorous ones I've seen before. They have jagged, toothy petals, larger than my hands, that sit propped open and waiting, crimson red insides looking too much like blood.

I draw my hand away, careful where I place them when I need to move a vine aside, and try not to let them slow me down enough to put too much space between me and the light.

On the ground, in places my gaze lands on strange clusters of flowers, moss and lichen, creeping across mounds in the ground. They're beautiful, in an unusual sort of way, and the blush flowers of bog laurel are present in each and every one.

The plants, vines and trees here all shine a bluish-green colour in the dim light, and the water, brown before, seems black here. At one point, I stop suddenly, a large pool of water stretching away before me. I am about to turn and go around it, sticking to solid ground, when I catch sight of small stepping-stones standing just barely above the surface. They are uneven and ragged, like someone dropped rocks long ago here in order to cross, but they will do well enough for now.

Who else has been here? There is little time for the thought, but it is there, haunting the back of my mind.

Holding both arms out to balance, I step on to the first rock, then the second. The third shifts a little, unsteady where it rests, and I have to move quickly on to the fourth one to keep from falling into the black water. Further out in the pond, ripples start to undulate towards me, one after another, quicker and quicker, as something below the surface is disturbed.

My steps quicken, but more of the rocks are unstable. Keeping from falling means I have to go faster, tripping from one to the next until I leap across the last three and land just barely on the ground, one foot slipping into the water as I trip and fall. I crawl forward on my hands and knees, out of breath, turning to see greenish eyes – human, I think, but it is so hard to tell – watching me from just above the surface.

The thing and I stare for a moment, my mind empty, heart running wild. I can see hints of dense, seaweed-like hair drifting in the dark water. As the eyes slowly begin to recede back beneath the surface, sending more ripples out towards the shore, I can think of nothing but how this place has existed behind our house for most of my life. This place with creatures and eyes and traveling lights – this was our garden since childhood.

Don't go into the Moss.

It was our one rule, the one we could never break. Now I wish I hadn't. I wish Eve hadn't. I wish Mom hadn't. I wish none of us had ever stepped foot into this godforsaken place. Because that is exactly how it feels: forsaken, like everything in the world has completely and utterly abandoned this place, leaving behind only the things that dwell in darkness.

I scrub at my face, the shaking just barely beginning to calm. Run a hand over the hard earth, as if to convince myself that I did in fact make it off the stones.

I am not given long to rest on the shore of the pond, not if I am to keep up with the light. But I am tired and sore, and I do not know how long I have been in here, when every minute feels like hours. Days. My heart is tired of beating so hard. My lungs ache from breathlessness and fear. I want nothing more than to lie down somewhere and sleep. At least if I am sleeping then I cannot see what things move about around me.

Once I can pull myself to my feet again, I follow the light through the forest of giant trees, less careful when I push away the vines than before. I cannot remember ever being this tired, like every moment in here drains a little more of me away.

"I have to rest," I say to the light. I still don't know if it can hear me, or understand me. But even if I have to abandon it altogether, I need to lie down. Every bone in my body is aching like it is about to break.

Ahead, through the bent and gnarled arms of the great trees, a structure is visible in snatches. Small hints of dark stone, half-hidden by vines. My feet slow when I see it, afraid of what might lurk inside, but as we move steadily closer, I see that the windows and doors are all gone, and it looks long abandoned. The sense of desolation is almost enough to warn me away, but sleeping inside enclosed walls will be better than sleeping out here. Or maybe I won't sleep, but merely rest my sore limbs. I will feel better having a stone wall to my back.

The light lurks outside now, like we've reached a waypoint and it will at last stop for me. I step inside slowly, holding on to the doorless frame. Grass grows on all the floors, and piles of rocks stand randomly beside tumbledown walls. Here and there a roof still hangs overhead, though it looks ready to fall at any moment. To the right, through another empty doorframe, is a smaller room with more of an intact roof than the others. An old stone fireplace sits on one wall, and the roots of a tree have begun to grow through another. But it will do for now.

Lying my backpack down to use as a pillow, I curl up in the corner and cross my arms over myself. The air in the Moss has always been damp and slightly warm, but here it is chilly and sharp, less humid.

My eyes close quickly, the long day bearing down on me. But before sleep can find me, my thoughts go to my dad. Does he already know I am gone? How long has it been? Will he come to look for me here? He has been in the bog before, but never mentioned any of this strangeness. Could he not see it, or did he simply not want to tell me?

The questions are useless. They just pile up around me like the stones falling out of the walls.

Emma.

A girl's voice, soft. My eyes shoot open. The voice is louder and clearer than it has ever been before. Previously it has always been mottled and muffled, like the buzz of noise on an old TV.

I am here. But you should not have come.

It sounds like Eve. For the first time ever, there are traces of her voice running along the words. I sit up and look around, but, of course, I am alone.

Ssh, she says. *Rest. Here. Let me help.*

There's a pause, but only for a moment.

> *I'll not leave thee, thou lone one,*
> *To pine on the stem.*
> *Since the lovely are sleeping,*
> *Go sleep now with them . . .*

The words are downy soft and sweet like honey, pulling me

into a gentle sleep. She may not be with me, or anywhere close by, but there is the quiet sense of peace around me, like my sister is singing me to sleep.

So I let sleep take me.

thirty-seven

IT IS STILL NIGHTTIME, the darkness thick and velveteen around me when my eyes open. I am certain there was a sound that awoke me, but as I lie here as still as I can, and listen, there is only the buzzing of unfamiliar insects outside. It is a sharp and discordant sound, not like the soft hum of crickets I am used to.

Then it happens again. The same sound I heard on the fringes of my dream: a soft rustling, maybe a flapping, coming from the direction of the fireplace. The room is lit only by the faintest glow, from the light bobbing up and down in the air outside the house. Relief settles in that it has not abandoned me while I slept. And the light is enough to be certain that there is nothing visible in the room with me, but little else.

Pulling myself to my knees, I crawl towards the hearth, slowly, listening. Imagining what sorts of other creatures make their home here in the Moss.

My fingers reach the stones of the hearth and I stop, tilting my head to listen better.

Flutter. Flutter. Tap. Tap.

The sound carries on again, then pauses – then, without warning, something flies from the chimney and into the room, brushing past my face. A yelp escapes my chest and I fall backwards into the grass, shaken, but am relieved to only see two bats zipping around the room. No long teeth or red eyes or any other strangeness in sight.

My heart races, reckless and wild, but begins to calm.

It's as good a sign as any to leave the house and press on, so, once I have caught my breath, I collect my backpack from the corner and leave the house.

The light greets me outside, darting suddenly as if it too is waking up, before quickly pressing on through the trees. My limbs are still slow with sleep, and for some reason all I can think about is how much I would love some coffee, but I am at least thankful to have been given some time to rest. Time is impossible to pin down. I don't know if I slept for two hours or three days, but dwelling on it will do me no good.

Night in the Moss is worse than the day, even though there is little difference. The darkness is just more complete, thick and inky and all-consuming, and I keep closer to the light than I did last time. There are sounds in the trees sometimes, footsteps or scratchings of things unseen, and I have no desire to see what causes them.

The landscape is shifting again. The large trees thin out, leaving grassy hills and slopes, and a river runs to my right. It isn't wide at first, narrow enough to throw a stone across it, but it grows wider as we carry on. There are the remnants of an old stone bridge, but it has long since tumbled into little more than a useless heap of rock.

The light leads me along the river, always further into the Moss. I know by now it should have come to an end. The end as far as the state of Maine knows it. But now that I'm inside, I don't think the limits of the Moss work the way they should. I think once you're in, it is endless, stretching and expanding like a balloon.

A steep slope rises up to my left, but we follow a narrow pathway that runs along the edge of the river. The rushing sound of the water grates against my soul. It brings back thoughts of ghosts. Of Simon and his daughter, and their voices in my house sometimes. How hard I worked to ignore them – and now, here I am. Deep in the bog, the rules meant to keep me out all shattered and scattered behind me.

As if my thoughts of him have conjured his presence, Simon's voice fills my head.

We have been waiting for you.

I stop walking, and ahead of me the light stops too.

I pull in a long, slow breath, remembering the feeling of his hand keeping me underwater, of how my body ached and burned without air.

"Did the light lead you to me?" I ask.

A pause. *What light?*

Now it's my turn to hesitate. Perhaps he can't see it, after all. Perhaps it only reveals itself to some. Or perhaps I am merely imagining its presence at all. Nothing makes sense here.

I shut my eyes and return to his first words: *We have been waiting for you.*

"Who is we?" I turn around to search for any sign of him. I find him standing under a tree, mostly hidden by the shadow of night. There are hints of a man in his face, or what I can see of it in the shadows. Decaying flesh, hollow eye sockets, like a body found after considerable time. But the longer I look, the more grass and moss and fungi I see.

The Moss. Myself.

"The Moss isn't a person," I tell him, even though it has always felt like one.

Is it not?

I cannot answer that, so I stay silent, hooking my thumbs through the strap of the backpack and standing as tall as I can. He has a way of making me feel small, even from a distance.

You know nothing of what it is. How long it has been here. What it wants.

"And I don't care. I am here for my sister. Nothing else."

A low laugh. *No one leaves the Moss. Not once they have come this far.*

"The Moss hasn't met me before."

He laughs again. *You will be no different, Emma.*

Now I laugh, but it's a harsh, breathy sound, born from anger. "You have spent enough time in my house to know what I have suffered, Simon Lark. Lurking around in the shadows, haunting the corners like a cobweb. Riding in on thunderstorms and lingering like dew. You know that for years I have been able to do nothing but survive. I am good at it, whether I want to be or not." A thought strikes me. "The bog laurel in my sister's bedroom. Was that you, too?"

He laughs a little, which I take to mean *yes*. Then there is the hissing sound of him heaving a sigh.

There are two ways to die in the Moss. Drown, and your soul remains here for ever. Or wander so long that it consumes you to your final breath, and your soul remains here for ever. Either way, you are here for ever.

A shiver racks my body, but I hope he doesn't notice.

I wanted to drown you, but the Moss does not care which way you die. So I think I will let you wander, like I let your sister wander. Like your mother wandered. Watching hope die over the years. Watching the last shreds of your soul and sanity forsake you.

I step forward, my hands reaching out as though I will tear him limb from limb, but he vanishes like a lightbulb switched off, and there is nothing left of his presence except for the smell of damp, rotting earth.

A sob makes my chest heave as I turn away. Back to the waiting light that bobs up and down expectantly.

"I want to see my sister," I say to it, as though it doesn't already know. "Please."

The river rushes on, turning rough and white in places, and gentle in others. I once found the sound of a rushing river to be soothing, but now I am afraid of it. Now it's like nails on a chalkboard, grating in the background, and I grind my teeth.

The grassy shore I'm walking along slopes down until it kisses the edge of the water, sometimes steep enough that I have to work carefully to keep my balance. Ahead, a bend in the pathway disappears around the side of a hill, making it impossible to see where it leads. There's a sense of unease any time I can't see the road ahead, a tremble setting into my hands. I trudge on, keeping as close to the light as I can, although the faster I walk, the faster it moves, always keeping a healthy space between us.

Then we round the bend and ahead is a large grove of birch trees, not unlike the copse of trees that Eve and I used to hide in.

They grow right down to the water, thick grass and moss growing beneath them. Sprinkled everywhere are the pink flowers of bog laurel, familiar and awful and beautiful in the same breath.

And my feet stop.

The world stops.

My heart and lungs stop.

There is a large growth of flowers between two trees, bog laurel and moss twining together to partially cover something – someone – lying on the ground. The blossoms rise and fall with breathing, like the ground itself is alive.

A soft and familiar voice reaches me, beautiful and comforting like a tonic for the soul.

> *When true hearts lie withered*
> *And fond ones are flown*
> *Oh! Who would inhabit*
> *This bleak world alone?*

She hasn't seen me yet, and I can't take one more second of it. Lurching forward, I stumble across the distance to her, letting my backpack fall to the ground somewhere along the way.

My voice is small at first and comes from far away. A whisper from the darkness around me – because everything falls into shadow except for the girl covered in flowers, lying under the trees.

"Eve. Eve . . ."

The flowers shift and her head rises, a crown of blossoms encircling her hair.

"Eve!" A shriek this time that splits the air.

She's startled into silence, unmoving for a time. Maybe unsure if it's me or some working of the Moss, but she slowly sits up and pulls the hungry flowers and moss away, the roots ripping away from her clothing. Her eyes don't move or blink, just stare at me as I stumble over and drop to my knees.

The freckles I remember are still there, but they are faded and fewer than before. Her dark eyes search into mine, as though trying to see reality after being trapped for so long in a dream. Her once rich brown hair that used to shine almost a deep fiery red in the right light has dulled some, as though this place has drained away much of her life. Her soul. Her essence.

"Emma," she says in a cracked, tired voice.

Words feel meaningless now. Nothing I can say will matter as much as holding on to her will, so I just wrap her in my arms, crushing flowers between us, and let the hug linger for so long I might grow my own roots and stay here for ever. There is only one thing that matters now, and everything else can die away.

I found her.

thirty-eight

"**EMMA.**" **HER VOICE CATCHES.** I pull away, the scent of flowers filling up the air. "I thought you might be here."

"I heard you," I tell her. "Everywhere. Well, not everywhere. Certain places, at certain times."

"You went to the Fort," she says matter-of-factly, plucking flowers away from her body. The sight makes me feel a little bit sick, but I don't want to look away from her.

"How do you know?"

"I could feel it. See you there, almost. This place . . . it's nearly impossible to communicate with anything outside, once you come in. It uses water, and places you have a strong connection to on the outside, and in-between times, like dawn and dusk. Midnight, when one day melts into the next. Everything here is *almost*. In-between. I think your soul leaves little breadcrumbs in the places it visits, and you have a stronger connection with the places you visit more frequently."

Understanding seeps in.

"I went to the harvest party this year. It reminded me of you so much, and then I thought I saw you, and there was someone in the trees, but I couldn't find you."

Her steely eyes stare out over the river, and she nods. "I felt you go there. I tried to talk to you, but it's so hard. So tiring. And I was sad because I couldn't believe it had been a year."

"How long has it felt to you?"

She bends her legs to rest her elbows on her knees, and I'm afraid to look away from her in case she vanishes again. Her hair is unbrushed, her boots are worn, and her eyes long for rest, but she is here, whole and alive.

"Like days, sometimes. Sometimes like decades. There is no sunlight in here to mark the passing of time. Just dark, and then slightly less dark." She pauses. "You shouldn't have come, even though I missed you. So much." Her lower lip quivers. I lay a hand on top of hers.

"How have you . . . stayed alive?" I don't see any food around her. No bags or anything to show how she has survived.

"I guess you don't really need food in here, or water, even though there's enough of it." She says it with an annoyed hiss. "That's part of the curse of it all. It keeps you alive, just barely, for so long that you just start to wither from your soul."

She peels away some moss from her leg and throws it into some nearby bushes.

Swallowing, I finally ask, "What's happening to you? What is all of this?"

She looks down at the flowers and growth covering most of her body. "It happens when you spend too long in one place. It grows over you and keeps you here, and eventually you don't mind so much. You get tired, trying to find a way out."

There's a shattering feeling in my heart at the thought of how tired she must have been to lie down and let the Moss grow over her. It makes me start picking away the flowers and vines one by one through blurry eyes. "Does it hurt?"

"Not really. It just feels . . . strange. Kind of soothing."

"And all the mounds of flowers and moss I passed on the way here?" I whisper, fearing her response.

"Barrows, I assume," she answers distantly, staring at nothing. "Others who have given up. Their souls are still here somewhere, but there's so much space, and the longer you spend here, the deeper you go. Like Mom."

I look up at her, a flower still pinched between my fingers. "Is she here?"

"Somewhere. But I've never found her." She reaches down and yanks a vine of something that looks like ivy from around her waist. "I told myself one of the barrows must be hers. So I picked one, and I brought it flowers sometimes, and I sat with it a while. But if not, wherever she is now is further in the Moss than I've had time to go."

"I can't imagine there being anywhere else to go. It already feels endless. Inescapable."

"There is so much more. I think at some stage, you cross the point of no return. And crossing is a bit like dying. You're here for ever. But before then, *if* you can find a way out, then you can still leave. But it tries its best to trap you here."

"I hate it. The Moss. After this is over, I never want to see it again."

My body trembles again and I return to pulling the flowers away, blinking back all the tears that want to fall.

"And you," I say. "Did it trap you here?"

She looks up at me, her eyebrows pressed together. Nods. "You can't leave, Emma."

I shake my head, throwing a handful of blossoms into the grass. "You can. I took mental notes on everything we passed. The house and the giant trees, and I dropped coins along the way for us to follow. We just go back the way we came. Retrace our steps until it looks more like the Moss again. The one that you can see from the house. And then we leave."

She laughs a little, and my stomach sours. "I haven't spent the past year sitting here doing nothing, Emma. I've walked in every direction I can think of. Done it a hundred times over. Retraced my steps, again and again, carved markings into trees to guide my way. The Moss just doesn't end once you're inside it. You'll double back around and wind up back where you started, passing the same things over and over again. And if that isn't enough to drive you mad, there's always the Sedge Man lurking in every shadow, ready to plunge you under the water with very little provocation."

My fingernails dig into the dirt around me and the soft scent of rot wafts up to my face. "We've come in before and left. There is a way out, Eve. We just haven't found it yet."

"Stepping in a short way is not the same as what we've done. We are *deep* in the Moss, Emma. It is a prison. A maze. It is designed to keep you in."

I look around us, at the thin trees and the rushing water and the pressing, grey sky above. There is always mist, everywhere, coiling and twisting about. "What *is* it? How is any of this possible?"

Eve shakes her head. "It doesn't matter what it is. I've spent years thinking about it. Questioning it. Wondering and wondering and wondering. It's a predator. Ancient. Twisted. A crack in the world, and once you fall in, there is no climbing back out."

"I don't understand."

"Neither do I. But there are parts of the world no one can understand. Things that will never make sense. Things no one has seen. The Moss is old, hungry, and it feeds on the people who respond to its call. Not everyone does, as far as I can tell. Dad doesn't hear it. Most of the people in Scarrow don't hear it. I don't know why some people do, but they do hear it calling and once it starts, it will never stop."

I remember coming home from the airport with Jordan, standing outside and taking in the bog for the first time since I went away.

Come play, it had said. I'd heard that before, many times over the years, but there were ghosts I could easily chalk it up to. But perhaps it was the Moss itself. Calling to me. Pulling at me. Luring me in. Using its own voice, deep and heavy and malevolent, and not of this world.

"To most people, it's just a bog," Eve continues. "Just a pretty, unique part of Maine. But to some, it is something else entirely, and that's how you end up here. Maybe we spent too long near it. Maybe it got into *us,* somehow." She taps her temple.

The chat with Sally comes back to me; it is never very far from my thoughts.

"I met with Sally," I say. "She used to live in the house, before us. Her daughter came in for three days, and it ruined her. She left the country to escape it."

She looks at me with an aching sadness in her eyes. "Jesus."

"She said the longer you spend in the house, close to the Moss, the worse it gets. It seeps in and stays there, like an infection, and the only way to cure it is to leave for ever."

She looks out through the trees. "We should have left a long time ago. Long before Mom disappeared."

"We can leave when we get out." I look around. "Simon. The Sedge Man. Sally said he helps pull people into the Moss. A hunter, like you said in your letter. Have you seen him much?"

She lets out a scoffing sound, like she has had quite enough of him. "All the time. He thought his daughter was a witch because of her obsession with the bog. Because it called to her, and she couldn't ignore it. So he drowned her in it to be done with it all, and for a while, it worked. But Sybil started to call to him from the Moss, pulling him in over the years until he drowned in it as well. Now his soul is stuck here, but he can visit the house during rainstorms or through the water, to try to bring in more of us. More of those it calls to. He does the footwork for the Moss, and to him, he's ridding the world of more of us *enchantresses*." The last word sours her face.

My head swims, so I lie back in the grass and close my eyes.

"How do you know all this?" I ask quietly.

"I've spoken to Sybil. I saw visions, before I came here. Back at the house. They grew more frequent in the time before I left."

I rub at my eyes with the palms of my hands. "I wish we had never moved here," I murmur. God, how much easier everything could have been. How much simpler. How much happier, without this godforsaken place weighing every moment down like an anchor. Of all the houses to pick, it had to be this one.

"Well, here we are."

I open my eyes and sit up again, unsteadily, turning to look at her. "You came in for Mom, didn't you?"

She nods a few times. "I thought I could hear her. Thought

maybe she was still alive. But I waited too long, and by the time I got here she was beyond reach. I've spent a year looking, but she's somewhere I can't find. Not without spending many more years here."

"You won't."

"Well." She says it like she definitely doesn't believe me.

I look back the way I came, towards the green hill and the path. "We should go, before it's too late."

Eve drops the grass she's been playing with and shrugs. "Go where? There's nowhere to go."

I close my eyes, trying to organise my thoughts. "I'm not going to wait here until you get eaten by flowers, Eve. You've been stuck here for a year, but you've been stuck here alone. Let me help you this time."

"You'll just get tired and wither away faster, and for nothing. I'd rather sit here than keep pretending I have hope. I had it for so long; I was convinced I could leave. But it wears you down over time, and you can feel the pieces of you falling away, and it's more painful than just letting the flowers grow through you."

She is so starkly different to the girl I have always known, the one who seemed built from sparks and fire. I came here looking for my older sister. The one who often held so much confidence. Who seemed so sure, even when the strangeness became something almost unbearable. But right now, in this moment, Eve needs an older sister. Someone to take her hand, pull her out and keep her safe.

My jaw tightens, chin rising a little.

"I almost died, Eve. I nearly drowned. And all I could think about was seeing you one more time. I saw your face, as the world

247

grew dark, and I wanted to hear your voice one more time. I have waited for you for a year. Waited, and wondered, and grieved. And here I am. I came here to bring you home, and that is exactly what I'm going to do."

Eve watches me, her chest heaving some. She shakes her head, her eyes going glassy. "I don't want to leave her."

Something in me softens, and I look around us like our mom might come walking out of the trees. But she doesn't. And unlike with Eve, I've never thought she would. In all the time I've spent missing them both, wondering what happened, longing to find it, it was only ever Eve's presence I could feel. Under a barrow or in another part of the Moss, I know, deep down, that my mother is beyond reach.

"Neither do I, Eve. But you can't reach her. And what about Dad? He's still out there, waiting. Worried. He deserves you. He deserves us."

Eve just cries a little, quietly.

"Look. Wherever Mom is, I hope it's beautiful. I hope there is birdsong, and light, and that she knows we are safe, and together. She would want nothing more than that." I wait a moment, stroking her hair. "Come with me. Let's get you home."

"You can't. I've tried."

"Then prove it to me. Let *me* see that there's no way out. Then I'll believe you."

She sighs, heavily, like it's the first time she has truly breathed since she came to this place. "Fine. I'll go with you. But listen to me, Emma. You will walk, and walk, and walk, and you'll always think you're on the right track, but the path just never ends, and days go by, or maybe months, and . . . And then you'll realise that the best thing for you to do is to just lie down and let the Moss grow around you, because it's peaceful and quiet and you sleep a lot—"

"Eve," I interrupt her. "It's OK. So we end up in the middle of nowhere, and maybe *nowhere* only grows bigger. Maybe it really does never end. So we wear ourselves out. That can't be worse than this." I point down to all of the growth around her. "And at least we will be together."

Neither of us moves for a moment, and I take one long, lingering look at the trees around us. And I don't quite feel Mom's presence, but there's a warmth around me suddenly, and I know that as hard as it will be to leave her, she would want this. More than anything.

It feels more like a goodbye than I ever got to have before. Eve is crying softly now, and I brush a few tears from her face.

"Come on." I stand and hold out my hand, hauling her to her feet when she takes it. "Let's go."

"This is a bad idea."

"Maybe."

Eve hesitates, and stares off through the trees, another single tear running down her face. I squeeze her hand and look with her, letting our silence act as a kind of goodbye. I think one day I'll look back on this moment and feel sad. Feel all the things I should be feeling right now. But I am happy to see Eve, and afraid of what is to come, and overwhelmed by everything she has said, so my feelings are out of order and confusing. And for now, that's OK.

Still holding her hand, I turn us away and lead us back on to the path I came in on, around the hill and along the river, until, slowly, the trees disappear behind us.

thirty-nine

I HAD LOST TRACK of the light for a time once it brought me to Eve. But as we walk on, it soon catches up to us. It travels behind us, rather than leading us – I'm not sure why, but it isn't worth asking since it's not like it can talk.

We keep a quick pace, but not so fast as to wear ourselves out too quickly. Especially if we have as long a walk as Eve reckons, though I privately hope we don't.

"What is it that calls to us?" I ask, almost in a whisper. We have been walking for a long while – hours, I think – in silence. "In the Moss, I mean. Is it the bog itself, or something in it?"

She looks around us, perhaps checking if we are alone. But everywhere I look there is nothing. No one else. Even though I have seen other living – or perhaps dead – things since I entered, there is always the never-ending and crushing sense of being alone. It's strange, after years and years spent living beside it, where it always felt so alive, watching and waiting. Only to get inside and feel more like I'm drifting through outer space.

"I don't know. I've already told you everything I know. If there is something else here, I haven't seen it."

"Simon would probably know," I say darkly, then regret it in case my words conjure him up again.

"Probably not. He died a few hundred years ago, but to the Moss that might as well have been yesterday."

The words induce a shiver. I hug myself as we press on.

Soon, I can see the giant forms of the trees ahead, but even reaching their outskirts takes what feels like hours more. By the time we pass the first of the trunks, my feet ache desperately and light is beginning to fade from the sky.

"We'll have to sleep," I say presently. "I found a house on my way to you. Well, half a house. It's mostly falling down, but it's a place to rest."

"The stone one. I slept there too."

It explains why I felt a connection to her when I laid down.

The house is where I left it, and as we climb inside I feel a pang of optimism that I will be able to lead us back out. No shifting landscapes yet. No walking in circles.

We lie down in the same room where I did, the bats no longer in sight. With our heads close together and the yellowish light shining softly outside, there is a sense of comfort I didn't feel the last time.

"Who do you think built this house?" I venture.

I can hear Eve shake her head softly beside me. "No idea. Maybe someone else who got stuck here, a long time ago. Maybe lots of people, before it was their time to cross."

We walk quietly for a time. "I went to California. Well, Dad sent me to California for a while, to get away from it all, after you vanished. But all I could think about was how much you would love it. So you should come, when we get out."

Eve laughs a little, like she just can't believe how persistent I am. "*If* we get out of here, Emma, then we'll go to California."

"Deal."

My eyes are heavy now, and the conversation dies away. I let sleep find me as we lie there in the room, bathed in a pale yellow glow from outside, and, finally, together again.

Sleep is a murky black thing, dreamless, and broken only by Eve's soft voice waking me up.

"Emma. Wake up." She shakes my shoulder softly, and I sit up on one elbow. The room is still dark, no grey light outside to signal that it's morning, or whatever passes for morning in the bog.

"What's wrong?" I ask, rubbing the sleep from my eyes. My thoughts are still fuzzy, unclear.

"We should get going. I don't like it here."

That wakes me up. "Why not?"

"I don't know, I just don't. I keep hearing sounds in the chimney."

"They're just bats," I tell her through a yawn. "I saw them last time."

"I still don't like it."

I'm awake now, and if Eve wants to move on I won't stop her. She has been here far longer than I have. Once we've collected our things, we leave the little house behind and press on again. Light starts to seep into this grim world, though there is never any visible sun or sky. There aren't even any definable clouds. Just a mantle of dull, ashy grey above us that leaches all the colour from the world. The giant trees surround us, their crooked limbs reaching and grabbing as we pass by.

"I remember coming here a few times," Eve muses as we walk. She trails a finger along the mossy trunk of one of the trees, and from her touch sprouts a handful of pink flowers. She doesn't seem to notice, or if she does, she doesn't care.

Confused, I lay a hand on the wide branch of another tree. Small sprigs of green start to slowly grow, but no flowers. Perhaps I haven't spent enough time here yet.

"It won't be too much further," I tell her, catching up again.

She sends me a look that I know is meant to highlight her opinion that we will not be leaving the Moss, but at least she doesn't say it.

We walk, endlessly.

The landscape shifts as we go, the large trees disappearing, replaced by familiar, boggy wetland.

We have to hop along the solid ground from time to time and retrace our steps when we reach a watery dead end. I keep an eye out for the coins, but there are no signs of them yet.

Step. Hop. Catch your breath. Walk. Walk. Hold that tree and shuffle around a deep pool.

Walk, walk, walk.

The day slips by like hourglass sand.

Lose your footing, and a shoe splashes into the water.

Walk.

Walk.

Walk.

"I told you," Eve says after hours and hours of walking. "It doesn't end."

A slippery, nervous feeling has been creeping in, making me cold despite all the movement. None of this looks familiar – and yet somehow all of it does. I can't tell if we are walking in circles or if the bog is just growing and growing, endlessly expanding as we walk. There is no sign of the house, no sign of the garden, no sign of anything that might signal an end. There is only more bog, more water, more reeds and grasses. More Moss.

"If there is a way in, there is a way out," I tell her, hopping carefully across another deep pool of inky-black water.

"That isn't always true," she says. "Some places in the world are only one way."

"This isn't one of them."

"How do you know that?" she snaps, stopping walking altogether and yanking my shoulder until I face her. My eyes sting with tears, but a sharp sort of anger kindles as well. "We've been walking since yesterday morning because you wanted to. I told you what would happen, and you didn't listen, and now here we are, in the middle of nowhere and with nowhere only getting bigger, and you still won't believe that we are never getting out of here."

"Because I don't want to believe it," I tell her shakily, adjusting my backpack just for something to do. "Because I don't want to be in here. I never wanted to be in here. You and Mom just couldn't leave it alone, and now here we are. And maybe we are stuck here for ever, but I don't want to give up as quickly as you did."

Her eyes narrow with hurt. "*Quickly?* Do you know how long I spent trying to get out of here? Trying to get back home. Telling myself 'just a few more minutes, a few more minutes and I'll be there' – for days on end. Camping out here by the water, sleeping alone in the dark, hoping I would wake up and see the house in the distance. You have no idea how hard I tried."

Guilt sets in, even though my anger is still hot.

"You're right, I don't. I'm sorry."

"Just because you want to get out of here, doesn't mean you can. I wanted to go back home when I realised Mom wasn't leaving, and I couldn't. But wanting something doesn't make it happen."

"Eve—"

Something moves behind her suddenly, and I break off. By the time I've realised what it is, it's too late – I don't have time to warn her before Simon's arm yanks her backwards, sending her tumbling into a dark, deep pool.

forty

I **SCREAM AND JUMP** forward, losing my footing and nearly falling in myself. I kneel down on the edge of the pool while her arms thrash out, searching for purchase.

Across from me, Simon just laughs.

You should listen to your sister.

"Get away from us."

My work is finished. I brought you here. But it is amusing, how hard people work to try to leave. Hope is a funny thing.

"What would you know of hope?" I hiss at him, giving Eve a hand to pull herself up with. "You thought your daughter was a witch. But isn't it you who ended up in hell?"

Silence, for a moment. *This isn't hell.*

"It isn't heaven either."

He hisses, and the coldness around him grows. *You will not leave this place, heaven or hell.*

I can feel something in me snap then, like a dry branch in the winter. I spin to face him as Eve climbs out of the water, crossing the distance between us in a few quick steps. The air around him is frigid and dark, and my skin prickles and crawls, but I don't move away.

"If I cannot be free of this place, then I will let it devour me, like it has devoured you. I will rot and wither and putrefy until grasses grow through me and the dirt has reclaimed me, like it has reclaimed you, and then I will torment you, Simon Lark, for however long forever is. I will let this place ruin me, and then I will use that hate and loathing to make every day for you feel like a lifetime. You will wish, more than you do now, that heaven had taken you, and not this place."

The coldness about him contracts and writhes, his anger spilling into the world. I wait, unmoving, for him to speak, but instead Simon departs in an instant, vanishing into nothingness and leaving us alone.

Eve coughs out brown water, still gasping for air, when I return to her side. When she's had some time to catch her breath, I lean in close so she can hear me better, about to say I'm sorry for what I said earlier, but something she said comes back to me.

Wanting something doesn't make it happen.

I'm not sure why, but I go back to the day in the car with my dad, reading on my phone and then in the library about death rituals and sacrifice and old bog legends – and how some thought will-o'-the-wisps showed you what you wanted to see most, leading you towards it.

"I wanted to see you," I say suddenly, turning to see the light hovering nearby.

Eve looks from me to the light. "What do you mean?"

"I wanted to see you, and it led me to you. The wisp. It showed me what I wanted the most, because all I've wanted for a year is to get you back."

Eve shakes her head, not following me, but she eyes the wisp and I think something starts to make sense.

"I asked it to take me to you, because it was what I wanted most in the world. But right now, what I want the most in the world is to go home." The light bobs a little, like it's listening. "I want to go home," I say again. "I want to go home." Tears begin to run down my face as I say it, because if this doesn't work then the Moss will never, ever, let us go. I can't stomach the thought of spending one more hour here, let alone for ever. "I want to go home. Please. Take us home."

There's a pause while all of the air leaves my lungs, the seconds dragging into an endless wait . . .

And then, for the first time since I found Eve, the light moves in front of us, instead of following us. My chest heaves with a sob of relief, even though it could be leading us anywhere, and Eve scrambles to her feet. I steady her by her elbow, and then we both follow the light as quickly as we can over the rough ground.

The Moss looks no different as we press on, and my feet and legs are aching and there's a pinch in my back from carrying the backpack for so long, but hope stays alive as the light leads the way.

"Do you think it understood?" Eve whispers presently. It could be minutes or hours later.

I shrug. "I don't know. But it led me to you. I have to hope it can lead us back out."

"I never thought to ask it for anything," she tells me.

"It didn't take you to Mom?"

"No. I wandered and wandered for ever, until I finally found the island."

"God. You must have been lonely."

She looks down at the ground as we walk. "You have no idea."

I squeeze her hand as the ground widens enough for us to walk side by side. "You won't be alone any more. Whether we make it out or not."

A coldness suddenly reaches out from behind us. I can feel the air shift.

"He's back," I say, just as Eve turns to look.

Those who enter can never leave. He's behind us now, his black coat dripping with cold water.

"This is your hell," Eve tells him. "Not ours."

No one leaves.

"I warned you to leave us alone," I bite out. The words escape me like a thunderclap, making him go silent for a moment.

I cannot let you leave.

Before I can reply, another voice, so distant it could just be a breeze, reaches me. Eve tilts her head, listening.

"Emma!"

We look at each other, wondering, hoping – is it? No. It could be. But probably not.

At the same time, we both turn and start running after the light, stumbling over the uneven ground and dodging pools of water with only inches to spare. The light quickens its pace before us, wending its way along, ever onwards. Onwards. Onwards. Simon suddenly here, then there, before and behind.

"Emma!" The voice comes again, painfully familiar and sweet. Jordan, I think. It's still so far away, but I'm almost certain it's him. My soul reaches towards it – hoping, praying.

"There's someone there," Eve calls beside me, her voice brimful of tears. "There's someone there."

Another voice joins, equally beautiful and welcome. "Emma!"
Dad.

Something yanks me back suddenly, tugging at my hair and throwing me off balance until I topple head over feet into a nearby pool.

Water surrounds me, thick and dark and drowning out all light. There is too much mud to see anything and my arms flail wildly, searching for anything they can grab on to. It's all so horribly familiar and cold.

But something presses down from above, just like before. Just like the girl I watched drown by our house. A hand, holding me under. Waiting until my lungs fill up and my body goes still. Waiting, waiting, waiting.

I have learnt to be patient.

I reach for the hand and squeeze, push, pull, but I have no leverage, my feet hanging loose in the water, and I am powerless to fight back.

I cannot let you leave.

The voice drips down from above, oozing into my mind through the mud.

I cannot die here, I think. So close to the end. So close to home. Just on the edge of the Moss, with freedom almost in reach. So close. So terribly, awfully, beautifully close.

Tick. Tock. Tick. Tock. I keep hold of his hand, even though the cold bites sharply into my skin, and wait. My legs hang in the water. There is nothing to do but wait, either for rescue or death. I wonder what Sybil's last thoughts were. If she awaited rescue, or if she knew that it was the end. I hope not. I hope she had some hope, until the very end.

Simon's grip on my hair loosens unexpectedly, and my body jolts with the sudden freedom. I reach around again for anything I can grab, and a moment later, a hand meets mine. Not the Sedge Man's – smaller, trying to catch hold of my fingers. I claw at it, frantic, desperate for a breath of air, and rise up, up, up and above the surface.

Mud clings to my eyes, but I try furiously to rub it away. Eve is pulling me further on to the bank, asking me over and over again if I'm OK, but my ears are still full of water, and everything feels dark and fuzzy. Like the last few moments of a dream before you wake up.

"I'm here, Emma. I'm here."

But she isn't the only one there. The deer is back, or the thing that is almost a deer but also something else. It has Simon pinned against a tree with its antlers, as Sybil stands limply nearby, watching us. Her gaze is locked on mine, unwavering, like she knows something. And I think I know what.

"Tell me you're OK," Eve begs, still holding my hand. "Emma, tell me you're OK."

"I'm OK," I say, still holding Sybil's gaze. Her eyes fall to my backpack, then lift back up to me.

Do it, she says. *End it all.*

Simon looks from me to her, then back again. I wonder how she knows. Wonder if the sounds that woke me up in the small house not so very long ago might have been someone rifling through my bag.

"I will," I tell her. "I will."

Eve pulls me to my feet and I stand, unsteadily.

"Come on," she says. "We're almost there."

With the creature still holding Simon in place, we turn and follow the light again, quickly, the land around us growing ever more familiar. There are clumps of trees everywhere – but I'm certain I've seen *that* clump before, from the house. Certain I recognise *that* cluster of bog laurel, and the way those vines wind around that old stump. My heart quickens, racing, like my feet against the ground.

"Emma! Emma!" Jordan's voice is louder, clearer, and much closer.

"I'm here!" I call back, my lungs still aching after my time underwater. "I'm here! I'm here!"

"Emma!" This time the voice is flooded with relief. Disbelief. "I can see her!"

Up ahead, beyond some thin trees, I can see two figures standing in the bog. Dad and Jordan. Beside me, Eve lets out a scream that erupts straight from her heart, running like she's just sprouted wings and might soar into the air at any moment.

Dad stands still, staring, his eyes wide as a full moon, his mouth open. I don't have the energy to run after her, so I have a good view as she runs headlong into Dad and throws her arms around him, sobbing in a way I haven't heard before. The kind of sobs borne from a homecoming, from a dream coming true, from the grief of time lost, and the newfound, fragile hope of things to come.

He holds her, staring dumbfounded at nothing, saying *"no, no,"* to himself again and again as if he can't make himself believe it. As if he has dreamt of this so often that he can't be certain it's real.

Jordan reaches me, finally, and grabs me by both shoulders, leaning down to look into my eyes.

"Emma! Oh my god. What happened? We searched the bog for you. I don't know how we could have missed you. Were you in there the whole time? Oh my god. It doesn't matter. I'm so glad to have you back. Jesus Christ." And he pulls me in for a kiss that I melt into, closing my eyes and just letting it consume me. Hello hugs and kisses are always so much better than goodbye ones, and I never, ever, ever want to say goodbye again.

Eve is still crying, explaining a dumbed down version of what happened to our dad, so Jordan doesn't hear the worst of it, but I move away a little bit, letting my backpack slide off into my hand.

"Where are you going?" Jordan asks nervously, moving to follow me.

"I'm not going anywhere," I tell him, unzipping it. "I just have something to do. I'll be right back."

I walk a little further back into the Moss – not enough to get lost, but enough to put some distance between myself and the others. Far away, I can just make out the shapes of Sybil, Simon and that wretched, twisted deer.

Still watching and waiting.

From the backpack, I pull out a large handful of firelighters I took from our house before I left, and a lighter I'm hoping isn't too water-damaged. I work quickly, before anyone can stop me, or I can find a reason not to do it.

I know there are things that live here in the bog, but they are only dead things, or things that do not belong in this world. Things trapped here by an ancient place that lives and breathes malice. That calls to people, draws them in, and drowns them in a nightmarish, empty world. No birds or mammals have ever lived here. They knew enough to stay away.

So I make a pile of the firelighters on the driest part of the ground I can find, flick the lighter until an orange flame appears, and drop it on to the heap with a smile.

It starts slowly, the flame turning into a small blaze, until the whole pile of firelighters is alight. The tall grass around it catches quickly – all thanks to this goddamn drought we've been experiencing. *Everything feels like a tinderbox, even with so much water around.* Isn't that what Jordan had said?

Even the rainstorm before I left wasn't enough to keep the earth damp for long. Not after such a long drought.

And if I know anything about bogs, and I do, it's that they are full of peat, and peat burns long and slow, nearly impossible to put out because it burns underground. It will take time, but eventually the Moss will be nothing but ashes, blanketing the world outside my window like freshly fallen snow.

Thank you, comes Sybil's voice from further in the bog.

I stare at her across the distance, smoke slowly starting to block her from view.

"You're welcome. And I'm sorry."

At my feet, the flames grow and spread, grass catching like kindling and sending the fire further and further. Behind me, I can hear Jordan asking me over and over again what I've done, what I'm doing, but I don't answer or turn around.

I just watch as the beautiful, malevolent Moss slowly goes up in smoke.

forty-one

WE AREN'T MEANT TO be anywhere near the Moss. Not with the fire and smoke still devouring it, even under the ground. But me, my father and Eve all know something that the others don't. That the fire department doesn't know. That the police don't know. That the news stations, curious as they are, don't know.

That my mother, in one form or another, is still somewhere inside the Moss. Even if there is nothing left of her, or who she once was. Somewhere, deep inside, a part of her is still there. Buried under a barrow of flowers, hopefully at peace.

I toss the last armful of flowers on to the pile as Eve sits nearby in the grass, hugging her knees. The closest we could get is the edge of the driveway, near the road, and even here, the smoke is thick and heavy. We won't stay long. Although, given the way my father stands facing the bog, eyes glued to it by tears, I worry we'll have to pull him away.

I look down to the makeshift flower barrow we made for her, using all of her favourite flowers. Sunflowers, chrysanthemums and daisies. Even the smell of them conjures an image of her, smiling in a sundress, sipping tea and telling stories of when she used to work as a florist. I can feel her now, somehow, and I wonder if Eve can feel her too.

"She's here," I say, joining my sister on the ground. "Somehow."

She looks over at me, and nods. "I know." Her eyes turn to the flowers, and she breathes in a long, deep drag of the scent. Closes her eyes, where a few tears shine. "She's happy we got out."

"How do you know?"

Eve shrugs. "I just know. Maybe my time in the Moss gave me some sort of connection to her. Or maybe I just want to believe it."

But I can feel it too. It's the same feeling as when you recognise someone you know, or that wash of familiarity when you walk into your own house. A sense of just *knowing*.

Dad turns and comes back to us, bending to pick a couple stubborn dandelions still growing in the grass and tossing them gently on to the barrow. "Are you guys ready?"

Eve and I both nod and pull handwritten letters from our pockets. Eve opens hers to re-read, wiping at her eyes a few times, but I just turn mine over in my hands. I have read it enough times to commit it to memory. All the things I wish I could have said to Mom in the time since she's been gone. All the things that happened that I wished I could tell her about. Stories from California. What it was like finding Eve again. I poured it all out like a dam had broken and the words rushed over the page at reckless speed. Pages and pages of them.

After a moment, Dad hands Eve a lighter, and with a small shudder of a sob, she lights the corner of her letter on fire and tosses it on to the barrow. The flowers are too fresh to catch, but the paper is consumed within moments. Ash rustling away in the breeze.

Dad pulls a small letter of his pocket and turns away quickly. I can tell he's wiping his eyes and doesn't want us to see, so I look away to give him some privacy. My soul wants to cry along with them, but I've cried so many tears over the past few days, both happy and sad, that I feel as dry as summer grass. Ready to catch fire like the paper.

In another minute, Dad's own letter has gone up in flames, the blaze quickly dying away and leaving nothing behind.

My turn.

I spin the letter a few more times, taking the lighter Dad offers me. But even before I can catch the corner alight, an idea grips me, firm and unrelenting.

I stand, gripping the letter, and move past the barrow. Past Dad and Eve – "Emma! Where are you going?" – and down the driveway.

Past the house and towards the garden that leads to the Moss. There are signs everywhere warning me away. Police tape to keep us out. The smoke is thick and dark. It's hard to breathe. But there isn't long to go now. I slip over what remains of the fence and stop before the first pool of water. The same pool where Eve and I brought the bird all those years ago. Where that thing watched us in the mist, and I got my first real inclination that there was something wrong with this place.

Gently, with a shaking hand, I drop the letter into the pool and watch as the water engulfs it. It floats, saturated, staring back at me from below. I let my eyes wander up again, to the bog that was once shrouded in mist but is now encompassed with smoke. I can't see very far, and I'm glad for it. That same cold, clammy fear has crept back in now that I've drawn so near to it – this time mixed with something else. There is a new kind of anger here. Anger at me, for what I did. For the blaze I started that no one can put out.

I smile.

Who are you? I imagine it asking as it watches me, the girl it tried to consume but failed. Who managed to claw her way back out with bloodied nails and a tattered soul.

"I am the end," I whisper into the smoke, then look down for one last glance at my letter.

But the letter is gone.

after

I **T HAS BEEN A** week since Eve and I came back from the Moss.

So much has happened since then, but it all feels so small compared to our time in the Moss. Compared to having her back after a year. Compared with the way the whole world seems to have changed, now that I know how little of it we really understand.

The bog is still on fire, so we are staying in a house across town that my dad rented, and I think it's for the best. There are too many memories bursting at the seams of that house, and we all need to be free of them. Put Scarrow into our rearview mirror and never look back.

No one told anyone else that I started the fire. Dad knew enough not to doubt me, and I told Jordan enough for him to understand. I'm not sure how much of it he really believes, but he says seeing us suddenly appear from nowhere in the Moss after they had searched it for days was enough to keep him from being too sceptical.

Dad says that once the fire is finally under control, we will sell the house, and I am glad for it.

I try to spend every waking moment with Eve. We are planning on visiting Aunt Freda in California over Christmas. Dad is coming too, and I'm excited to show them all the places I ended up falling in love with while I was out there.

Everywhere, there is the sense of newness. Of a fresh start. I know that's what Dad had intended for me when he first sent me away, but this time, it's sticking.

The Moss will probably burn for years, and we can't sell it while it still burns. Once the fire reached the peat hiding underneath, it became nearly impossible for them to put it out. Fires that burn underground are hard to combat. They haven't let us go back to the house yet, but part of me wants to, just to see if the ghosts are still there. If Simon will be waiting, or if the fire took him away too.

Maybe the fire won't fix everything. Maybe I'll hear his voice again one day, or feel the pull of the hungry Moss as it calls to me once more, but I'm different now. I went in and I came out, and it changed me. I don't feel so afraid now, because the Moss is the only thing that ever truly scared me, and I set it on fire. So now, I feel like the one to be feared.

Jordan is thinking more about studying physics, and I hope he does, because leaving the bog and seeing a starlit sky again made me realise it is one bit of beauty I will never take for granted again. And anyway, the stars deserve his fire. That light energy that makes you always want to be around him.

Eve is back. Sometimes I still worry that it was all a dream, so I go to her new room all the time just to poke my head in and make sure that she's there. Dad does it too, for both of us, and though Mom never came back out, seeing both of his daughters again patched up most of his missing pieces.

Eve is *back*. The Moss is on fire, and will be for years and years. I don't know what it is, or how it got there, or whether it will still be there after the fire. But I know that neither me nor Eve will ever step foot in it again. In a way, that feels like winning. The Moss wanted us. Lured us. Dragged us in and pulled us under. But we found a way back out, and that is what matters.

Dad was right. There are places in this world that no one understands, and maybe that's for the best. I don't have to understand the Moss to know that darkness pooled there like rainwater on the street. There are some things that only fire can cure.

So I'm happy to let its darkness burn, and let the starlight and sunshine and the light that comes with hope flood the shadows until they vanish like frost in the dawn.

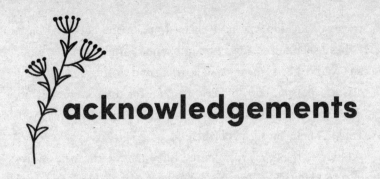

acknowledgements

As always, huge thanks go to my agent, Silvia Molteni, for her tireless work and dedication. This book wouldn't exist without her.

I'm so thankful to Hazel Holmes, Kathy Webb, the students, and the entire team at UCLan. They've worked so hard to bring this book to life, with care and kindness every step of the way.

Thank you to my husband, Thomas, and my son, Atlas, the brightest stars in my night sky.

Thank you to my parents, for loving me and putting up with me for all these years. To my siblings, near and far, I love you. Nieces, nephews, in-laws, and to my wider family: thank you to all of you, for everything. Always.

Thank you to all of the friends who have supported and encouraged me when writing was hard (it's always hard, but sometimes it's *really* hard). I'll be forever grateful for all of you. Especially Claire Donnelly, who has always been there, and always will be, and Schuyler Rees. Twenty years of friendship, and counting.

A special thank you to my aunt, Kathy, for being one of the strongest, best people I could ever know. Forever an inspiration, and forever a hero. *You go, girl.*

A big thank you to the new friends I've made since I began

screenwriting, and who have cheered me on and kept me going. It's been such fun to adventure into a new form of writing, and I can't wait to keep growing and learning and writing new things.

Not a person, but I'm very thankful for the state of Maine, which has been one of the most inspiring places I've ever lived. I couldn't help but set a book here.

I have to thank my cats, Jeffrey, Riley and Xanthe, who always seem to know when I'm stressed or have writer's block and need their affection the most. They never seem to want to sit in my lap more than the moment I pick up my laptop to start writing.

And thank you to anyone who reads this book, which I started (a very early draft of) at the beginning of the pandemic. The early days of the pandemic coincided with one of the hardest times I've ever had in my life, and the combination created such a dark, desolate place in my mind. Finding the light often felt like an impossible task, but it happened slowly, over time. And through it all, books kept me going, so here's one I hope you'll love.

Thank you.

about the author

Lisa Lueddecke has spent her life moving between four countries and five states, having been born into an Air Force family. *A Shiver of Snow and Sky*, the first instalment in her debut fantasy series, was published by Scholastic UK in October 2017. Its sequel, *A Storm of Ice and Stars*, came out in October 2018. *The Forest of Ghost and Bones*, a new standalone novel aimed at young adults, was published in October 2020, followed by *The City of Lost Dreamers* in October 2021.

IF YOU LIKED THIS, YOU'LL LOVE . . .

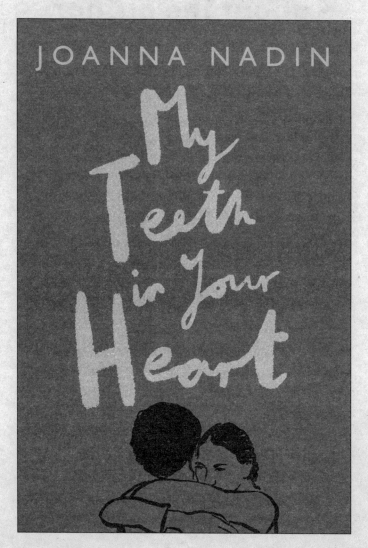

JOANNA NADIN

My Teeth in Your Heart

ROSE EDWARDS
This whole kingdom floats on a sea of blood
Plough the fields and it comes seeping up
The HARM TREE
"A rich, compelling epic" MELINDA SALISBURY

'Delicious and gruesome – will ignite a new generation of vampire fans' LAUREN JAMES

MINA
and the Undead

MYSTERY

Be Kind
Rewind
◄◄

Amy McCaw

YA

VHS